THE SNOWDROP GARDEN

Martin Baxendale

© Copyright 2009 Martin Baxendale.

Published by Silent But Deadly Publications,
21 Bisley Road, Stroud, Glos, GL5 1HF,
England.

ISBN 978 0 9550500 9 1

Printed in England by Stoate & Bishop Printers
Ltd, The Runnings, Cheltenham, Glos.

For Ivi with love

...

About the author

Martin Baxendale has written more than twenty successful
humour books, including 'Your New Baby - An Owner's Manual'
which has sold over half a million copies in the UK and more than
a million worldwide in nearly twenty languages and is now a
classic gift for new parents.

He has been collecting, growing and breeding snowdrops for over
twenty-five years, following in the footsteps of his parents, who
have been lifelong snowdrop enthusiasts.

This is Martin's first novel.

Guns and Snowdrops

"Hey! You out there! Stop shooting at us! My wife's pregnant...with *twins*!"

Beside me, Lady Cherrington jabbed her sharp little elbow into my ribs and jerked her head towards the dirty, broken window and the shrubbery beyond.

"And!?" she whispered loudly, jabbing me again, this time with a hard, bony finger.

"Ouch....and try not to step on the *snowdrops*!"

Crack! Another bullet splintered through the wooden side-wall of Lady C's ancient, crumbling barn-like garage and thwacked into an old metal watering can hanging from a beam behind us. It swung wildly then crashed to the floor.

"Buggers are getting closer," muttered Lady C's equally ancient and crumbling toad-like husband, the Colonel, as he eyed the latest in a line of small bright holes letting in thin streams of winter sunlight along the timber wall.

"That was my favourite watering can," grumbled Lady C, her bent little figure quivering with anger in the dusty gloom.

I moved closer to the window and yelled at the bushes again.

"Will you *please* stop doing that! You can't shoot at a *pregnant woman*!"

As I stepped back to re-join the others, I noticed the Colonel slyly creeping sideways until Katka and her huge nine-month-pregnant tummy were between him and the bullet holes. There was a burst of coarse male laughter from outside and the answer came back:

"No? But they are making bigger targets! Easier for hitting! Ha, ha, ha!"

Bulgarian gangster humour.

The Colonel's pale, balding head popped back out from behind Katka like a startled tortoise from its shell. He blinked nervously then hastily crept away from her again, a lot further than before. Meanwhile Lady C glared from her punctured watering can to Katka's pregnant tummy and out at the garden. Unbending from her bullet-dodging crouch and stretching to her full height of four-foot-ten-inches, she glowered furiously at the window. Now positively shaking with rage, she looked like....well, like an incredibly ferocious version of the little Jedi alien Yoda from the Star Wars films. Then she bellowed in her scariest cut glass Cheltenham Ladies' College voice, usually reserved for people who ignore the sign saying 'Private Area - No Visitors Beyond This Point' on her garden open days:

"Fuck you, you fucking nasty motherfuckers! I'm going to fucking blow your motherfucking heads off for that! You see if I don't! Oh, you've made me really motherfucking angry now!"

You wouldn't expect someone of Lady C's generation and background to be a Tarantino fan, certainly not at the age of eighty-nine, but then life's full of surprises. At least it was that particular day, and there were more to come.

I looked down to see her angrily jamming fresh shotgun cartridges into the Colonel's double-barrelled twelve-bore and slamming the breach closed before shuffling sideways towards the window, the gun to her shoulder, ducking and weaving like a demented little octogenarian Bruce Willis on hormone replacement therapy.

"And if you've trampled all over my motherfucking snowdrops, I'll let you have both barrels up your motherfucking backsides!"

As Lady C peered manically through a hole in the window pane, searching for a target, the Colonel snapped rattily from the shadows in the furthest corner of the dark, cavernous garage, where he'd retreated in his haste to put as much distance as possible between himself and the tempting target that Katka had apparently now become.

"Steady on, Primula old girl. Don't waste the ammo. We've only three cartridges left. Oh! Hell and damnation! That bloody hurts!"

"Did they hit you, Oliver, dear?"

Lady C glanced back towards the Colonel's dim and dusty hiding place, not sounding anywhere near as concerned about the possibility of him being shot as she was about her snowdrops being trampled (or, for that matter, her favourite watering can being hit). In fact I could have sworn there was a slight note of hope in her voice. And if you'd ever met the Colonel, you'd understand why.

"No! Damn, bugger and sod it. Stupid bloody thing. Completely forgot it was there. Think I've fractured my bloody knee on it. Hang *on* though….maybe we could escape in *this*."

Katka squinted into the gloom at the far end of the garage. It was huge even for a double garage, a massive barn of a place with piles of junk everywhere and rickety steps up to a cobwebby second storey. The sole illumination was from the one tiny window half-obscured by dark laurel leaves, where Lady C was tottering on tiptoes trying to see over the sill.

"I thought your car was being mended after you made Alfred ram it into that school bus coming home from your pub lunch last week," said Katka.

"Not the bloody car, woman," grumbled the Colonel. "*This!* Look, over here. Dammit, where's that light switch? Ouch! Buggeration! Bashed my *other* knee now!"

There was a click and a light bulb came on, dimly illuminating the building's far-flung corners, in one of which the Colonel could now be seen hunched over, rubbing both knees, beside a military armoured personnel carrier. Very old, dusty and covered in cobwebs, rust and pigeon shit, but indisputably an armoured personnel carrier; or as we would have called it in my childhood days of playing soldiers, an armoured car. The Colonel pulled up his trouser leg and began examining a frighteningly thin, chalky-white and blue-veined leg for cuts and bruises as he shot Katka a bleary-eyed glare.

"And I did *not* make Alfred crash the bloody car. The damn fool had plenty of room to overtake that bus. Ouch! My blasted knee's *broken*, I'm sure it is."

Katka frowned back at him.

"Well from what Primula told me, you were hitting Alfred on the head from the back seat with a rolled-up newspaper and shouting at him to overtake on a corner. You nearly pushed the bus into the hedge. Those poor children were terrified. It said so in the newspaper. And poor Alfred will probably lose his licence."

"Can you *drive* that, Colonel?" I asked, pointing at the armoured car and trying not to look or sound amazed. After all, this was the garage of a pretty bonkers retired Colonel and his lady wife.

"Doesn't look like it's been moved for years, Colonel. Has it got petrol in it? If it hasn't, Alfred usually keeps a can of two-stroke fuel in here somewhere."

Katka, one hand on her pregnant tummy and the other on her back, walked slowly towards the ugly lump of rusting British Army hardware in the corner, running her eyes over its dirty armour-plate and half-deflated tyres. The Colonel watched closely as she walked around the armoured car, then he snapped at me.

"Two-stroke? Bloody two-stroke? It's a military bloody vehicle, not a lawn mower, you arse. And don't be so bloody silly, I haven't driven *anything* for over 50 years. Always had a *man* to do that. Ah! Good point. Alfred! Where's Alfred?"

The Colonel straightened up and threw his shoulders back in a commanding military pose (while still holding up his trouser-leg with one scrawny hand) before bellowing loudly.

"Alfred! Alfred! Where the sodding hell *is* the stupid man?!"

"Out here, sir! They took me prisoner, sir! Remember, sir?"

We all looked at the window as Alfred, the Colonel's ageing gardener/chauffeur and former army batman, shouted back in a high, trembling voice. Twigs cracked and dried leaves crunched underfoot as a short struggle broke out in the shrubbery, followed by thumping noises, an Alfred-sounding moan and more cheery Bulgarian gangster backchat:

"And you will all come out now or we shoot him dead...or maybe we shoot up his backside first and *then* in head, eh Mrs Lady Cherringtons? You throw out your gun now.....*please*! Ha, ha, ha!"

The Colonel frowned and looked from the window to the armoured car and back to the window, memories of recent events visibly seeping back through the whisky-befuddled haze that passed for thought-processes in his balding old head.

"Ah! Yes. Bugger. Forgot about that. Well can *anyone* around here *apart* from Alfred drive one of these?"

"I can, I think. Should be quite similar to Soviet armoured vehicle."

Katka was beside the armoured car, struggling to get a leg up onto its thick metal hide and reach a hatch, her free hand pressing into her lower back and her pregnant tummy bumping up against the grubby beige-green metal.

"They taught us in the Pioneers in Slovakia. Also how to shoot a Kalashnikov machine gun and how to stop NATO vehicles with petrol bombs. Why are you all *staring* like that? And can you please *help* me? I *am* having *babies* you know."

I couldn't help looking up at Katka admiringly as Lady C helped me push her bum up the steps of the armoured car.

"Don't look at my bottom like that!" she hissed over her shoulder.

"I didn't say anything. It's a lovely bottom. I never said it was big. Anyway, I *like* big bums. For God's sake, we've been over this before. You're pregnant. What did you expect? That it'd get *smaller*?

By the way, your Slovak Pioneers sound much more exciting than our Cubs and Scouts. All they ever taught me in the Scouts was how to tie knots and burn sausages on a stick. I wouldn't have been much use if anyone had invaded *us* during the Cold War. You're just so amazing. I really love you."

Katka smiled down as she swung open the hatch.

"That's nice. I love you too. But I was talking to the Colonel. He is always staring at my bottom."

After a brief struggle to get her tummy through the hatch, Katka disappeared inside. The Colonel, meanwhile, gazed innocently at the wooden rafters, his mouth pursed in a silent whistle. He never saw Lady C's handbag coming. It hit him on the back of the head with a loud thunk, making his eyes bulge out of their sockets and his thin, bony frame shudder.

"You really are disgusting, Oliver. And take your hand out of your pocket. I know you're interfering with yourself in there," snapped Lady C.

Who in their right mind runs for their life from their home, dragging a drink-befuddled old git of a husband behind them, firing a shotgun at pursuing armed Bulgarian gangsters and *still* finds time to grab their handbag from the hall hat-stand? Not that this was the weirdest part of today. Not by a long chalk.

Lady C heaved open a door at the rear of the armoured car and we pushed the Colonel inside before clambering after him. He sat huffily on one of the narrow benches, rubbing the back of his head as Lady C slammed the hatch shut and shouted through to Katka.

"Can you get it started, dear?"

There was a moment's silence, then the starter motor whined and the engine coughed and roared into life, rocking the ancient armoured car on its creaking, corroded suspension springs. I slapped a hand over my mouth and nose, trying desperately not to breathe in.

"Oh Christ! We're being gassed in here! What the hell *is* that? Do you have *chemical weapons* or something in here, Colonel? Oh dear God, open the door!"

The Colonel smiled maliciously as I gagged and retched,

while Lady C gave me an apologetic half-smile.

"I'm sorry. It's Oliver. He was eating pickled eggs again last night. I usually hide them from him. Could you try to hold it in, Oliver? It's a little close in here, and that was one of your more impressive ones."

I thought I was used to the Colonel's horrendous farts by now but in the circumstances, and combined with the stink of diesel fumes from the engine, the particularly sulphurous post-pickled-egg stench at such close quarters and in such a confined space had panicked me. Any further discussion of the Colonel's chronic flatulence problem became impossible as the armoured car lurched forward in a series of alarming and teeth-jarring jolts, bouncing creakily on its springs as it crashed through the wooden doors of the garage. Katka yelped excitedly from the driver's compartment.

"*Yes*! I remember how to do this. Wheeeee!"

But Katka's glee was short-lived. The armoured car crunched over the gravel of the long, curving driveway and swerved sharply to the right, heading straight for the garden gates across the carefully manicured front lawn. Then the engine back-fired twice and we ground slowly to a halt as it died. We could hear Katka swearing in Slovak as she hit the starter again and again, turning the engine over slower and slower as the battery went flat.

"I don't suppose there's ammunition for the machine gun is there, Colonel?" Katka yelled through the bulkhead.

"No, he used it all up on the pigeons in the vegetable garden three or four years ago," Lady C shouted back, frowning at her leaky husband, absent-mindedly scratching his crotch on the opposite bench-seat. "The poor things didn't make nearly as many holes in the cabbages and cauliflowers as *he* did!"

The Colonel grinned and chuckled to himself, silently miming wild bursts of machine gun fire and exploding brassicas like a gleeful child until his watery eye caught Lady C's disapproving stare.

Just then Albert, the ageing gardener/chauffeur, piped up from outside the vehicle, his voice sounding shaky and almost tearful.

"Lady Cherrington! One of 'em's kicked all the flowers off of your best clump of 'Bertram Anderson'. That big clump under the pink magnolia tree. Done it on purpose, he did."

At this point I'd like to say that Lady C is a lot stronger than you'd think. At just four-foot-ten and almost ninety years old, you could be forgiven for thinking it wouldn't take much to keep her in her seat. Well you'd be wrong. Which is why she managed to burst out of the rear door of the armoured car less than ten seconds later, shotgun to her shoulder, despite the best efforts of both myself and the Colonel to hold her back. Nursing my ribs where she'd cracked me with the gun butt, I clambered out after her. Behind us, the Colonel's shiny white head glistened briefly in the winter sunlight as he leaned out to pull the hatch closed again with a loud clang.

"Thanks Colonel!" I shouted. "Good of you to back us up!"

From inside the armoured car came what sounded like another fart followed by the Colonel's muffled voice.

"Always keep your command and control position secure. Important rule of combat. Report back to me at regular intervals; one bang on the door for all clear, two bangs for they're still here but trying to get in by making you pretend they've gone. Got that? They can't hear this, can they?"

"Oh do shut up Oliver," Lady C shouted over her shoulder, then stopped dead as, across the shotgun sight, she saw Alfred kneeling on the grass holding a bunch of battered snowdrop flowers in one hand. A Bulgarian gangster stood beside him with an automatic pistol pointed at Alfred's head.

"My 'Bertram Anderson'! They were looking so good this year! You utter sodding bastard! How could you? You unspeakable little shit! You despicable low-life, fuck-witted little turd of a man!"

For a moment the Bulgarian looked a bit un-nerved by this furious verbal onslaught and Lady C's unwavering aim, but quickly recovered when the second gangster crept around from the front of the armoured car, tiptoed up behind Lady C and snatched the shotgun from her. It must have hurt like hell when she kicked him in the shins, but I guess Bulgarian gangsters are used to much worse and he actually smiled as he hobbled over to join his friend, plucking a snowdrop flower from Alfred's hand and flicking it towards us. Lady C bent to pick it up and held the battered bloom like a wounded bird in the cupped palm of her hand as she let loose an even worse torrent of abuse at the gangsters that included at least half-a-dozen f-words and a c-word that I didn't think she even knew.

Eventually the gangster with the shotgun started to look bored and slowly raised the gun in Lady C's direction with one hand while poking at his ear wax with the little finger of the other. At this, even Lady C must have realized that, as lovely a snowdrop as 'Bertram Anderson' is, it's really not worth getting blasted at close-range with a twelve-bore over it, and she finally shut up.

I mean 'Bertram Anderson' *is* a stunning snowdrop, one of the biggest and best of the large-flowered hybrids, with a huge, shapely flower and a strong stem. It makes a very showy clump and is certainly one of *my* favourites. Maybe not one of the very rarest and most expensive snowdrop varieties around, but really very nice indeed, a real classic, and a favourite with most snowdrop growers and collectors.

Then again, you'd only pay about ten or twelve pounds for a bulb of 'Bertram Anderson', and you can buy it from a number of specialist growers, so it's not actually *that* costly or difficult to get hold of. Not compared to some of the most expensive snowdrops that might set you back forty or fifty pounds a bulb; or a couple of hundred pounds or more for a single bulb at auction if it's a *really* rare new one. And then there are those that are so rare you simply can't buy them, but have to swap with other specialist growers and collectors, if you have something rare and desirable enough to offer in exchange. And lovely, showy and garden-worthy as 'Bertram

Anderson' is, it's not one of those.

But it *is* a superb snowdrop. And that was one of the most impressive clumps of snowdrops in the garden, putting on a wonderful display that year with well over a hundred of the big glistening white flowers. I knew it had taken Lady C many years of careful lifting, dividing, replanting and general cosseting to produce such a fantastic show, only to have a clumsy Bulgarian gangster put the boot into it. Well, you would get a bit cross, wouldn't you? I certainly would.

In addition, Lady C always was especially sentimental about 'Bertram Anderson'. It was, after all, named in memory of a very special gardening and snowdrop-loving friend of hers, found and selected after his death as probably the best snowdrop seedling in his Cotswold garden, not far from Lady C's own garden at Westcombe Manor, on the front lawn of which we were now standing...oh, right! Sorry. The gangsters and the guns, and the pregnant wife in the armoured car with the stinky old Colonel, and the doddery old gardener about to be executed on the lawn?

Yes, well...as Lady C stopped ranting, everyone turned their attention to Alfred, kneeling on the grass at the gangsters' feet. Seemingly oblivious to the gun pointing at him, he'd carefully placed the handful of battered snowdrops on the lawn, taken a trowel from the pocket of his ancient waxed gardening jacket and, unnoticed by us all, had started digging out a stubborn, deep-rooted weed from the neat turf.

"Come out you little bleeder. Ah! Another one! Bleedin' dandelions."

Alfred tried to lunge forwards after the second weed but was held back by an incredulous gangster grabbing his frayed collar. The trowel flailed and stabbed uselessly in the air inches from the weed as the gangster tightened his grip on the grubby jacket, pressed the barrel of his gun to the side of Alfred's head and growled bad-temperedly.

"Colonel will come with us now or idiot man dies. Is final word. Now I am counting. One...two...uh...is to ten I count, then idiot man dies. One…two…three…five…"

The second gangster shook his head.

"No. Is four. One, two, three, *four*."

The first gangster glared at him.

"Is four that I said!"

"No, you say five. Is you that is idiot man."

"Shut fuck up, or I shoot *you*."

Clang! The hatch at the front of the armoured car fell open and Katka's head and her large pregnant boobs popped out. I mean they popped out of the hatch, not…*out*. Although in that dress, well, they were always threatening to burst the top button. I really liked that dress. Apparently the gangsters did too. One gave an admiring whistle and the other stroked his moustache as they both flashed macho gold-toothed grins at her. She struggled briefly in the tight opening then stopped and smiled broadly at Lady C and me.

"Yes! Contractions, they start! Must be because I bounce up and down so much inside tank. Please help with getting out. I go to hospital at last!"

Katka's English, normally very good these days, started to slip a little with the excitement of the imminent births (the last half-an-hour's gun-toting madness, by comparison, had barely seemed to fluster her). She struggled a little more, getting her arms out and pushing as she tried to wriggle through the hatch, then she stopped and frowned, her huge tummy still inside the armoured car.

"Except I am *stuck*! I cannot get free! Twins must have moved. I think maybe I am different shape now. I could get in here but now I cannot get out."

Katka's predicament seemed to have distracted Alfred from his frantic attempts at weeding and he let out a loud moan as he stared at the armoured car.

"No! Oh no! Oh dear, dear, dear! No! Dreadful!"

Katka stopped wriggling and looked down at him.

"It's all right, Alfred. Don't worry, I will be okay."

But Alfred pointed past her with a trembling finger at the

muddy tyre-tracks across the neat, close-cropped grass behind the armoured car.

"Oh dear! Them'll take some fixing! I'll 'ave to re-seed or get some turf in!"

Alfred tried to get to his feet but once again was restrained by the gangster with the pistol, who raised his gun as if to hit him. But before the blow could land, a very large, very shiny, very black, very menacing limousine with darkened windows rolled in through the garden gates, followed by a very shiny, very black, even more menacing four-wheel-drive with blacked-out windows.

Everyone froze and stared as the two cars came to a halt on the neatly-raked gravel and sat there, across the lawn from us, their engines purring and exhausts steaming in the winter chill. Slowly all the car doors swung open and one large full-length black coat after another stepped out onto the gravel, until seven big black coats and seven pairs of very dark sunglasses were facing us across the wet grass.

"Oh shit! Not *more* Bulgarians!" I heard myself groan.

The tall, broad-shouldered and black-coated men stared back at us and exchanged a few quick words amongst themselves. I could barely hear them, but Katka was watching them closely, her hand shading her narrowed eyes from the low sun, and listening carefully.

"No, not Bulgarian. Russian…I think," she corrected me.

Lady C squinted into the sun and she too shaded her eyes as she looked across the lawn.

"Are you sure, dear? Excuse me! We weren't expecting you! Are you here to see the snowdrops? I'm afraid we're not open to the public today! Sorry!"

The black coats simply looked at her in silence.

"Well, Russian or not, they're very *rude*!" she muttered.

With a wave to get their attention, Katka shouted across.

"Zdrastvuitye! Vy Ruskiye?"

All the black coats glanced at her, jammed in the hatch of the armoured car. One, a little shorter, less broad-shouldered and with hair less short-cropped than the rest, stepped forward and started walking towards us.

"Yes, that's right. We are the Russians!"

With a curt wave of his hand, he indicated for the rest to follow. Katka frowned and curled her lip disdainfully.

"I thought so. Then welcome to the party. I hope you bring your own guns."

Halfway across the lawn, the leading black coat stopped and gave his followers another quick hand-signal, in response to which they lined up across the grass on either side of him, reaching into their coats and pulling out very large and business-like hand-guns.

"But of course. It would be very rude to turn up at a party empty-handed."

He smiled at Lady C as he walked forward again, then looked down at Alfred, still kneeling with a gun to his head, and finally up at the two Bulgarians. Pointing to Alfred, he frowned at one of the gangsters and shook his head.

"But this is not the Colonel."

I spoke to Katka out of the corner of my mouth, too worried about all the guns to take my eyes off them.

"Oh bloody brilliant. It just gets better and bloody better. First a garden full of Bulgarian gangsters and now *Russian* gangsters too. Katka? Are you okay?"

Katka's eyes were closed and she grimaced before letting out a long, slow, shuddering breath and muttering angrily.

"No, not okay! I am stuck in this tank. I am having babies. *Two* of them. And it *hurts*. Contractions are…owwww!...very strong! Bože môj! Sprostý chlap! So no, definitely not okay."

Black coat leader looked around him, then back at the Bulgarian gangster holding his gun on Alfred.

"So where is the Colonel?"

The Bulgarian looked apprehensive then smiled nervously.

"We are not told you will come here. This is not agreed meeting place for exchange. But it is good. You can have Colonel right now. We have him. He is in there, but soon he must come out or we will shoot stupid garden man and Lady Cherringtons. You bring money? You can show us?"

The Russian turned to face Katka and the armoured car.

"The Colonel is in *that*?"

The Bulgarian nodded and waved his hand towards the armoured car as if inviting the Russian to inspect it and its contents. Slowly the Russian walked over and rapped on the armour plate with his knuckles.

"Colonel? You are in there? Hello? Colonel? You can hear me?"

Silence. Then, a little muffled through the thick metal, the unmistakable sound of the Colonel yet again nervously breaking wind.

Katka groaned with pain, then giggled.

"Well, I am stuck having twins in bloody tank, but at least there is plenty of *gas*!"

The Russian looked up at her, puzzled. Then his stony face broke into a smile and he started to laugh.

The Slovak 'Maybe'

It was about fifteen months before all this Bulgarian and Russian gangster stuff that I saw Katka for the first time, towards the end of October 2006, at the Frankfurt Book Fair. On the Saturday of the book fair week I was supposed to take over for a couple of hours from my UK publisher's marketing director, who was manning a stand in the British and American hall at the sprawling concrete-and-steel Frankfurt Messe exhibition centre. But, as often happened, I'd overslept and was very late getting in.

Katka and another, older woman were just inside the stand, looking at a book Katka was holding. They were turning the pages and smiling but not laughing, which was a bit disappointing since it was one of *my* cartoon books, and one of the funnier ones at that. The long, straight, glossy dark hair halfway down her back was the first thing I noticed as I walked up behind Katka - okay, that and a very nice bum - then those amazing almond-shaped green-brown eyes that glanced up as I reached the stand and quickly flicked back to the book. A little *too* quickly for my liking. And I still wasn't hearing any laughter.

James, the marketing director, was pacing up and down between the shelves of books and catalogues, silently fuming.

"Where the sodding hell have you been? You were supposed to be here at ten so I could walk the halls. I'm gasping for a smoke. You know I don't like leaving the stand unattended."

"Sorry, I was out with the guys from that Australian book distribution company that we met on the hotel-boat. It was nearly two by the time I got to bed."

But James wasn't listening. Turning on his heel, he started marching towards a side-door, irritably patting the pockets of his pinstripe suit for cigarettes and lighter. As I yawned loudly behind him, he stopped dead and spun around in the middle of the aisle.

"Stop *yawning!*" he hissed angrily. "How do you think it looks to clients if they see you yawning on the stand? I've told you before, don't do *anything* that makes it look like you're *bored* when you're on *my bloody stand.*"

Which was a bit rich, since I was actually doing him a favour. I wasn't being paid to sit on a chair at his stand. I was mostly at the book fair to meet my German publishers, with whom I deal directly, and to do some book signings for them. *James* was supposed to be looking after the stand, as he did each year. And, as I did every time I went to the book fair, I was helping him out a little.

"I suppose having a *wank* would be out of the question then?"

James froze. He'd turned to stalk off again, but now his pinstriped back was rigid. He swivelled slowly back to face

19

me, his face purple with suppressed rage.

"*What* did you say?!"

It was an open goal, and I just couldn't resist it.

"I said, I suppose having a wa…"

James looked like he was going to explode.

"Shut up! Shut *up*! Don't say it *again*!"

He glanced at the neighbouring stands to see if anyone had overheard, then hurried out through the hall doors, pulling a broken cigarette from the crushed packet in his clenched fist.

That's when I realized that Katka and her friend were still standing there. They replaced my book on the shelf and left, glancing back over their shoulders and whispering to each other. Across the aisle, the woman on the religious publications stand was sipping her coffee and trying desperately not to catch my eye.

The second time I saw Katka was that afternoon, when I'd finished a book signing at my German publishers' stand in another hall a long way from the British one.

I just happened to be taking a look around the Eastern European hall on the way back when…well, yes, I think maybe James *had* mentioned, when he returned in a better mood from walking the halls and visiting various bars along the way, that he'd seen the same two women who were at his stand that morning. They were apparently in charge of a Czech publisher's stand and were offering visitors small cups of very strong coffee and small glasses of even stronger plum brandy, both of which James had felt obliged to sample a couple of times during his circuit of the hall.

Anyway, there Katka was, surrounded by glossy coffee-table books about Czech castles, countryside and flowers, stirring a pot of coffee and humming to herself.

"Hello! I saw you reading one of my cartoon books at my publisher's stand this morning in the British and American hall. I hope you liked it."

She looked up and gave me a brief, slightly embarrassed smile.

"Yes, I remember. This was your book? Was very funny."

Her English wasn't quite as good then as it is now, and her accent was stronger and very sexy in a breathy sort of way.

"What a coincidence bumping into you again in this huge place! So, you're Czech?"

"I am Slovak," she sighed and started to explain patiently, like she'd done it many times before. "From Slovakia, to east of Czech Republic. We…"

"Used to be part of Czechoslovakia, but you split up in ninety-two or ninety-three, right? A few years ago most English people would probably have mixed you up with Slovenia, or had no idea at all. But we do know a *bit* more about Eastern Europe now. Well, some of us do. Anyway, now I can practice my Slovak. I speak a little. Actually, not that much. Just a few words, from when I was in Bratislava a few years ago…dobry den. Is that right?"

I grinned, pleased that I'd managed to dredge up a couple of words. I was never very good with languages.

Katka sighed again.

"That is 'good day' in *Czech*."

"No, it's Slovak. I learned it in Bratislava. From a…um…Slovak girl that I met."

She stared at me. This wasn't going as well as I'd hoped. Why did I have to say it was a Slovak *girl*? Showing off? Shit! I *was* showing off, and she knew it. I could see it in her eyes, in the disdainful curl of her lip, and in the tapping of her fingers on her folded arms.

"No, it is *Czech*. We say dobrý deň in Slovakia, but Czechs say dobrý den."

"Okay…but that's the *same*. I mean you just said the same thing twice. Anyway, aren't Czech and Slovak virtually the same language?"

"No. Similar, but *not* same. We say dobrý deň. They say dobrý den."

"But you did it again. You just said exactly the same thing twice. You said 'dobry den' and then you said 'dobry den'

21

again. Are you making fun of me? Or is this a Slovak joke? Sorry, but I don't get it."

Katka gave me a slightly annoyed, vaguely pitying look that I was to come to know well over the months that followed, then sighed yet again. It had been a lovely sigh the first time; very light and charming, even sexy. But now it was starting to get on my nerves.

"Please listen to difference. Dobrý den...dobrý deň! Czech 'den' has *hard* 'd' and *hard* 'n'. Slovak has *soft* 'd' and *soft* 'n'. Did your Slovak girlfriend not teach you this?"

"What's a soft 'd' and a soft 'n'? A 'd' is a 'd' and an 'n' is an 'n', isn't it?"

I grinned. She had to be pulling my leg. And there was that sigh again.

"In Slovak, we have hard conso...consonants? This is right word? Those sound same as English consonants. But we also have *soft* consonants. Sound...*softer*. Please listen to difference *carefully*..."

I listened carefully, nodded slowly and thoughtfully...then shook my head.

"No. Sorry. Can you do it again?"

The sigh was *really* starting to bug me now, but after another two or three attempts, with Katka heavily emphasising the - to an English ear - very slight differences, I was starting to hear it; the soft 'd' halfway between an English 'd' and an English 'j', and the soft 'n' more like a 'ny' than a normal 'n'.

"Now *you* say it.....no! That is still Czech! Make 'd' and 'n' softer."

"Look, I've got an idea! Why don't I buy you dinner tonight, and you can teach me some more about soft and hard consonants?"

Katka frowned and shook her head.

"I have better idea. You go away and you practice. If you come back and say it right, then perhaps...*perhaps* we talk about dinner."

She turned away and started rearranging the books on a

table with her back to me, and it didn't look like she was going to turn around again until I'd gone.

I was at the end of the aisle, heading for the hall doors when Katka's older friend from that morning clutched at my arm, out of breath and pink in the cheeks, struggling to catch up in a tight skirt and very high heels.

"Excuse me, please! Hello! My name is Elena. I am friend of Katarina."

I took her outstretched hand.

"I'm sorry? Katarina? Oh, on the stand back there? Katarina? Yes, of course. You were in the British hall with her this morning. I didn't know her name. Nice to meet you."

"Please, you like coffee?"

She pointed to a small coffee bar in the corner of the hall.

"I may speak to you about Katarina, yes? I know her well. I am Slovak also. We are only Slovaks in our office in Praha...in Prague. All others are Czech, so we are *special* friends, you understand."

Elena blew gently on her espresso to cool it and looked around as if checking we weren't being watched. Then she shook her bright red dyed hair and leaned in close as I tried very hard not to look down her - really very impressive - cleavage.

"Katka is...sorry, Katka is small name for Katarina, short name, you know this?"

I shook my head.

"So, Katka is...hmmm...sometimes *difficult*. Very special person, very lovely person, very nice after you are knowing her better, really, really, very special girl. I love her very much, like mother almost. But she is...*difficult* sometimes."

Elena shrugged as if to suggest it was really quite a minor drawback in the grand scheme of things.

"I hear you are talking with Katka. I am in next stand looking at book of...oh, does not matter...I hear you and Katka talk."

She frowned and waved an admonishing finger in my face.

"It was not good. It was really quite bad. But she likes you. Do not smile! I *think* she likes you. Quite a lot before, but perhaps now not so much after all of that rubbishness! She thinks you have nice hands. You are artist, perhaps?"

"Cartoonist. I draw cartoons."

Elena nodded and sipped her coffee.

"Mmmm. She thinks also you are very funny."

It was my turn to shrug.

"She said she thought my book was funny, but you weren't laughing when you were reading it, so I guess she can't think I'm all *that* hilarious."

"Ah, it was *your* book with cartoons we look at? Yes, we thought this was funny. But no, I mean after we leave your stand in British Hall, we look for word 'wank' in English dictionary. When we find it, first Katka screams then she laughs. She thinks it is very rude what you say to your friend but also very funny. I am different generation. For me, I think it is mostly rude and just little bit funny. But your friend he was being rude to you, so it is okay you make fun out of him, I think. It is fair."

Elena reached into her shoulder-bag, brought out a half-litre bottle with a brightly coloured label and poured a shot of clear liquid into her coffee before reaching across to my cup.

"Slivovica! It is very good plum brandy, the best make. For guests to our stand. You were guest at our stand, but did not drink, so I bring this for you. No? Okay. So, Katka. You must understand, she is really not *easy* girl…"

I could feel my cheeks starting to burn.

"No, no, of course not! I never thought she was *easy*! I wasn't trying to…"

Elena frowned.

"…not *easy* girl to make *happy*. She likes you, but you have lot of work to do. You want to take her to dinner? I will help you."

She swallowed a mouthful of the coffee and plum brandy then took a pad and pencil from her bag.

"First we practice soft consonants for 'dobrý deň' then I teach you little more Slovak to help make better impression. How much do you know of Slovak language from before in Blava? From being in Bratislava?"

"In Blava? Oh, right. Bratislava. You call it Blava? I hadn't heard that."

Elena tapped her teeth with her pencil and nodded.

"Sometimes, yes. Is short name. How much Slovak? How many words?"

"Well, apart from dobry den…how was that?"

Elena nodded again.

"A little better. But not much. Actually, still quite bad. How many Slovak words?"

"Um, well…oh, yes…please is prosim, isn't it? And thank you…that's um…no, sorry, I've forgotten. Pivo! Yes! Pivo is beer."

Elena was resting her elbow on the coffee bar and her head on her hand, watching me with a mixture of disbelief and incredulity.

"How long you were in Blava?"

"About three or four weeks. Why?"

"And during complete whole month in Blava, *with Slovak girl*, you learn 'good-day' and 'beer please'? That is *all*?"

She put a lot of emphasis on 'with Slovak girl' and shot me a look, not dissimilar to the one Katarina had given me.

"Well, she did most of the talking for me. She spoke very good English."

"Yes. It is very good that everyone speaks English so well, I think, or you English would have only yourselves to talk to on holidays. Okay. First the soft 'd' and soft 'n' then we work at some vocabulary. Perhaps we think of polite and nice words for you to say to Katka after 'dobrý deň', because you cannot ask her for beer. She is not waitress, and we have only slivovica on our stand, no beer."

Twenty minutes later we had the soft consonants in 'dobrý deň' pretty much nailed. Even Elena seemed pleased with my efforts. Or maybe it was the second slug of slivovica she'd despairingly helped herself to after one of my less successful attempts.

"So, now I will write down more very useful Slovak words. I will also write for you how these *sound* in *English* to make it easy for you to learn to speak them. You will not need to write them…no, I am sure Katka will not ask you to *write* Slovak for her…no, certainly not. Well, I hope at least. With Katka, you are never quite sure! First, 'ako sa máš?'. This is 'how are you?'. 'Prepáčte'. This is 'excuse me'. Say this first, then 'ako sa máš?' Okay? Hmmm. This is enough for now. Enough to show you properly learn some Slovak in Blava. Or to make Katka *believe* this."

The slivovica was really starting to take effect now as Elena gave me a huge lopsided smile and, with a dreamy look on her face and her voice slurring slightly, added:

"Oh, and also, perhaps…'Máš krásne oči' is 'you have beautiful eyes.' I write this for you also, but mention beautiful eyes only if she is seeming to like you very much. Perhaps after dinner and when she has drunk some wine. Men are not good at this, I know, but please, please, *please* try to wait for best time…not straight as soon as you sit at table. Okay?"

She reached across and squeezed my knee with a conspiratorial smile.

"So, good luck! You will need it. Perhaps not so much with those nice blue eyes you have, but you will certainly need *some* luck…every man does with Katka!"

I grinned back at Elena as she slid the piece of paper towards me.

"So what's Slovak for 'I love you'?"

Elena's smile instantly turned to a frown.

"What? No! Too soon! Silly boy! You will scare her away! Bože! Men are as stupid from England as from Slovakia!"

"Oh, so I can say she has beautiful eyes, but not that I love her?"

Elena's frown deepened.

"Yes, because Katarina *does* have beautiful eyes. But you do *not* love her yet! You do not *know* her! She is not silly little girl you get to your bed with drinks and 'I love you'. She is educated woman, with master's degree from university in Blava, who speaks *five languages*. She is very clever woman, not stupid tart from Ukraine!"

"Sorry, no, look…I was just joking. I'm not really that daft. It was just a joke. I'm the funny guy, remember? Cartoonist? That's what I do…I do funny."

"No, it is not funny. Last night in hotel bar, Italian guy gets drunk and asks Katka to go to bedroom. He says 'I love you' and he touches her zadok…her bottom. Katka makes him wear his beer. So no, is not funny. Do not make such big mistake. Do not be masturbator. Katka will not like you if you are masturbator like Italian guy."

A woman further along the bar almost choked on her coffee then stared at us.

"I think you mean 'wanker', Elena."

She swung her bag over her shoulder and slid, a little unsteadily, off her stool.

"Yes, wanker. We also find word 'wanker' in dictionary. This means 'person who masturbates' and is also slang word for 'very stupid man' yes? You cannot say 'masturbator' in same way as 'wanker' to mean 'stupid man'? It is not less rude to use more formal word? No? Okay, this is not important. Most important is to remember this…no 'I love you', and no touching zadok. German beer is very cold! Oh…wait…"

Elena turned and tottered back to the bar on her high heels, took my crib sheet of Slovak words and phrases, and scribbled one last sentence.

"One more: 'Prepáčte, som sprostý Angličan'. There, that is to say when you mess up things, say wrong Slovak words, do or say stupid things men always do and say. Okay?"

With a cheery wave and a tug at her bra-straps, she was off. And after an hour practicing my new Slovak vocabulary on a very uncomfortable modern bench outside in the pale autumn sunshine, I reckoned I was ready.

Elena disappeared into a little cubby-hole at the back of their stand as soon as she saw me arrive, so it was just me and Katka. At first Katka ignored me, busying herself with some brochures and glancing towards the curtains that Elena had disappeared through, as though willing Elena to reappear and deal with me. But she had to look up when I launched into my prepared Slovak speech.

"Prepáčte, prosím. Dobrý deň. Ako sa máš, Katarina?"

For a moment her expression was distant and business-like, but then she smiled.

"This is better. Your Slovak actually sounds quite good. You even make soft 'd' and soft 'n' quite well…for foreigner. You speak with terrible foreign accent, but yes quite good. And you remember more Slovak words. Excellent."

The curtain at the rear of the stand twitched and Elena's fist stuck out, thumb up. I couldn't help grinning, and unfortunately Katka followed my look. Elena's thumbs-up disappeared back behind the curtains, but Katka had already seen it and her smile disappeared too.

"Elena! You will please come out here! Now!"

As Elena re-emerged, looking a little sheepish, Katka turned back to face me.

"May I look in pockets?"

Before I could answer, Katka's hand dived into one jacket pocket after another, finally pulling out the evidence she was looking for. Unfolding the sheet of paper and reading it, she rounded on Elena.

"So, your old matchmaking tricks again? Elena, how many times do I say, please do not do this, giving to men papers with Slovak chatter-up words? You remember what yesterday when you try to put me together with Italian man? It is never ending well, Elena, so please stop doing this."

It looked like I'd really dropped Elena in it, though she didn't seem that bothered, folding her arms, rolling her eyes at the ceiling and sucking her teeth throughout Katka's ticking-off. Still, I felt I should try to put things right.

"I'm sorry, Katarina. It's my fault. I saw Elena at the coffee bar and I asked her to help me with some Slovak words to say to you. I just wanted to talk to you again."

Katka turned back to me and held out the paper.

"No, *I* should be sorry. I apologise. I should not look in pockets. Excuse me, please."

She started to walk away but I reached out and touched her shoulder.

"No, wait. It really *is* all my fault...prepáčte, som sprostý Angličan."

Katka stopped and turned back again. Her mouth was still serious, but her eyes seemed to be smiling, and then she was laughing.

"No, no you are not. Really you are not. It is nice you try to be blamed for Elena's meddlings, but I do not think you are stupid Englishman."

Elena was putting on a coat and reaching for her bag. I tried to give her a look that said "So, 'som sprostý Angličan' means 'I'm a stupid Englishman'? Thanks for that!" She shrugged and grinned back, a little tipsily - I guessed she'd been at the bottle of slivovica again. This seemed like a good moment, so...

"Listen, Katarina. Can I call you Katka?"

She nodded.

"I'd really like to buy you dinner. Or maybe have a drink, go to the Jazzkeller or something? Elena, why don't you come too? I don't think James has a meeting tonight. That's my colleague from our stand. James *loves* the Jazzkeller, and there's a good band on tonight."

Elena shook her head.

"No. Thank you, I have other invitation tonight. You both have nice time, yes? Was nice to meet you!"

Reaching around Katka to offer her hand, Elena was off up the aisle in a cloud of strong perfume and slivovica fumes, a little unsteady on her heels as she waved goodbye, her bag clinking as she walked. Katka watched her go with a wry smile.

"I think I must count our slivovica bottles again."

She started to re-arrange books and brochures, tidying the stall ready for the end of the day.

"So, Katka, if Elena's got a date does that mean you're on your own tonight? If you're not doing anything, how about dinner? I could still ask James to join us. You'd like him. He's a bit stuffy and old school tie, and tells terrible jokes, but he's okay when you get to know him."

Katka was watching me out of the corner of her eye as she dusted a low table with a cloth.

"No, I have no plans for tonight. It is just Elena I am with in Frankfurt, no other people from our company, so…maybe."

"What? You'd like to have dinner?"

Katka nodded.

"Mmm, maybe."

She continued tidying and polishing as I followed her around the stand.

"We could have dinner, then go and listen to some jazz? You, me and James. Does that sound okay?"

"Maybe."

Katka straighten up from her cleaning, smiled at me and headed for the curtains at the rear. I took a deep breath and let it out slowly before trying again.

"So, do you want to go?"

I raised my voice as Katka disappeared behind the curtains, and she raised hers back. I was trying not to make mine a 'getting-a-bit-annoyed' kind of raised voice.

"Maybe!"

That's when I got annoyed and left. Halfway up the aisle I turned to go back, thought better of it, turned again and finally found myself back at the stand feeling like a complete idiot. Which I assumed was how Katka wanted me to feel. How had Elena described her? '*Sometimes difficult*'? Bloody right! She was giving me the brush-off and trying to make me look like a desperate, needy prat while she was at it. So why was I back here for more? I turned to walk away again.

"Okay, now I am ready. Where do you go? You do not wait for me?"

Katka had appeared through the curtains, her coat over her arm. I stopped and stared.

"What? Sorry, you *do* want to have dinner then?"

"Maybe."

This time I was really going. I was almost at the end of the aisle and heading for the hall doors when Katka caught up and tugged at the sleeve of my jacket.

"Do you always walk very fast? It is difficult to stay up with you."

"What? I'm sorry, but what do you *want*? Don't you think you've taken the mickey enough for one day? With your soft 'd' and soft 'n', 'come back when you can say it right', and 'maybe, maybe, maybe'?"

Katka stopped and stared at me, smiling a little awkwardly.

"Look, I'm sorry I thought you were Czech, but you were on a Czech publisher's stand. It said it right there on the front of the stand…Prague, Czech Republic. It's a mistake *anyone* could have made. I just wanted to talk to you, ask you out for dinner. But this has turned into the most tortuous, mind-bending, confusing and humiliating encounter I've ever had with a woman. And I've had a few odd ones over the years. Admittedly that's mostly been my fault, but in this case I'm prepared to share the blame. If you didn't want to have dinner with me, why not just *say* so?! A simple 'get lost' would have done the trick…it always has in the past."

Katka's smile had faded away, to be replaced by a puzzled frown.

"But I *do* want to have dinner with you. I *said* yes. And what is 'taking mickey'?"

I can honestly say I'd never, ever been aware of my mouth actually dropping open until that moment. I mean, mouths don't, do they? Not unless you're in a cartoon or something.

But I swear mine did right then. I just looked blankly at Katka for a good four or five seconds as the power of speech slowly seeped back.

"*When* did you say yes? I never heard you say yes. You just kept saying *maybe*."

"Maybe *means* yes."

"No it doesn't! Maybe means maybe. It means perhaps. It means I haven't made my mind up, I'll let you know, I don't want to say yes but I'm too polite to say no. It does *not* mean *yes*!"

"I am sorry. I always think 'maybe' is same as 'yes', not same as 'perhaps'. In Slovak 'možno' is 'perhaps'. But 'môže byt' is 'maybe'. This means what you ask *may be*, is informal way to say 'yes, it *may* be'…is really quite *definite*…just like to say 'yes', but more like 'yes, it *will* be'. You understand? A way you would say 'yes' to a friend, not very formal.

But, thank you. Knowing this mistake is making me understand some problems I have before with some English people, and big problems with some English boys I meet in Praha. Hmmm. Yes, this is explaining a lot. Thank you. So, you will give me name and address for restaurant for tonight, yes? And what time we are to meet?"

She took a small notepad and pen from her coat pocket and held them out to me, smiling again now.

"Okay. So you meant 'yes' every time you were saying 'maybe'? See, I thought you were saying…okay, never mind. The restaurant? Yes, um, why don't I pick you up in a taxi? What's the name of your hotel?"

Katka shook her head cheerfully and pushed the notepad at me.

"No, I like to walk. In foreign city it is shame to sit in taxi when you can walk and see things properly, hear, smell, feel everything properly instead of looking through taxi window. We will meet at restaurant. It will be *long* walk I hope, yes?"

I took the pad and pen and started writing.

"Yes, it's quite a long way from the centre, but just about

walkable I suppose. Depends where your hotel is. It's not a fancy touristy place, just a small family-run neighbourhood Italian restaurant that James and I go to a lot when we're here, but very good food. Very authentic. Do you have a map? I'll give you my mobile number in case you get lost."

Katka took the pad and glanced at the address.

"I am never getting lost. Even in deep forest in Slovakia I am never lost. It is a good ability. When we train with Slovak Pioneers I was always one to have trust of map-reading, in forest and on mountain, and I never make my Pioneers group get lost. Also I was very good at shooting Kalashnikov machine gun. I win regional Pioneers shooting prize in grammar school."

"A Kalashnikov? An AK47? Really?! How...um...*old* were you?"

"Fourteen, perhaps fifteen years. Was during communist regime. What time shall I be at restaurant?"

"Fourteen?! Bloody hell! Well, is eight o'clock okay? That'll give us time to go on to the Jazzkeller later if you like. I'll phone and book a table, and I'll see if James wants to go too."

Katka took back the pad, held out her hand to shake mine then turned to walk off.

"Oh, Katka! Sorry, I never told you my name! It's..."

"It is okay, I know your name."

She reached into her inside pocket and pulled out a book.

"It is on your book. Elena went back and got copy for me from your stand, probably when you were busy learning Slovak soft consonants and new Slovak words."

"Really? James *never* gives out free samples."

"Elena is very persuasive woman."

Katka grinned and shouted over her shoulder as she disappeared into the crowd heading for the front of the Messe building and the main doors.

"I think it is perhaps your friend James who she meets tonight. So we will be on our own together. It will be nicer."

"Right, yes much nicer! Okay. See you at the restaurant then? At eight, yes?"

"Maybe!"

Dumplings, Hapchees and Lost Keys

Thanks to a hotel receptionist forgetting to order the taxi I'd asked for, I was half-an-hour late getting to the restaurant. I'd planned to arrive early and be at the table waiting for Katka, relaxed, cool and sophisticated, browsing the menu and chatting impressively to the waiters in what little Italian I knew I could muster. Instead I hurtled through the door, hot, flustered and half expecting to find she'd been and gone even though I'd phoned ahead and left a message. I was kicking myself for not exchanging mobile numbers with Katka and quite prepared to find I'd blown the whole thing.

But there she was, looking relaxed, cool and *very* sophisticated in a little black dress with her hair up, chatting with the proprietor's wife in what was obviously pretty fluent Italian and with just about every waiter in the place hovering around her table, topping up her water and trying to look down the front of her low-cut dress. She smiled and waved aside my breathless apology.

"It is okay. I have been talking to waiters and restaurant owners, practising my Italian. Also answering questions in quiz for 'relationship compatibility' in magazine."

Katka pushed a battered old copy of an English women's magazine across the table.

"I find it in hotel. Very interesting questions-quiz...*Are You And Your Man Made For Each Other*? I answered for both of us. I have very good mark. You have not so good mark. In fact, you perform quite badly in this quiz. It seems we are not very compatible at all."

"What? But you can't answer *for* me! You don't even know me. What did you put?"

Katka slid her notepad across the table as well, so I could compare her answers with the magazine questions.

"Well *that's* not right for a start! I'd *never* say that. And I'd never do *that*, not in a million years. Can I have your pen? Thanks. *You'd* do *that*? Really? That's interesting. Very interesting. On a first date? No, of course not. I see. That's the answer to the next question. Oh, no, no, no! I don't think *that*. Why would you think I would? I'd have to be really *horrible* to think that. But of course I'd do *that*, and I agree with *this*..."

By the end of our starters we'd managed to work our way through my 'answers', as anticipated by Katka, and put most of them right, although Katka insisted on over-ruling me on a few where she felt she 'instinctively' knew better than me what my answers really *should* be, despite what I might think.

Turned out Katka had got it wrong. Hah! We *were* quite compatible after all. Not cuddly-bunny, kissy-wissy, Mr and Mrs Perfect compatible, but not bad. According to the author of the quiz, we'd at least make it through the honeymoon and quite possibly the first couple of years without necessarily maiming or emotionally scarring each other excessively. Katka said women usually find it very difficult to get men to do a questionnaire like that with them, and I can't say I'm surprised. Most of the questions were pretty stupid, and what do the people who write magazine quizzes know anyway?

Now Katka was tucking into a plate of gnocchi with the chef's special tomato sauce of the day and shavings of Pecorino cheese, while I was eating my favourite wafer-thin fried liver with Parmesan potatoes but with a lot less enthusiasm than usual; in fact trying to pretend I wasn't really enjoying it at all.

Katka pointed at my meat with her fork.

"It is good?"

"Sorry, Katka. If I'd known you were a vegetarian I wouldn't have ordered this."

She shook her head and waved her fork in an "eat up" gesture.

"It is okay. I eat meat when I was child before I decided to be vegetarian. And I come from Slovakia where almost every meal is meat and dumplings, meat and potatoes, almost never with vegetables, so it is not problem for me."

She scooped another forkful of potato dumplings into her mouth.

"And every year when I was child at home in village we keep and feed our own pig, so after pig-killing each year, my mother and father would make sausages for smoking, which I loved in those days. Only kind I really did not like were special sausages made with rice and pig's blood. They were my father's favourite for eating at pig-killing feast, but not favourite to me. Very delicious sausage, I am told, and great delicacy, but after seeing our pig's throat cut with knife and so much blood pouring from neck into bucket I did not like to eat them. You are not hungry?"

I put down my knife and fork and pushed my plate away.

"Not any more, no. I know you said you don't mind, but I always feel uncomfortable eating meat in front of a vegetarian, even when they say it really doesn't bother them. I worry I might…y'know…*put them off their meal*."

I glanced at the liver going cold on my plate, then at Katka's dumplings. No, I mean her gnocchi! Not that her…y'know, with that low-cut dress…weren't very nice too, as the waiters were very much aware (we were getting the most attentive service I'd ever experienced in a restaurant).

"I once went out with a woman who was vegan and I didn't eat meat, cheese, anything to do with animals for six months, not when I was eating with her anyway. She even bought me a membership for a vegan society that she belonged to. I used to get newsletters every month. I just didn't like to say. But your gnocchi are okay? They make them fresh of course, not from a packet. They're really light and fluffy, aren't they? Mmmm. I should have had them instead of the liver."

I was half hoping Katka would offer me a forkful, especially as I hadn't been able to finish my own main course. They really were very good, and the sauce was incredible; James and I had it the first night of the book fair. But Katka didn't take the hint - or chose not to notice it - continuing instead to shovel the dumplings into her own mouth.

"Yes, they are very nice. I must go to kitchen and tell them. Almost as good as my father's knedle. If you like potato dumplings, you must try my father's. His restaurant in Tatra Mountains is famous for traditional Slovak dishes, and his potato dumplings are my favourite food since I was little child. Every time I go home to Slovakia, Bryndzové halušky is first thing I ask for in restaurants and in my mother and father's kitchen. It is small potato dumplings with Bryndza sheeps-cheese sauce. You did not eat it when you were in Blava? It is Slovak national dish."

"No, I don't think so. I was with a bunch of Slovak students most of the time. They were more into junk food, plus they were partying a lot because they'd just finished their final exams, so there was generally more booze than food. I'd just split up with my girlfriend in England. We'd been living together for seven years and were supposed to be getting married that year, but she met someone else and…well, I was in the mood for a party, and I went to a lot of them that summer in Bratislava. Um, sorry, that was probably a bit more information than you needed. You just wanted to know if I'd eaten Slovak dumplings, didn't you?"

Katka leaned her elbow on the table and rested her chin in her hand, lifting her glass and sipping some wine.

"So, how did you come to Blava? To Bratislava? It was for holiday?"

"I was in Germany on business, trying to interest a German publisher in licensing my first couple of cartoon books. I was publishing and selling them myself in England before I got a big English publisher to take them on. I'd set up my own small publishing business working from my spare bedroom.

Anyway, I was staying with some German friends who I'd met at a snowdrop-growers gala in England and who knew some people in the publishing business in Germany. I know a lot of people who grow snowdrops. You know what snowdrops are? Galanthus? In German they're called…"

"Yes, of course I know galanthus. We have these in Slovakia and Czech Republic, and I studied botany at Commenius University in Bratislava as part of Master's Degree for Environmental Sciences.

You say in 'compatibility quiz' you are interested in gardens. And you like galanthus? Snowdrops? Yes? I also like very much. My grandmother has many in her plum orchard, and they grow at some places in forest behind our village. My sister and I like to pick them when we are children. In Slovakia they are called 'snežienky'. It means something like 'little snow women', because galanthus flowers look like little women dancing in white dresses. It is nice idea, I think. So, you grow snowdrops in your garden in England?"

"Yes. I collect them, actually. I've got somewhere between three and four hundred different named ones so far, and lots of new seedlings that I've raised and selected. Some of them are special and unusual forms of wild snowdrops, but most are garden varieties and hybrids. I *know*…it sounds a bit bonkers, having a *snowdrop collection*; a bit 'mad English eccentric'. You can laugh if you like. I won't mind."

I have to admit I didn't really expect Katka to *actually* laugh. But she did. Pretty loudly too. Not a little behind-her-hand snigger but loud enough to make people at nearby tables stop eating and stare. Usually when I go on about snowdrops, people grin and look at me like I'm a bit odd. Sometimes, if they're keen gardeners, they get interested and ask questions, or they might grow a few different snowdrops themselves and we get a discussion going. What they don't, as a general rule, do is laugh out loud like bloody hyenas. Or make loud bloody snorting noises with their noses. Not usually.

"You *collect* snežienky? *Snowdrops*? Not football

magazines or mats for beer glasses? Or stamps, coins, little models of cars? These I know men like to collect. It is little bit crazy, I always think, this madness of men for collecting things. But to collect snežienky is *really* quite crazy! *Four hundred different snowdrops*!? This is not possible! There are only few species, not hundreds, and all look almost same. You really *are* crazy Englishman! Or perhaps you make fun of me?"

"No, it *is* possible. And I don't have nearly as many varieties as *some* people. A few of the really keen collectors I know have nearly *twice* as many as me. Someone told me recently that there are over one thousand five hundred different named snowdrops now, and more every year."

Katka shook her head and smiled in disbelief.

"I cannot believe this! *How* they are all different? All are white, yes? Or do you have different colour snežienky in England? Would be horrible, I think! Please tell me you do not make garden snowdrops with red and blue flowers! It would be terrible! Sneiženky should be white. It is their colour. If they are not white, they will not be *snow*drops! Not little snow-white dancing women! Please tell me you do not do this to them!"

Katka was starting to look and sound genuinely worried and upset, so I was quick to reassure her that English gardeners *weren't* breeding multi-coloured snowdrops; that she didn't have to worry about anyone raising red or blue seedlings. The gene pool in galanthus doesn't run to anything more than the usual white flowers with green - or sometimes yellow - petal markings. You could breed them forever and probably all you'd ever get in the way of colour variation is slightly whiter or creamier petals, darker or paler green marks and brighter or less bright yellow marks.

What attracts and interests collectors is the almost infinite variety of often quite small differences between flowers. They come in a wide range of slightly different shapes and forms, with lots of variations in the green and yellow markings on the inner petals, and sometimes on the outer petals too. All these tiny details are fascinating to a keen snowdrop grower, just as Victorian fern collectors were enthralled by the minute variations in the fronds of the hundreds of different varieties of ferns that they grew.

It's especially interesting to study the different snowdrop varieties close up. Some have double flowers, with dozens of petals instead of the usual six, and there are tiny ones with miniature flowers that are good in pots or trough gardens, while others are tall and large-flowered, really good garden plants that anyone would enjoy having in their beds and borders.

"I'm not boring you, am I, Katka? Just say if I am and I'll shut up."

Katka stopped yawning, smiled politely and shook her head.

"Okay. If you're quite sure? The all-green snowdrops are amongst the rarest and most sought-after, and one of my seed-raising programmes is aimed at breeding new varieties of those, bigger and better…"

At this, Katka started to look concerned again.

"You said you were not making snowdrops with coloured flowers except white with some marks, and now…"

"Yes, I know. I forgot about the virescent ones, but they're perfectly natural. The very first ones were found amongst wild snowdrops, and they're not really *completely* green. Usually the outer petals are *almost* completely green, with some white around the edges, and generally the same on the inside petals. It might sound horrible, but they're actually very attractive. And expensive, too. Keen galanthophiles will pay a small fortune for the ones with the most green and the darkest green on the petals."

I noticed that Katka's eyes had started to glaze over, the way people's eyes do sometimes when I start going on about snowdrops, but she snapped right back at the mention of galanthophiles.

"Snowdrop collectors call themselves 'galanthophiles'?"

"Yes, sometimes."

"So what you do, it is galanthophilia, yes? You do galanthophilia in garden?"

Katka sniggered behind her hand.

"I suppose so."

"I am sorry. Ha, ha! But this sounds little bit like you do rude things with *dead* snowdrops in garden! Ha, ha, ha! I am sorry! It is just galanthophilia sounds like necro…"

"Yes, I get it! Very funny. And it's 'in *the* garden' by the way, or 'in *a* garden', not 'in garden'. Actually I wouldn't have quite so many different snowdrops if my mum and dad hadn't given me their collection as well when they went to live in New Zealand. They'd been collecting and growing snowdrops for years before I started."

Katka had stopped laughing, put down her wine glass and and was leaning towards me.

"I am sorry. What did you say about garden? I did not hear."

"Probably because of all the laughing. I said it's 'in *the* garden' or 'in *a* garden', not 'in garden'. I noticed you keep missing out 'the' and 'a' when you're speaking English. Look, I'm sorry, I didn't mean to be rude. I know we English can't really complain about people not speaking our language properly, given how crap most of us are at other people's languages. It's just that I noticed you keep saying things like 'in magazine' when it should be 'in *a* magazine' or 'in garden' instead of 'in *the* garden' or 'in forest', when it should be 'in *the* forest'. Elena kept doing it too."

Katka looked serious and nodded.

"Yes, thank you. I am happy you point this out to me. I really must remember to use definite and indefinite articles when I speak English. This is problem for all Slovaks, you know, because we do not have words for 'the' and 'a' in Slovak language."

"Really? What? No 'the' and 'a'? How does that work

41

then? By the way, you did it again just then. You said 'this is problem' when it should have been 'this is *a* problem.' Sorry. Just, y'know…"

"We do not have these words in Slovak. We do not say 'give me *the* menu.' We say 'give me menu'."

"Actually we'd say 'could I have the menu'. It's a bit rude to say 'give me the menu'. And it's not a good idea to be rude to waiters. If you do, you end up worrying whether they've gobbed in your soup in the kitchen or sneezed all over your steak."

"In Slovakia also we would be more polite if really asking. It is just example I give you, like…"

She smiled, rested her arms on the table and leaned across her plate towards me, gesturing with her hand for me to do the same. When our faces were just inches apart, she looked into my eyes, slowly licked her top lip and whispered huskily:

"…give me a kiss."

"What!? Now? Here? It's a bit…well…"

Katka sat back in her chair, grinning widely.

"That is what you say in English. But in Slovak we would say only 'give me kiss', 'daj mi pusu'. There would be no 'a'."

I sat back too, feeling my face turn bright red.

"But I do wish to make my English better. I read a lot of English books and magazines and have really quite good vocabulary, I think, but I do not have much opportunity to *speak* English in conversation. I just need more practice and little bit of help to stop making silly mistakes. So please tell me when I do not use definite and indefinite articles. I will try hard to remember, but I would also like to have your help in this. Okay?"

"Well, actually when you said 'it is just example' just now…that should have been 'it's just *an* example'. I suppose you don't have *'an'* in Slovak either. No, of course you wouldn't if you don't have 'a'…"

But I was talking to myself. Katka had turned her full attention to the pudding a beaming waiter had just slid in front of her. She'd passed on the Italian desserts and gone for a very German dark chocolate confection with even darker bitter chocolate sauce and chocolate ice cream. She squealed with delight before attacking it with her spoon.

"Bože môj! I love dark chocolate! Mmmmm! This is like Heaven! Please, try some!"

If she'd been reluctant to share her gnocchi, she made up for it by pushing spoonful after spoonful of the chocolate dessert into my mouth. Maybe she was just too full to manage it all on her own after the dumplings. Incidentally, Katka eventually came to regret asking for my help with reminders about using 'a' and 'the' in English. For a while she would sound quite grateful whenever I pulled her up over it, and that happened a lot at first. It was obviously a difficult language adjustment for Slovaks to make. But I stuck with it, and as she got better at remembering, she started resenting my reminders a little, then more and more, until after a few months our conversations would often end something like this:

"It's 'going to *the* supermarket', not 'going to supermarket', Katka. Remember?"

"Oh shut up! I know! I know! Shut fuck up!"

"And it's 'shut *the* fuck up' , not..."

"I know how to kill you and make it look like accident! They teach us in Pioneers, you know! Is really quite easy!"

"You do realise it should be 'in *the* pioneers'...ouch, that hurt!"

As for me, over time I've found it a very handy little verbal tool to have to hand during arguments with Katka. It's perfect for throwing her off track and changing the subject whenever it looks like she might be about to win a disagreement or make a telling point. A quick "that should be 'put *the* toilet seat back down', Katka" or "it's 'you are *an* idiot', remember?" will generally throw her off balance just long enough for me to steer the discussion in a different direction or get out of the room while she's re-gathering her thoughts. Of course occasionally she'll just hit me with something, but that's a risk worth taking.

Katka put down her spoon and started transferring the last streaks of chocolate sauce from the plate to her mouth with her finger. When there wasn't a trace left, she gave the empty plate a final wistful look and sighed.

"Why did your parents go to New Zealand? That is very long way from England to go and live, I think. Yes, thank you! That is *a* very long way. Actually, it is not *really* necessary for you to tell me *every* time I forget, if it is trouble for you."

"No trouble. I'm happy to help."

"Mmmm. Okay. Thank you. But really…"

"That's okay. Happy to do it. You were asking about my parents? They moved to New Zealand four years ago when my dad took early retirement, to be near my brother and his family. He went to live there ages ago, and my mum and dad wanted to see the grandchildren more than just once a year. They had to leave their snowdrop collection with me, to add to mine, because importing plants into New Zealand is almost impossible. They have to be quarantined, chemically treated, stuff like that. Half of them would probably have died."

"Hapchee! Hapchee!"

"Are you okay, Katka?"

"Yes, thank you. Hapchee! Excuse me. Hapchee! I am sorry! Hapchee! I have small allergy to dark chocolate. Always I sneeze after eating it. Hapchee!"

"Why do you eat dark chocolate then?"

"Because I love it. Hapchee! That is stupid question. And sometimes I sneeze only once or twice, but that was very, very dark and very, very nice choco…hapchee!"

"Why do you say 'hapchee' when you sneeze?"

"Hapchee! Because that is what we say in Slovakia when we sneeze. We say 'hapchee'! I think it is stopped now."

"Why don't you say 'achoo'? That's what a sneeze sounds like. 'Hapchee' doesn't sound like a sneeze."

Katka sniffed, took a tissue from her bag and dabbed at her nose.

"To *Slovaks* it sounds like sneeze. Yes, thank you...sounds like *a* sneeze. Please stop doing that now. I promise I will try *really very hard* to remember for rest of...*the*...night! I promise! Okay?

What I was saying? Oh, yes, in our publishing house in Praha, when we are translating some English books for children, we have found that many sounds are different in English and in Slovak. It was very interesting for us. For an example...what? That is correct, yes? I should say 'for *an* example'? No? Why not? My God! Your English language is...never mind."

Katka took a swig of her coffee, as if to give her strength.

"*For example*, we find that English dogs say 'woof-woof' or 'bow-wow' but in Slovakia dogs say 'how-how', and English cockerels say 'cock-a-doodle-doo' but in Slovakia they make 'kikeerikee' sound, while trains in English children's books say 'choo-choo-choo' and 'chuff-chuff-chuff' but in Slovakia the sound for a train is 'shee-ta-ta, shee-ta-ta, shee-ta-ta'..."

"Hang on, Katka. Dogs don't go 'how-how' and trains certainly don't go 'shee-ta-ta, shee-ta-ta'..."

"In Slovakia they do."

"Okay, well maybe that's just how Slovak people *hear* them. Just different sort of, well, phonetic interpretations of sounds."

Katka smiled as I gave the waiter my credit card.

"No, I don't think so. Well, perhaps that is some small truth, but also I think dogs and cockerels do *sound* different in Slovakia. That *is* really how they sound. My sneezes, they sounded like 'hapchee' to you, just like they sounded to me, yes?"

"Yes, but that's because you *said* 'hapchee' when you were sneezing."

"Of course. That is what all Slovaks say when they sneeze.

45

That is what sneezes in Slovakia sound like."

"Yes, of course they do. Because that's what you're all *saying*."

"No. Because that is what sneezes *sound* like."

It was at this point, as our voices were starting to get a little raised and - I have to admit - I was probably starting to sound just a tad hysterical, that the owner's wife bustled over with my credit card slip and our coats before escorting us to the door and out into the cold night air. She stood on the steps of the restaurant chatting to Katka in Italian as I looked around for a taxi, then she gave her a huge hug and waved as we walked off down the dark street.

"You should come to Slovakia and hear our dogs and cockerels for yourself. Then you will see, they *do* sound different than in England. I promise, it is true."

"Well...maybe cockerels, I guess. You might have different breeds in Slovakia that make a *slightly* different sound, I suppose. That's possible. But surely they wouldn't sound all *that* different? And I still don't see how a *dog* can make a different sound. Dogs *bark*, and a bark sounds like a bark wherever you are. I mean you have the same sort of breeds of *dog* as everyone else, surely?"

"Yes of course we do. But you will see! Would you not like to see...I mean hear...for yourself? Would you not like to visit Slovakia again? Did you not enjoy your first visit to my country, to Bratislava? How long ago was it that you went? Things have changed very much in recent years. Maybe you will like it better now. Hotels are better, and there are more restaurants, bars, nightclubs, many changes. But of course countryside, forests, mountains, lakes and rivers, these are all still just as beautiful. Did you see these also, as well as the city?"

I was standing at the kerb, looking up and down the road for a taxi. Katka pulled a tourist map from her coat pocket and started unfolding it.

"Please, do not try to find taxi. I am sorry...*a* taxi. I would like to walk. This is *the* first time I am in Germany and it is my almost-last night in Frankfurt, so I would like to see more sights. Especially I would like to see *the* river. It is also better for environment to walk than to take taxis everywhere, and anyway I do not see a taxi nowhere around here."

"Fine, we'll walk. You're not too cold? It's bloody freezing. I've never known it this cold in Frankfurt in October."

"I heard on television at hotel that whole of central Europe is forecast to have very, very cold weather because of unusual Arctic air mass moving down across Russia. Maybe they will have snow in Tatra Mountains in Slovakia very early this year."

"In *October*?"

"Perhaps. It is quite usual to have the first snow of winter in some parts of Slovakia in middle of November, and in Tatra Mountains, where my mother and father's village is, it is possible even at end of October if weather is very cold."

"Your winters must be pretty long. We don't usually get much snow in England, especially these days, with global warming and everything. We hardly seem to have a winter at all any more. Just wet, windy autumns that go on until spring. If we do have snow, it's usually gone again the next day. By the way, sorry to be the language police but you did say you wanted to know when you got stuff wrong, and you can't say 'I don't see a taxi nowhere around here.' It should be 'I don't see a taxi *any*where around here.' Sorry."

Katka gave me one of her looks, then reluctantly nodded agreement.

"Yes, I know this also, but sometimes I forget, just as with definite and indefinite articles."

"It's what we call a double negative. You just can't say it in English."

"Yes, yes, I know. We were taught this in English lessons at school, but you see in Slovak language it is quite common to have such 'double negatives'. We would say in Slovak, for an example, 'nikde tu nevidím taxík' which means literally 'nowhere here I don't see taxi'. It sounds quite natural to Slovaks. Also, for 'no-one is here' we would say 'nikto tu nie je' which is literally 'nobody is not here.' Actually..."

"No, no, no! You can't say that either! The 'nobody' and the 'not' cancel each other out, so what you're *really* saying is 'there *is* someone here'.'"

"I understand how this works in English, but really it does not sound strange in Slovak. Actually, this sentence is part of very funny, very old Slovak joke about someone who knocks at door of toilet and asks if anyone is in there...but no, I do not tell jokes well. You should really hear my father tell it. He is very funny and he knows many jokes, especially old ones from time of the communist regime.

It is one reason he lost his job as engineer at factory in our local town, Poprad, when I was child, and had to work in hotel and restaurant kitchens instead. Also, he refused to join Communist Party, which was other reason. But it was good for him, he says, because he discovers his love for cooking when forced to do kitchen work."

"It was that bad? You could lose your job just for telling jokes?"

"If they were about communist regime or our leaders, sometimes, yes. My father and some friends made a small magazine with funny articles and jokes, and some cartoons, about regime and life in Czechoslovakia in those times. Local Party leaders discovered he was one of writers of this magazine, so his job at factory was taken away.

He already had some problems from saying he would not be forced to join Communist Party. They tell him he must do it to be promoted, but he said he would not if it was *requirement*. So he worked for many years without promotions before losing his job. But in end he was much happier doing that kitchen work and eventually becoming chef. Now he has his own restaurant and is really happy man. You should come to see his restaurant in Tatras. You would like his food *and* his jokes."

We crossed over a busy road and headed into the glass towers of the financial district on our way to the river. Katka surprised me by slipping her arm through mine and clinging onto it as we walked.

"Sounds like it was very repressive under the communists."

"Yes. Even at school we know it is important to always keep our heads down. That is what you say in English? We have similar saying in Slovakia. Political system was very tough, especially after Russians invade in late sixties to suppress moderate government of Dubček, who wanted to make 'communism with human face'. They stay until end of communist regime after Velvet Revolution in eighty-nine.

Some Russian soldiers had base near our village. They came just before I was born and I grew up seeing their trucks on road past our house. They would whistle and wave to me and to my sister. They were nice boys, very young and very lonely, I think, so far from their homes.

There were many anti-Russian demonstrations, and later a lot of anti-Russian jokes. My father knew many very rude ones. Actually, only one I remember which was *not* rude is 'Those Russian digital watches are very good. You can even take your lunch to work in them.' Russian digital watches sold in our shops in those days were very big, like boxes, you understand?"

I grinned.

"Yes, our first digital watches were pretty awful too."

"But people then had to be careful what they say, even as jokes. Secret police were everywhere, even in our village. We were quite close to border with Poland, and we had a saying that 'Polish dogs come across border to Czechoslovakia to eat'…because Poland often had big food shortages…'and Czechoslovak dogs go across border to Poland to bark'…because communist regime was a little less strict there. It was funny, but reflected the truth of our situation. You, of course, did not have these kinds of problems in West during

Cold War."

"We had some civil liberties problems in Britain during the Cold War, and quite a few protests. I don't suppose you've heard of a place called Greenham Common? Huge American cruise missile base in England? Massive protests by thousands of women trying to get the American nuclear missiles taken away? No? Well I could tell you some stories about that, and about our secret service bugging the phones of anti-nuclear campaigners and left-wing politicians...but no, obviously nothing like it must have been for people in Eastern Europe."

Katka shook her head and pulled my arm tighter to her side as the freezing wind whipped around us.

"No, I do not know about this particular missile base. But I do remember about missiles which America sent into Europe to threaten communist countries. In school, our teacher organised our class to write letters to America's President Reagan asking him not to fire those new missiles at us. People were really worried that he would attack us. West was very threatening towards Russia and her allies at that time.

But you still did not tell me about your visit to Bratislava. You were with some Slovak girl? She was your girlfriend at that time? Did she take you to other parts of Slovakia, outside Blava?"

"No, just Bratislava. It was about eleven, no, *twelve* years ago...maybe thirteen, I'm not sure, and it was August, not October, and very hot. Like I said before, I'd been in Germany and I decided to go on to Vienna because I'd always wanted to see it. Then some people in a coffee shop in Vienna, an English couple, said I should get the coach to Bratislava, that it was only an hour or so from Vienna and worth a visit. So I did. And then I met Zuzana in a bar the next night with some other students. They were having a party to celebrate finishing university and they invited me to join them because I was on my own and they heard me trying to speak English to the waiter. Zuzana spoke very good English. She'd been studying something like environmental sciences too. That's what you said you did isn't it?"

Suddenly I was walking alone. Katka had let go of my arm and was standing staring at me.

"Zuzana? Very tall Zuzana with long blonde hair? Did you know her second name? Zuzana Kováčová? Was that it? Bože môj! I don't believe it!"

"Kováčová? Yes, that was it. You know her? That's amazing. But we weren't *together*. We were just friends."

Katka was still rooted to the spot, staring at me and frowning as if delving back into memories almost forgotten.

"I know. She told me. I mean she wrote to me. I went straight home to our village after final exams. I did not want to celebrate. I had just broken up my relationship of very long time with my boyfriend from school days. We were together for many years, but he had new girlfriend at his university in city of Brno, which I found out only from a friend of ours during exams. It was sad time for me. I was unhappy for very long time."

"You managed to finish your exams though?"

"Yes, of course. It was difficult time for me, but I got my master's degree. So, Zuzana, she wrote to me that there was nice English guy in Bratislava. We did not have telephone in our house in those days, or in houses of our neighbours, and no mobile telephones of course. She wrote to me many times during first month after exams, always asking me to come back to Bratislava. She thought I would like this English guy she met. I always wanted to visit England, ever since school days, and I spoke English just as well as Zuzana. You really did not become boyfriend and girlfriend in those days? You were there for almost whole month and Zuzana had no Slovak boyfriend at that time."

" Zuzana had just started to go out with someone that first night I met her in the bar in Bratislava. I can't remember his name. Micha? Something like that?"

"Michal. Yes, she married him year after our finals. They have two children now. He works in a bank and she works for

Slovak government. I did not know they started to be together so soon after our exams. Zuzana was, I think, hiding it from me in her letters so she would not make me jealous and upset about my own boyfriend problem. She was very good friend. She still is my best friend, except for Elena."

We started walking again, wending our way through the streets of central Frankfurt, heading for the more historic buildings around the Römer market square. Katka was rummaging in her bag, so I took out my mobile and switched it on.

"I'll just call James and see if the doors are still open at the Jazzkeller. It's a long shot on a weekend during the book fair. They're usually packed out by ten. But you never know. Do you fancy going there after we've been to see the river?"

I spoke to James and turned to Katka, who had found her keys and was now dangling them in front of me, shaking them so they jangled, her eyebrows raised expectantly.

"James says they've closed the doors at the Jazzkeller. And guess what? James *is* with Elena. Sounds like they're getting on okay, but I can't imagine they'd have much in common. Why are you doing that?"

Katka stopped shaking the keys.

"Elena is excellent jazz musician. She plays trumpet with band in Praha, one of best jazz bands in Czech Republic."

"Well that explains it. James is a *huge* jazz fan."

Katka was jangling her keys again, holding them at eye-level in front of me.

"You're doing it again."

"Look at the keys. Look closely."

"Are you trying to *hypnotise* me?"

"Did you lose something in Bratislava?"

"What? No. Oh…yes, I lost my keys. Is that my Snoopy…"

Katka nodded and grinned.

"Yes. It is your Snoopy cartoon dog key-ring. Zuzana gave your keys to me when I see her again in Blava at Christmas after you leave to go to England. I have also your keys at home, at my mother's and father's house. I liked very much your Snoopy dog, so I use for my own keys. Zuzana said you lose keys in Slovak National Uprising Square in Bratislava. You wave and shake them…"

"I might have been a little bit drunk that night. I was going home the next day and Zuzana had been telling me the history of the square, how it was named after the uprising…"

"Heroic uprising."

"Right, yes. The *heroic* uprising of the Slovak partisan fighters against the German Army towards the end of the Second World War. And it was the square that everyone chose to start your demonstrations against the communist government in…when was it exactly? Eighty-nine or ninety? I forget."

"In November eighty-nine. And it was students who began demonstrations. On November seventeen, which was National Students' Day under old regime. Normally we were made some small treat by our teachers and lecturers, such as no home-study, no home-work to do that day. This time we decided it was good day for something bigger. Student demonstrations started in Praha just before this, and rumours were that communist regime could fall soon."

"The demonstrations in Prague ended violently didn't they? I saw something about that on TV."

"Yes, some students were attacked in Prague and quite badly hurt. Some people say it was secret police trying to stop demonstrations. Other people say it was secret police starting some violence to get everyone angry enough to bring communists down, because secret police knew regime was not stable for much longer, so they wanted quick end to it. Whatever was truth, parents became angry that students were hurt, and even more people start to join student demonstrations, until we had our peaceful Velvet Revolution and communist regime fell."

"I think Zuzana said it was much less dangerous in Bratislava."

"Yes, was some small trouble, but not very much. Police by that time know things have to change soon. But we were careful anyway, not to give to police reasons for violence. Many thousands of students gathered in Slovak National Uprising Square after marching from campuses; also many older people who decided to join us as we marched. I was there with Zuzana and other friends from university. It was freezing cold, but we stand in square for long time, shouting for our freedom and…"

"Shaking your keys. Yes, Zuzana told me. It was…"

"To represent freedoms that we want. Freedom to travel where we like, think what we like, vote how we like. To show we do not want to be locked up like prisoners in our own country any more. It was lucky for us that in end regime goes quietly. It is of course why we say it was Velvet Revolution, not bloody one. And that is why you shake your keys in square with Zuzana?"

"Yes, she'd been telling me all about it, and we'd had a few drinks. Some of us started shaking our keys and they were shouting slogans from the Velvet Revolution. Until a police car pulled up. I thought I'd put my keys back in my pocket, but they must have fallen out. I didn't realize until later. We went back to look but couldn't find them."

Katka nodded in agreement and linked her arm through mine again as we crossed another busy road.

"Zuzana went to look more carefully next day and found them under bench at edge of square. She took them to your hotel but you had already left for airport in Vienna. She had your address in England and thought to mail them to you, but then she lost this address."

"I meant to write to her when I got back. But I was busy catching up with work. And it's not like we were, you know…"

"She waited for you to write but no letter came. So when I see her at Christmas, she tells me I miss wonderful chance to meet very nice, very good-looking English man, perhaps

54

chance to go to England, to see London. It is something I always wanted to do, but of course during communist days we could not travel to such places. Why do you smile? Ah! Because Zuzana tells me you are very good-looking English man?"

"Sorry. I wasn't being big-headed. I'm not the most self-confident person in the world, and it's always nice to hear a compliment about yourself. Even if it is twelve or thirteen years old. I've probably changed a lot since then."

Katka laughed.

"And now you are, how you say in English, fishing for more compliments. Yes, you *are* really still good-looking Englishman. I did not see you all those years ago so I do not know how much you change. Photographs Zuzana has from those after-exam parties showed you only once, and that was really just back of your head at table in pub. But I am sure Zuzana would still say same thing about you now."

We turned into Frankfurt's historic Römer Square. It was brightly lit and as busy with sightseers as it always was during Book Fair week.

"One day, after you do not write for long time, Zuzana gives me your keys. Mostly as joke, she says if I ever go to England I should look for you, give you keys and make up for lost chance of meeting you in Bratislava. Of course I leave keys at home, because I do not expect ever to meet you. But I carry Snoopy with me ever since, on *my* keys. You must have him back now."

Katka started to take the little plastic Snoopy off her key ring.

"No, don't do that, keep it. This is the Römer Market Square. And that's the old City Hall."

"Yes, I know."

"You've been here before? I thought you might not have seen it. This is one of my favourite parts of Frankfurt."

"I am glad to see it again before I leave. I love town squares. We have many wonderful ones in Slovakia. This is

55

veľmi pekné...very beautiful. I especially like these old buildings with the wooden pieces in the walls. Very old Germany, I think."

"Yes. A lot of old Frankfurt was bombed flat during the war but some bits, like this, survived. Although actually, James once told me those timbered buildings on that side were destroyed by bombs but were rebuilt after the war as almost exact replicas, using new materials. You'd never guess, would you? Of course, he could wrong, or pulling my leg. You never really know with James."

We were walking around the square, still with Katka's arm through mine, and she caught me glancing down.

"You do not mind that I hold your arm? It is quite common in Slovakia for friends to walk like this. Not in England? I know English people are quite formal. Does this embarrass you? It is too forward?"

"No, it's fine. You should see the square when they have the Christmas market here. It's incredible. They have a huge Christmas tree over there, taller than the buildings, must be eighty or ninety feet. And an old merry-go-round, a musical carousel thing for the kids, very traditional, with painted horses that go up and down. Loads of stalls with mulled wine, bratwurst, apple strudel, special Christmas sweets, gingerbread hearts..."

"Yes, I know these. They are made with ginger here? We have them in Slovakia also, but ours are honey-bread hearts, not gingerbread. In Slovakia honey-bread biscuits, medovníky, are very traditional for Christmas. They are made with honey and cinnamon. I love them. Every year when we were children, my father would let us...me and my sister...help to mix dough and cut into shapes ready for baking. After cooking in oven and cooling, we would hang on Christmas tree with little threads put through with sewing needles. We still do this every year."

Katka was gazing happily around the square with a dreamy expression on her face, her arm through mine and her hands clasped together in front of her.

"The river's down this way, Katka. You did say you wanted to see the river, didn't you?"

"Yes, *please*. When I was here in square with Elena, we had to go back to book fair and had no time to look for river as well. Also I did not have map that day, so we ask people for directions. I did not know river was near to this square."

"We just have to cross over this road. Watch out, the traffic's very fast here. Then we can walk along the riverside to…well, you'll see. It's another of my favourite places."

Katka looked out across the dark water of the River Main at the lights on the other bank.

"What is on other side of river?"

"That's Sachsenhausen, another old part of the city. Nice, but lots of bars and pubs, steak houses and stuff like that. Very touristy. I could take you there tomorrow if you can get away from the book fair for a bit. My flight isn't 'till the evening and I've only got a quick meeting at lunchtime…come on, up here."

We started climbing the steps to the bridge.

"You go back to England tomorrow? That is…oh, this is very beautiful bridge."

"It's the Eiserner Steg, the old iron footbridge over the Main. Now, look at the view from up here. Isn't that fantastic? I always think it looks a bit like a smaller version of Manhattan."

I pointed at the glass towers of the financial district on the north bank, back where we'd come from, their lights mirrored in the black water. Katka squeezed my arm and huddled up closer. The wind was even colder up above the river.

"Manhattan? New York? I have seen it on television. Mmmm. I see what you mean. Yes. It is beautiful how lights from buildings and ships shine on dark river. What are those ships? Do you know? They look like cruise ships."

"Boats, not ships. They're not big enough to be ships. They're the hotel boats."

"I am sorry. We do not have many ships in Slovakia. We have no sea coast, just River Danube, a little like this river. To me those look like ships. But they are also hotels?"

"They're river cruisers. Mostly German, although one of them this year…the one I'm staying on…is from Holland. They're the kind of boats that take people on holiday cruises along the Rhine. A few of them always tie up here at the Unter-Main-Kai for the book fair. The city hotels can't cope with all the visitors."

"You are staying on hotel boat? That must be very romantic. Which one? Show me."

"That one there, second from the end. It's a bit cramped, but fun; tiny cabins, and a bit noisy at night if you're too close to the generator room. But it's nice being in the bar after dark, looking out over the river while you eat or have a drink. James persuaded me to stay on one my second year at the book fair. He always uses them, and now I'm hooked on them too. Would you like to go back for a drink? The bar's usually open till one or two, and someone might be playing the piano since it's Saturday."

Katka didn't answer. Instead she leaned her head against my shoulder and stared at the lights of the hotel boats.

"When I find out at end of University that my boyfriend from school days was with another girlfriend, I spend much time by River Danube in Bratislava. One day Zuzana sees me by river and I am crying. Zuza says to me 'Katka, really you must stop so much crying into Danube or you will cause Hundred Years Flood.' This is huge flood we get, by legend, about every hundred years, where all rivers in Slovakia overflow. By strange chance, it happened few years later. There was great flooding all over Slovakia, Czech Republic, Hungary, Poland, Germany."

"I think I remember that. A few years ago? It was on the news. There was really bad flooding in Prague, wasn't there?"

Katka sighed deeply and seemed not to have heard me, too bound up in her own thoughts.

"I never want to be that sad again. My friends tell me it is why I do not keep boyfriends more than few weeks or months at most, then I find new one. Do you have girlfriend or wife now?"

"Me? No. Not right now. I mean, I've never had a wife, and I don't have a girlfriend just now."

"You were very sad when your girlfriend left you? You were going to get married, yes?"

" Yes. But I'm over that now. It was ages ago."

"Mmm. But you have never settled with someone else since that time?"

"There've been girlfriends. A few. Just no-one I wanted to really settle down with long-term, that's all."

There was a moment's silence from Katka, then she took her head off my shoulder, unhooked her arm from mine and stepped away.

"You have book samples on hotel boat?"

"Sorry? Book samples? You mean *my* books? Yes. Why?"

"You can give me samples, or I should wait for you to mail to us in Praha? I did not mention to you that Elena and I think our publisher would be interested in your books? He asks us to look for new kinds of books, to make a change from mostly nature and travel books which we publish. Especially, he asks us to look for humour books. Elena and I like your cartoon books. We would like to make proposal to our boss in Praha for a deal. You can also give me details of business terms? Advance payments, royalty rates? Or we should talk to James about this?"

"No, I can give you all that. I didn't know you were interested in the books professionally. What do you do at your publishers?"

"I am one of our publishing house's editors. Elena is editor-in-chief."

She leaned on the girder-railing of the bridge, rubbing her hands against the biting cold. I shuffled awkwardly by her side for a moment, scuffing my shoes, before speaking again.

"So, Katka, I didn't realise this was a business meeting. I thought…well, I mean I asked you to have dinner with me because…I thought we were…never mind. Yes, I've got samples of all my books on the hotel boat. It's *the* hotel boat, by the way."

"What? I am sorry. I did not hear. You speak very quietly, and wind is…"

"I said 'it's *the* hotel boat. You've been slipping a bit since the restaurant. You've been forgetting to say 'the' and 'a' quite a lot. Most of the time, actually. Sorry. You asked me to correct you."

Katka turned to me and pulled her coat tight around her, shivering a little and frowning.

"Yes. Thank you once again. You are very kind. How will I ever make my English perfect without you and your constant reminding? On *the* boat! Give me *the* menu! Give me *a* kiss!"

"You did *ask* me to…oh for Christ's sake, I'm sorry. Come on, I'll get you those book samples."

"Give me *a* kiss."

"There's no need to take the piss! I was just trying to help."

"Please give me *a* kiss."

"What? You mean…"

"Yes, I would like you to kiss me. And I would also like you to come with me to Slovakia. I have some holiday time after I go back to Praha, after I talk to our boss about book fair…*the* book fair. I will go to Slovakia to see my friends in Blava and to my home village to see my family.

We missed a chance in Blava all those years ago. I think we should take this second chance and travel to Slovakia together. Perhaps it will be big disaster, perhaps not; but whichever way it will be, I would like to show you my country, if you have some time to spare. Must you really go straight to England tomorrow?"

"Well, that's when my flight is. But I suppose…I don't know…I don't *have* to go straight back…I suppose I *could*…"

"Good! I go back with Elena to Praha after last day of book

fair, on Monday. You can stay at boat hotel for one more night? Yes? They will have room for you?"

"Are you sure? You really want me to come to Slovakia? Well, I know quite a few people are leaving tomorrow from our boat. And no-one new will be arriving this late for the book fair. So, yeah, I'm sure they'll let me keep the room another night. If you're really sure you want me to come with you."

Katka sighed.

"I have been asking it all evening. You have not noticed?"

"Not really. I mean, a lot of today and tonight has been a bit confusing. Like I said, I'm not the most self-confident person in the universe. Not since…well, not for a few years now. Yes, I know I come across as self-confident. Everyone tells me. But that's only the front I put on. Underneath, I'm hardly ever really sure of myself, or of others. For instance, I've always been crap at picking up signals. And you've been giving out a lot of mixed signals, which are the kind that I have the most trouble with. One minute I think you like me, the next I think…"

"You do not understand my signals? What does this…? Okay, I think I know. Give me your hand. I will give you signal you will not misunderstand. Give me your hand."

Katka took a felt-tip pen out of her bag and wrote on the back of my right hand in big black capitals 'I would like to sleep with you tonight.' I stared at it as she put the pen away again then looked at me with her head tilted to one side and her eyebrows raised, waiting for my response.

"You said in the relationship quiz at the restaurant that you wouldn't do that on a first date," I heard myself saying.

"I lied."

"Oh. I see. Right."

"Okay, it is true *usually* I would not. But I think this is not usual kind of situation. Do you think this makes me bad woman?"

"No! Of course not! And it makes you a bloody good first

date! Sorry. Just joking. Are you sure? We've only just met. I mean I didn't invite you out for dinner *intending* to get you into bed. Not on the first night anyway."

"I believe you. But we only have this night before you have flight to England. It might be that you change your mind and do not come to Slovakia and then this will really be our only night together. But I must tell you that I am getting sea-sickness sometimes."

"Really? Even on a river boat?"

"Yes, once on boat at Danube, once on boat at lake in Hungary, and even once when I was on canoe at river in Czech republic. It seems I get sea-sickness very easily. But your hotel-boat is tied to shore, yes? It does not move around very much?"

"Not unless it's very windy."

An icy blast whistled through the ironwork of the bridge and whipped Katka's coat around her legs.

Katka took my hand. As we walked, I looked down at the back of it.

"Is that *indelible* ink? Right. Okay. It's just that I'm supposed to be having lunch with James and an American publisher tomorrow. And if that felt-tip's indelible, this writing's not going to wash off."

Katka laughed as she pulled me towards the steps at the end of the bridge. Then I remembered something.

"Hang on, Katka…"

She looked at me expectantly as I struggled with my memory.

"No, sorry. It's gone. Hang on…"

I dug deep into my jacket pocket, pulled out Elena's cheat-sheet and read from it.

"Máš krásne oči!"

Katka laughed.

"I have beautiful eyes? Thank you, but I know. And how dare you read this to me now straight from Elena's 'how to make love to Katka' tips-paper? When I have already asked you to sleep with me. Are you really English idiot? Why you could not slip this into conversation at restaurant, or in beautiful market square, or when my head is on your shoulder and we are seeing beautiful lights in river?"

"I forgot. Sorry. But I didn't want to waste it. I spent hours learning those Slovak phrases."

"But you *forget* this one and have to *read* it to me!"

"Yes, well, okay, it didn't go quite right, but you *do* have really beautiful eyes, you know, *really*…"

Katka took my hand and dragged me down the steps and along the riverbank towards the hotel boats.

"Shut up now, and hurry before I change my mind. Typical man! Elena makes it so easy for you, and still you turn it to a mess."

I laughed as Katka went to hit me on the arm, assuming she was just being playful. But it turned out to be a suspiciously accurate and expert blow to the upper arm muscle and surprisingly painful and disabling. It was a good five minutes before I could use my hand properly again. Probably something she learned in the Pioneers, right after how to fire a Kalashnikov and disable a NATO tank with a hair-grip. For a second I wondering what I was getting into, then the freezing wind blasted around my neck and ears, and I was the one pulling Katka along as we ran for the shelter of the boats. Even then, I had a sneaky feeling she could race to the hotel-boats much faster than I ever could…if she really wanted to.

"Katka? Hang on. I'm sorry, it's just that…"

We stopped at the bottom of the gang-plank.

"…I don't have any…y'know…and there's no machine in the toilets. Not that I was *looking* for one. It's just that I thought 'That's odd, no thingy machine, on a *Dutch* hotel boat!' So maybe we should try to find a…"

Katka was staring at me, her hands on her hips.

"What? What is this now? We should try to find a *what?*"

"Well, a chemist's shop…or a pharmacy…for some…you know…unless *you* have…"

"Unless I have what?"

"Condoms. No of course you don't! Sorry! There's no need to hit me again! It's just that you did say you lied in the relationship quiz about…ouch! That really hurts, you know. Maybe you could hit the *other* arm sometimes instead of always the *same* one. Ouch! No, that hurts almost as much."

"Did I say we would have sex? I only say I want to sleep with you. You have never slept with woman just to hold each other, without sex?"

"Yes, but not on a first date. On a first date it's usually bed and sex or no bed at all. I don't think I've ever had a first date where bed and no sex was an option. So you want to stay the night but no sex?"

"I did not say that either. Perhaps we *will* have sex. I have not absolutely decided yet. On bridge perhaps I did, but then there was all that stupid 'beautiful eyes' thing that you say…that you *read*. Perhaps now I will change my mind."

"Okay. Well, how about a drink while you're thinking about it?"

In the bar I got the drinks while Katka sat at a window table looking out across the oily-black water and the reflected lights. The Dutch barman kept staring at my hand as I picked at the bowls of bar snacks, waiting for my beer. It was only as I sat down opposite Katka and passed her drink across the table that I realized he'd been looking at Katka's felt-tip message. I glanced over my shoulder and the barman gave me a big smile.

"Here's your drink, Katka. I suppose I could ask the barman if he has any condoms."

I looked down at my hand then back at the still beaming barman. Katka reluctantly dragged her gaze from the window to the bar.

"To sell to you? They do that? Dutch bar waiters?"

The barman was still smiling at me, and now he was winking as well. I was staring at him, and he was winking back. I looked down at the message on the back of my hand.

64

"Maybe not. Like you said, we're probably not going to have sex anyway."

I took a long swig of my beer and stared at the dark window. The reflection of the barman smiled back at me. Katka opened her bag and started rummaging.

"It might be that I have some in my bag…"

"Really?"

Katka stopped digging in her bag, blushed and took a sip of her Jack Daniels and Coke.

"It is possible, yes. But I do not know for sure."

She shrugged and took another sip before nodding towards her bag and shooting it a slightly annoyed look.

"Sometimes Elena will put some…of those…into my bag when she has tried to get me together with some man, or when she knows I am meeting with some man. It is sometimes very embarrassing. At start of book fair, I was meeting for drink in evening with guy from some Hungarian publishing house. I try to take handkerchief from my bag, and I pull out with it whole strip of packets, maybe six or seven. It was really *very* embarrassing for poor guy and for me. She behaves to me like mother - a little bit *strange* mother, who puts condoms in daughter's bag and gives boyfriends papers with 'You have beautiful eyes' written in Slovak. She cares very much for me and tries to look after me, but sometimes she causes problems."

"So we *might* be having sex? I'm getting confused again."

Katka grinned and looked at her bag.

"I think perhaps that will depend on Elena."

I reached towards Katka's bag but she slapped my hand away and laughed.

"We must wait to see. It will be surprise. Like Christmas. Did someone leave a present for us under our tree?"

"Or will we be sleeping in separate beds?"

"I am sorry. What?"

"Ah! I meant to say, the sleeping together and holding might be a bit difficult. My room - cabin really - has two single beds, well, more like bunks. Very narrow, on opposite sides of the room - cabin - not brilliant for two people wanting to sleep together. Then again, if Elena's let us down I suppose we *could* just *hold hands*. It's a very *small* cabin, a bit like a big railway compartment. You could probably hold hands across it quite easily…if there's no *present* under the tree that is."

I glanced down at the back of my right hand and Katka's message. The barman noticed and looked across. For a second I thought he was actually going to wave.

"You know, this writing really isn't going to come off. What if James or the American publisher sees it at lunch tomorrow? They might think it's some kind of a signal…that I want to…y'know…with one of *them*."

The barman was still smiling at me. Katka laughed, reached out and stroked the back of my hand with her fingers then held my hand. The barman stopped smiling, frowned and started noisily clattering glasses around.

"You could wear gloves to hide it."

"What, all through lunch? I can't eat with gloves on. They'd think I was mad."

"Then eat only with other hand. Keep this hand underneath table while you eat lunch."

Katka let go of my hand and started giggling.

"What?"

"No. This would not work very well, I think."

"Why not?"

"After what you say to James at book fair, he will probably think you are having *wank* under table!"

"Katka! Keep your voice down!"

The barman, now wiping down a table nearby, started to look interested again.

Eco-Terrorism and Other Misunderstandings

As we walked into the hotel boat dining room the next morning, Katka glared at me and muttered angrily.

"Yes, you *are* eco-terrorist! You do not care about environment and climate change!"

"But I *do* care about the environment, Katka. Anyway, I think you've got it the wrong way round. Isn't an eco-terrorist someone who *stops* environmental damage by sabotaging logging machinery to prevent forests being cut down, that sort of thing?"

"No! Well, yes, that is how some *governments* and *big businesses* try to call people who take actions to stop environmental destruction. But those presidents, prime ministers, big businesses, people who do not believe climate change happens and will not try to stop it, *those* are people who *really* should be called eco-terrorists. This is how I use word eco-terrorist; how everyone should use word eco-terrorist because it is much more true. Men and women who have courage to stand up against environmental dangers are eco-*warriors* who fight for our planet. You, on other hand, are really eco-*terrorist* for sure. I am sorry but that is my opinion. Where is coffee? I need coffee, even if it is weak hotel excuse for real coffee."

Frowning, Katka poured herself coffee at the breakfast counter. She didn't offer to pour *me* some, even though I was holding out my cup, so I waited for her to bang the pot back down then helped myself and followed her to a window table. She was buttering a croissant and gazing out across the river, now smooth and calm after the choppy swell that had buffeted the boat most of the night.

"I really *do* care about the environment, Katka. I recycle. I have a compost bin. I buy organic veg…"

"You are eco-terrorist! You really want to *fly on plane* to

Praha? To Prague? From Frankfurt? It is just as quick on coach, and this way you will not help to destroy planet. Do you *know* how much CO2 you will make on such a silly little flea-hop flight from Frankfurt to Prague? *Do* you?"

"No. How much?"

"I do not know, but must be huge amount. Exact quantity is not most important point in this case. Coach trip is much better for environment. *That* is most important point. It is only seven, perhaps eight hours and we can travel on night-coach, so we can sleep and not waste a day by travelling."

"Seven or eight hours on a crowded coach? How is that just as quick as a one-hour flight?"

"When you include time travelling to airport, checking-in luggage, going through securities, and waiting in departures place…"

"Where we can get a coffee, eat, do some shopping, stroll around, go to the toilet if we need to."

"There is toilet on coach. This is not Third World or Soviet times. There is also sometimes coffee on coach. And aeroplanes are not crowded? I think they *are.*"

"Yes, but we won't have to sit in a plane for seven or eight hours, and even with all the waiting around it's still going to be quicker than a coach. I wouldn't be surprised if it turns out to be *cheaper* than the coach if we get a low-cost budget airline flight. Do you know if Easy Jet fly from Frankfurt to Prague?"

"Eco-terrorist! Planet killer!"

"That's a bit harsh!"

"Is it? How many times did you fly already this year? How many more times next year? How many times *do* you fly every year?"

"Okay, how about I hire a car?"

"You want to pay small fortune to hire big, shiny BMW to race past little Czech and Slovak Skodas like fat western businessman, with air-conditioning, satellite navigation, television screen, refrigerator for cold drinks?"

"Actually I was thinking more of a Volkswagen or a…"

"Do you *ever* travel on coach or train in England? Or do you *always* drive car everywhere and take aeroplane?"

"I get the train to London sometimes. And I used to get the bus to school every day when I was a kid."

"Okay, we get night coach to Praha tomorrow! No more arguing! School bus! Hah! No arguing! Stop! Shut up now!"

The barman from the night before walked in and headed for the breakfast buffet. I tried not to catch his eye, but Katka gave him a smile and got a grumpy nod in return. When he'd passed our table, I leaned in closer to Katka and stroked the back of her hand for a bit while she tried hard not to notice.

"So, last night was nice, Katka. God, am I tired though! We couldn't have got more than a couple of hours sleep. You just couldn't *stop* could you? On and on, time after time. You were pretty *loud* too. I'm sure they could hear you in the cabin next door."

Katka was looking over my shoulder. I glanced round to see the barman standing just behind me. He rolled his eyes at the ceiling and banged his tray down onto a nearby table before sitting and jabbing at a sausage with his knife and fork, chopping it into what looked like an unnecessarily large number of very small pieces.

I really wouldn't have believed anyone could get seasick on a moored river cruiser, but Katka had. Within an hour of going back to my cabin, as the wind whipped up the waves on the river, she'd leaped up and dashed to the toilet and shower cubicle to retch and groan loudly - again, and again, and again, virtually all night long. It was almost dawn before the wind dropped and the rocking stopped, allowing us to finally get some sleep.

The very thought of it now was making me even more tired. I put down my fork and yawned, hiding my mouth behind my hand, which of course started Katka yawning too. For a minute or two we took it in turns, each starting the other off again, while behind me I heard the barman stirring his coffee loudly, banging his spoon on the side of his cup and rattling it in his saucer. I stifled another yawn, ignored the barman's derisory snort, and picked up my cup.

"This coffee *is* a bit weak, isn't it?"

Katka took a sip of her coffee and pulled a disgusted face.

"Yeugh! When we get to Praha, I will make you real cup of Slovak coffee, Turkish-style, very, very strong. Much better than this dishwater filter-coffee. You like good coffee, Stephen?"

"I'm sorry?"

"You like good coffee? I must have very *strong* coffee, especially in morning to start my day; at least two cups or I am impossible to be with, so my friends tell me."

"No, I mean you called me Stephen."

"Yes, that is your name."

"No."

"Yes."

"No! Okay, hang on. Look, my name isn't Stephen. It's *Ben*."

"Really? You are *Ben*? Not Stephen? Oh. That is embarrassing."

"We just spent the night together and you can't remember my name? So who's Stephen?"

Katka and I stared at each other in bemusement. Behind me the barman was sniggering. I glared at him over my shoulder, but he'd finished his breakfast and was standing up, a huge smile on his face. He bumped into my shoulder as he walked past but didn't stop to apologise, instead strolling jauntily out of the restaurant room whistling a cheery tune.

"I thought *you* are Stephen. Stephen Watkins is name on your book Elena brings for me from your stand at book fair. It was one which we thought was most funny from all books we look at."

"Stephen Watkins? You mean the books about animals playing football and golf and tennis and stuff?"

"Yes, very funny cartoon animals playing lots of different

70

sports. We liked those very much."

"I don't draw *animals playing football*! Didn't you look at any of *my* cartoon books? Mine are *much* funnier than Steve Watkins' stupid sporting animals. What about 'How To Kill Your Boss And Get Away With It', or 'How To Have A Happy Divorce'? You didn't like those? Or *any* of the Ben Brown books?"

Katka pursed her lips and looked away across the river.

"Yes, we saw them but those were quite unusual kind of humour to Czech and Slovak tastes. Very dry, very English style of humour I think. I like them, but Elena does not like so much, and she is chief editor, so…"

"Yes, well there's always a black edge to my humour. I don't do nice cutesy bunny-wabbit cartoons, or golfing penguins either. Did you see 'The Kama Sutra for Garden Gnomes'? That sold quite well through garden centres, though we did get a few complaints from shops who hadn't realised just how rude the cartoons would be. Also from a few of those weird people who *collect* gnomes.

One nutter wrote to complain that he'd been given a copy as a Christmas present by his grandson and that his *gnomes* must have got hold of it, because he kept finding them in '*strange and disgusting positions*' around the garden. I wrote back and suggested that maybe his grandson was having a bit of fun with him, but he replied that he thought one of his gnomes was starting to look pregnant and it was all my fault. Is that even possible? Aren't all garden gnomes *male*? I mean, I drew female gnomes in my book, obviously, for the joke, but in real life aren't all garden gnomes male…y'know with beards? He still writes to me apparently, with photos of his gnomes, but I asked my publishers not to pass the letters on any more. It was all getting a bit disturbing."

Katka was gently tapping her buttery knife on her plate, pursing her lips even more and gazing at me with a strangely pitying look in her eyes. She shook her head as if to clear it, then pointed her knife at me.

"I *showed* you book. I took it from my pocket at book fair after you invite me for dinner. You try to tell me your name, but I say it is okay because I already know it from cover of book. Why do you not say then that this is not your book, not your name?"

"I wasn't really looking that carefully at the book, Katka. I was looking at *you*. It was just a book. You said it was one of mine and I must have assumed it *was*."

"You said that you saw us looking at your book on stand. That was book we were reading when you come to stand and talk to your friend James."

"No it wasn't."

"Well we look at many books on stand before you arrive. Elena says this is one we read as you talk to James. Perhaps she makes mistake. Perhaps she is talking too much with James and does not think enough about which book she brings back for me. But this is very good. I am really happy now."

Katka clapped her hands together and beamed at me. Now it was *my* turn to purse my lips and give *her* a look. I shook my head vehemently.

"No, it's *not* good. So it's Steve's books you want to publish in Czech, not mine?"

"Well, perhaps your books as well. But mostly those very funny animals playing football and other sports. They are really *very* funny. I am sorry, Ben. It is not so important if we like Stephen's books or your books best. What is important is that we finally meet after all these years and have our second chance. Or do you really think who makes funniest books is more important?"

"No of course not. Us meeting after all this time is amazing. It's just a pity you couldn't have liked my books best *as well* as us meeting again and…ouch! That hurt! And you've got butter in my hair!"

Katka looked thoughtful for a moment then put her butter knife down, smiled and poked me playfully in the chest with her finger.

"Ben. Yes, this name is much better. Ben, do you not want to know *why* I am happy about this name business? *Why* I think it is so good?"

"I want to know why you keep trying to *hurt* me! D'you think you could ease up on the arm-punching and the whacking with buttery knives and the poking with sharp finger nails? Or is it your Pioneer unarmed combat training coming out? Are you subconsciously constantly probing and checking for special one-finger killing-points or something?"

Katka stared at me.

"You think I would try to *kill* you with breakfast-table knife or finger-nail? I was Slovak Pioneer, not Special Forces soldier."

"Just joking! That's me, the jokey, funny cartoonist guy, remember? Not as funny as some *other* cartoonists apparently, but...will you put that knife down! It's still got butter on it, and this is my best suit. Plus I still have a sneaky suspicion that you might know how to use that for a lot more than just spreading butter and jam. I don't know exactly *why*. It's just a feeling I get. And while it has its sexy side, it's also sort of worrying. So why *are* you so happy that you got my name wrong?"

"I am glad your name is not Stephen because I hate this name. Actually, I hate Slovak version, which is Štefan. Really it is surprising that I still like you even when I think your name is Štefan...I mean Stephen.

You see, at our little village school really horrible older boy called Štefan bullied me quite a lot. He calls me names and every day he pulls my pigtails and makes me cry. Always he waits for me on way to my home, to shout names and throw stones at me."

"You had pigtails?"

"Yes, my sister and I often put our hair in pigtails when we are small children, and even when we are teenagers. I still sometimes have pigtails in my hair now. But this stupid schoolboy makes me very unhappy..."

"You still put your hair in pigtails now?"

"Yes, sometimes. Not often, but sometimes I still like to do it. Anyway, to make long story shorter, Štefan did stop after quite long time, but since then I have always not liked this name at all. Ben? Are you listening? You look like you are having daydream."

"Pigtails? Really? So did he just get fed up and stop bullying you eventually?"

"Yes, but of course my sister and I first have to hit him with school-bags which we fill with stones from field. Then, while he is confused by hitting, we take away his trousers and underpants and we throw him onto farmer's dung-pile. After this, he does not do bad things to me ever again."

"I'm not surprised."

"So it is very good you are not Stephen. I am happy that you are Ben instead. Pleased to meet you, Ben Brown! *My* full name, by way, is Katarina Krásnohorská."

Katka held out her hand for me to shake.

"Katarina Krásnohorská? That sounds more interesting than plain old Ben Brown."

"Krásnohorská means 'of beautiful forest'. It also means 'of beautiful mountains'. So of course it is family name from people who live in these kinds of places long ago. My father's family live for very many generations in same couple of villages in forest on lower slopes of Tatra Mountains, so this makes plenty of sense I think."

"Hang on, Katka. You have the same word for forests and mountains? Isn't that confusing? What if you say you'll meet someone in the forest and they end up hanging around for ages on top of a mountain looking at their watch and…"

"No it is not confusing. It just happens that in this case word 'hora', from which name Krásnohorská comes, can mean some kind of forest or some kind of mountains. It is rather complicated. We have many forests and many mountains in Slovakia. And we have different names for different kinds of mountains and forests, for deep, thick forest, for less dense forest, for forest on hillside or mountainside, for mountains with high peaks, mountains with rounder tops, mountains on their own or together in ranges..."

"A bit like the Eskimos and their forty or fifty different names for different kinds of snow."

"I think I read that this is not actually true. Also I think they are called Inuit now, not Eskimo. But yes, I suppose is same principle. Why do you smile? Oh, you can have hundreds of different *snowdrops* in England, all with different names, but in Slovakia we cannot have few different kinds of forests and mountains and different names for these?"

"Sorry, Katka. Of course you can."

"Thank you. In England you do not have different names for different kinds of forest and different kinds of mountains?"

"Not really. A mountain's a mountain, unless it's too small to be a mountain and then it's a hill. And a forest is just a forest. Not that we have much real forest. Most of it was chopped down centuries ago. I once drove through Nottinghamshire and saw a road sign that said 'Welcome To Sherwood Forest'...you know, Robin Hood's forest...and there wasn't a tree in sight. Well maybe one or two, and some hedges, but that was it. So you have a *lot* of forests and mountains?"

"Of course. Almost three quarters of country is forested, and some areas are very ancient, deep forest, very special and exciting."

"Hansel and Gretel territory? Gingerbread houses and evil witches?"

"No, of course we do not have witches in Slovak forests. Only scary things are bears, and sometimes wolves. But we do make little gingerbread houses...actually little *honeybread* houses...at Christmas, for the children, with walls and roofs and chimneys of baked honeybread, and sugar-iced windows and doors, and dusted sugar powder for snow. Also, usually little honeybread people standing in snow.

When my sister and I are children we love to eat first the

little people. My father, he tries sometimes to make the honeybread people very ugly, with big noses and pointed ears; like ugly gnomes, short and fat, with wide mouths and sharp honeybread teeth, so we will not eat them before Christmas Eve. But always we *do* steal them away and eat them, even if they are horrible looking. One Christmas he even makes them to look like our granny and our granddad. 'These are your grandmother and grandfather' he tells us, 'so you cannot eat them'.

We steal them anyway, but we take them to our granny and granddad's house and we give to them as Christmas present, for them to eat. We laugh so much when they eat themselves. We were not hundred percent nice children, my sister and I. So, what does *your* last name mean? I know Brown is name of colour but does it also mean something else? Where does this name come from?"

"No idea. Maybe I come from a long line of sewage workers."

"Sewage? What is…oh! Yes, I know this word. It is another of your funny jokes."

"Probably would have been funnier if there'd been a footballing penguin involved."

"This 'who is funnier cartoonist' is *really* very important to you?"

"No. Sorry. Look, do you want to go back to my cabin before we head off to the book fair, and you can show me what you look like with pigtails?"

"We do not have time. We are actually very late. And I do not have ribbons."

Katka looked at her watch.

"As matter of fact we must hurry or Elena will worry where I am. I did not go to hotel last night so…well, perhaps she will *guess*…but we should hurry anyway."

"Maybe they'll have some ribbons on the boat somewhere. I could ask someone."

"*Who* would you ask? Man from behind bar last night? You

think perhaps he has ribbons in his cabin?!"

"I wouldn't be surprised."

"Ben, I hope you are not anti-gay. I have friends who are gay and it is not easy for them. In Eastern Europe there is not so much tolerance of this as in West and gay people are often still really *hated* and even attacked. In Slovakia this gets a little better, but very slowly, especially in smaller towns and villages."

"I don't think it's exactly easy being gay anywhere. And no, of course I don't have a problem with gay people. My best friend is gay as it happens. I do, however, have a problem with *grumpy* people. And that barman...well...grumpy must be his middle name."

Katka grinned.

"I think he likes you, Ben."

"Well he's got a funny way of showing it. Talking of grumpy, have you heard the joke about the seven dwarves sitting in the bath, all feeling happy? Happy got out, so they all felt grumpy."

"We really do not have time for very bad jokes, Ben. Can we please go now? We are really quite late."

"You're sure you don't want to show me how you look with your hair in pigtails?"

"No."

"You could have another shower and wash your hair this time, so it doesn't stick up all funny on one side like that."

Katka took a hairbrush from her bag.

"No, just brushing isn't doing it, Katka. I really think it needs washing to make it lie down right. Do you really want to go out in public with it looking like that? I'm not saying it makes you look like a clown, but you don't want to be mistaken for a street entertainer do you? Ouch! Again, I know you're just being playful, but you have a curious aptitude for causing pain with everyday objects. Are you *sure* you didn't have any kind of *special* communist Pioneer training?"

Katka shook her hair, put the brush she'd just jabbed me

with back into her bag, got up from the table and marched out of the dining room.

"Wait for me, Katka. You're going to have another shower then? I'll ask the woman at the reception desk if they have any ribbons lying around."

Twenty minutes later we were walking down the gangway to the quay, Katka pulling her coat collar up to protect her still-damp hair from the cold morning air.

"Shame I couldn't get any ribbons, Katka. Why didn't you take a bit longer to dry your hair properly?"

"Do you *know* how late we are, Ben? Book fair has been open for more than one hour already."

"Then let me get reception to phone for a taxi."

"Eco-terrorist!"

"Okay, can we not start all that again?"

"You always want to take taxis and aeroplanes! You are eco-terrorist!"

"Can you stop saying that? There's a policeman over there starting to look at us funny. Even if he doesn't speak English, which he probably does, I'm sure he'll recognise the word 'terrorist', especially when you say it right after 'aeroplane'. And could you slow down a bit. You walk awfully fast."

"Ben, global warming is *ticking bomb*! Why do you not care?"

I looked back at the policeman, who was now staring after us and talking into his radio.

"Katka, slow down. It might look like we're running away. And *please* don't shout 'bomb' at me right after calling me a terrorist. Are you still annoyed about the shower thing?"

Katka stopped, her fists on her hips, and glared at me.

"You tried to get into shower with me!"

"People do that sometimes. Y'know, get in the shower together and…"

"Not when shower cubicle is just half-metre square! I have never seen such small shower before."

"Well it's on a boat. Everything's a bit cramped. I thought

it'd be sexy."

"Ben, we were *stuck*! You start to shout for help! Was very lucky we manage to get free before someone comes to cabin."

"Sorry, I had a bit of a panic. I get claustrophobic in confined spaces sometimes."

The policeman was following us now, so I took Katka's arm and got her walking again.

"Come on, Katka, don't just stand there. We're late, remember?"

By the time I got to James's stand, the book fair had been open for nearly two hours and I fully expected him to be in a foul mood. I'd said I'd keep an eye on the stand again so he could have one last dash around the halls before our lunch meeting and my flight home. Why he couldn't leave the stand unattended for an hour or at least nip out for a quick smoke like other exhibitors did...but he was paranoid about people nicking the books. Once, just for fun, a couple of years before, I'd taken every single one of the books off the shelves while James was away from the stand and hidden them in the cupboards at the back, then pretended to be fast asleep in my chair when he returned. I thought he was going to have a heart attack when he frantically shook me awake and I told him I vaguely remembered some German schoolchildren looking at the cartoon books just before I nodded off. He goes some strange colours when he's really angry, but I'd never before seen him turn quite such a wide range of hues in so short a time, shifting rapidly from shocked, chalky white to a sort of sickly puce with livid plum-purple patches, to a volcanic crimson-scarlet, like some sort of furious public school chameleon sprinting across a lava flow.

Today, though, he was strangely calm and almost - hard to believe - happy. He didn't dash off for a ciggie the moment I arrived. Didn't even mention my lateness. Just sat there quietly humming snatches of jazz melodies and staring up at the concrete and steel ceiling with a scary smiley sort of expression.

"Good night at the Jazzkeller, James? Hello? James?"

I stepped slowly away from the stand, staring at James staring at the ceiling.

"Okay, James, you're mad at me for being late again and now you're trying to lure me into a false sense of security so I'll come close enough for you to get me. Well it's not going to work. Why is your hand in your jacket pocket? Have you got your stapler in there? I haven't forgotten that time you tried to staple my ear to the table, you know."

James's gaze drifted slowly down from the ceiling.

"Ah, Ben, you're here. Good chap. What was that? Your ear? Stapler? Oh, yes, I remember. But that was *two years* ago, dear boy. Isn't it time you got over it? After all, you did trick me into thinking all our books had been stolen from the stand on the first day of the book fair with no way for me to get hold of replacements. One *could* almost say you were *asking* to have your ear stapled to the table."

"Okay, yes, with hindsight I agree you had every right to be pissed off with me about that. I was bored stiff sitting here on the stand all afternoon and I thought you'd see the funny side of it. Obviously I was wrong, and I'm sorry about that. But that was still no reason for you to shove my head down on the table and try to staple my ear to it. You promise you haven't got your staple gun in that pocket? Take your hand out and show me."

"Ben, you should have heard her. It was wonderful."

"What? Heard who?"

"Elena. She brought her trumpet along to the Jazzkeller last night and the warm-up band let her jam with them a little. Christ, she was good! She was so good that the main band asked her to join them for a number during their set. Then they wouldn't let her sit back down. She played with them all night, and she was bloody brilliant. Best trumpet player I've heard for a long time. The proprietor invited her to play again tonight. You *have* to come, Ben. She'll make you want to cry. The woman's a genius."

James leaned back in his chair and sighed. I stepped into the stand and patted him on his pin-striped shoulder.

"Sounds like you had a really good time. I'm sure Katka would like to go to the Jazzkeller tonight. Did I tell you…"

That was the moment James chose to whip a large staple gun out of his jacket pocket and lunge at me with it.

"Two bloody hours late, you inconsiderate bastard! You said you'd be here at nine! I was supposed to meet that French publisher at her stand an hour ago! Give me your bloody ear!"

Luckily I was rescued by Elena just as James had pinned me against the wall of the stand and was trying to staple my ear to a poster showing one of Steve Watkins' stupid cartoon penguins playing table tennis. Elena had popped round to see if James wanted to go for a coffee, and her arrival distracted him just long enough for me to grab the staple gun and shove it down the front of my trousers where I knew he'd never go after it - a product of the public school system James might be, but I knew he prided himself on his heterosexuality and would never do anything that might even remotely be mistaken for a homosexual advance, such as rummaging in another man's trousers.

As Elena dragged James away, I told him I'd look after the stand until lunchtime. He was still fuming and glaring over his shoulder at me, tugging his ear and making stapling motions as they disappeared up the aisle towards the coffee stand. Across the other side of the aisle, the lady from the religious publications stand was returning with a coffee and a bratwurst in a bun. I gave her a smile as she sat down at her table, but she took one look at the prominent bulge in the front of my trousers, glanced down at her bratwurst, turned bright pink and hid her face behind a large book.

The rest of the day went fairly quietly. I got the stapler out of my trousers and hid it in a cupboard, and by the time James returned, smelling of Elena's perfume and slivovica, he seemed to have forgotten about the whole incident. So when one of the guys from the travel books stand next door came round to keep an eye on things for us, we headed off to one of the exhibition centre's many cafés to meet our American contact. While we were waiting for her to arrive and reading the menu, James did jokingly click a paper hole-punch beside my ear, which gave us both a good laugh. Actually, James laughed and I hit my head on the floor as I fell backwards, tipping my chair over in sheer panic. But that was the only reference he made to his earlier outburst and the ear-stapling attempt. After that, he really cheered up and couldn't stop praising Elena's prowess on the trumpet, repeatedly insisting that Katka and I absolutely *must* make it to the Jazzkeller that night to hear her play again.

To ensure that we did, without any danger of me and Katka detouring for more sightseeing or back to the hotel boat for what James elegantly described as 'a quick jump', he insisted on phoning the Italian restaurant himself and booking a table for the four of us for seven-thirty, so we could eat early and get to the Jazzkeller before the music started. This time Katka chose pasta and I had the potato dumplings, which she immediately started helping herself to from my plate. I tried to order her the dark chocolate pudding again, insisting that James should see the effect for himself. But Elena - who knew about Katka's chocolate allergy - said it was cruel to make fun of her and sternly forbade the waiter from bringing anything so rich in dark chocolate anywhere near our table. As we ate our vanilla ice creams and watched the last available portion of the dark chocolate pud disappearing into another diner, Katka kicked me hard under the table.

Outside, after another long farewell between Katka and the proprietor's wife, involving half-whispered exchanges in fast Italian, amused sideways glances at me and a couple of actual out-loud laughs, we walked off into the dark. I limped from the pain in my ankle where Katka had kicked me, Elena was complaining about the freezing cold and James kept demanding to know *how* exactly one taxi ride to the Jazzkeller would make so much difference to the environment. When

Katka tried to explain, James huffily insisted that he was actually quite looking forward to England being as hot as Spain, and then no-one would need to fly abroad on holiday, which he imagined would be something Katka should welcome, shouldn't she? If Katka thought hitting him with her handbag was going to shut him up, well she didn't know James. By the time we reached the Jazzkeller they'd been going at it like cat and dog for a good twenty minutes.

"I'm an eco-terrorist," James proudly announced to the barman as we walked in. "Give me four large beers or I'll blow up a tree!"

Katka tried to hit him again, but by now James was getting used to it and easily dodged the handbag on his way to the toilet.

"Just going to point Percy at the porcelain, Ben. Pay for those will you? Good man."

But James had underestimated Katka's determination. She waylaid him as he came back out of the toilets, getting him in what looked like some kind of elbow-bending judo hold and steering him towards a corner table where she proceeded to lecture him about the real dangers of climate change until Elena felt well-lubricated enough to get up on the stage. She really was *very* good. She performed a couple of fantastic warm-up trumpet solos while the advertised band assembled behind her, then they joined in and helped her blow the roof off the place.

It was past midnight by the time Katka and I got back to the hotel boat. We were both shattered and ready for bed, but the bar was still open and full of people, so we went in for a night-cap to wash down the sea-sickness pills I'd bought for her.

"Thank God grumpy-guts the barman isn't here," I muttered, watching a stunningly attractive, tall blond woman in a tight white blouse and black pencil skirt pouring beers behind the bar. "Must be his night off."

"I told you, I think he likes you," Katka smiled. "It is not his fault he thinks you are nice and then realises you are with me and not available."

Katka caught the eye of the gorgeous barmaid, who immediately turned to her and asked, with a wide smile, what she'd like. I leaned against the bar and started to reach for the bowl of peanuts - until Katka kicked me for the second time that night, frowned and nodded at the back of my hand, the indelible writing on it still clearly legible.

I bent to rub my ankle, and when I stood back up Katka and the barmaid seemed to be enjoying a private little smile-fest, flashing their teeth at one another and shaking their long hair as they chatted. Without even looking at me, the barmaid plonked a cold beer in front of me then, with an extra big smile, leaned on the bar to give Katka *her* drink. For a moment the top of the blond goddess's blouse gaped open to reveal a truly superb cleavage before she straightened up again and took Katka's money. Turning back from the till, she handed Katka her change, placing the coins in the palm of Katka's hand then slowly sliding her finger-tips back across Katka's outstretched fingers and winking at her before walking off to the other end of the bar, swinging her hips in her short black skirt, to serve a slightly pissed group of Australians. Katka watched her walk away then turned to me, smiled and raised her glass.

"This Dutch hotel boat is very interesting place, Ben. Cheers!"

Slivovica and Slovak Bacon Butties

"Actually, Ben, I did have some small lesbian experience once, with girl at university in Bratislava."

I opened my eyes and stared at Katka, who was watching the lights of German villages slide past in the dark outside the coach window. I'd been trying to get to sleep for the last hour or so. Despite the engine noise, Elena snoring loudly in the seat in front of me and the fact that I'd never in my life managed to fall asleep sitting upright in a moving vehicle, I was so tired that I *had* actually started to nod off. But now I was wide awake again.

"You had a lesbian relationship?"

"Not relationship. Experience. Once only. After New Year's party in university dormitory building."

"Why are you telling me this *now*?"

"Last night on hotel boat you ask me why woman behind bar was so friendly to me. You keep asking if I was flirting with her."

"Well it did *look* a bit like the two of you were flirting. She was definitely hitting on you, the way she leaned over so you could see down the front of her blouse, and all that stroking your fingers and winking, and wiggling her bum at you - *and* you looked at her bum as she walked away. But why are you telling me *now* that you had a lesbian thing when you were at college?"

"Because last night you keep asking…"

"No, I mean why couldn't you tell me *last night*, instead of *now*, when we're stuck on a coach with forty or fifty other people?"

"I do not understand. Why does it matter whether I tell you this last night when we are in bed or tonight when we are on coach?"

"Because…trust me, it just does! How far are we from Prague?"

"Must be still hundreds of kilometres. Why?"

"Never mind."

"She had very nice bottom."

"What? The girl at university?"

"No, woman behind bar on hotel boat last night. Very nice and roundy, so I look at it. What is wrong with this?"

"Oh God! Nothing! Just, you could have told me all this last night when we *weren't* hundreds of kilometres from the nearest available bed! Are you doing it on purpose? Are you winding me up?"

"You did not think she had nice bottom?"

"Stop it!"

"Okay, I stop."

Katka turned back to the window and I closed my eyes for a minute, then opened them again.

"So what did you do, you and this girl at university? Did you kiss?"

"Yes, at midnight on New Year's Eve. We both did not have boyfriends with us and all nice-looking boys at party are with girlfriends, so we joke that we should kiss *each other* at midnight. We were little bit drunk from too much vodka."

"You mean a proper kiss? On the mouth? Anything else?"

"This is private. It is not something to talk about to other people. Do you also want to know about sex with my last boyfriend?"

"No, of course not. But this is different. It's you and another *girl*!"

"That is great pity, because sex with my last boyfriend was really quite good. He had really very large…"

"Okay, I'm not talking to you any more. I'm going to sleep."

I closed my eyes and, after a couple of minutes, was once again surprisingly close to nodding off.

"Kissing only. But later we also hold each other and look at stars on balcony because we are both lonely. Also, we have to share same bed that night because so many drunk people sleep in our room. It was very crowded."

I was wide awake again.

"Really!? So did you…"

"I am sorry, did I wake you, Ben? Go back to sleep."

"I can't. Not now. Did the two of you…"

"I read in magazine somewhere that majority of women have some bisexual feelings, sometimes feel attraction to other women, but most do nothing about this. It is interesting topic to you? I do not bore you? You would not rather sleep?"

"You're trying to wind me up. You didn't really have a lesbian experience with a girl at college, did you? Oh for crying out loud! They're at it again!"

The two Czech teenagers on the long back seat behind us were snogging noisily and fumbling around with each other again. They'd been at it non-stop since we left Frankfurt. I peeked round the back of my seat then nudged Katka.

"I think they're actually having sex now. They're lying down with a blanket over them."

"Ben, please leave those kids alone. You will be thrown off bus for watching them."

"*I'll* be thrown off the bus? What about *them?* You know *we* could have nabbed the back seat if we'd got to the coach station earlier."

"Please do not start this again."

"I'm just saying, if we'd got a taxi at the start instead of trying to lug all our bags *and* the books from your stand halfway across Frankfurt..."

"Ben, we did get taxi."

"Only after half an hour, when my arms felt like they were going to drop off and Elena was threatening to throw the books into the river. We almost missed the coach."

"Well we did not miss coach, and if we took back seat, Elena would be on it with us. Now please shut up about this."

I glanced round at the young couple behind us.

"Y'know, I could get my coat down and put it over us..."

"Ben, we are not having sex on coach!"

"Oh, so *they* can shag all they want back there but...Katka? D'you want to go to the toilet?"

"No, I am okay thank you, Ben."

"I mean, do you want to *go to the toilet?"*

"What? Ben, toilet on this coach is really *tiny* small! I am *not* going to toilet with you! This would be repeat of getting-stuck-in-shower-cubicle incident. In case you forget, this is *not* aeroplane and it would not be 'mile-high-club' sex."

"No, I suppose 'three-feet-above-Germany-motorway-club' doesn't have quite the same ring to it."

"Go to sleep, Ben."

"I can't, and even if I do I'll only wake up again after a few minutes. I might nod off for a bit, but I just can't sleep properly sitting up. And what if we have a crash when I'm asleep? What if the driver dozes off at the wheel and we crash? If I'm sleeping, I won't know anything about it. I won't know to brace myself."

"Or throw yourself on top of me."

"What?"

"To save me. In this crash you think we will have."

"Oh, right. Yes, of course. I could throw myself on top of you *now* just to be on the safe side."

"Ben! Get off!"

"If I'm asleep and we crash, will I still see my life flash before my eyes? What if I don't. What if we crash and I die because you wouldn't take a 'plane, and on top of that I don't get to see my life flash before my eyes because I was asleep? There were some good bits I wouldn't mind seeing again. Not many, but some. And even if my life does flash before my eyes, if I'm asleep I might just think it's a dream and not take much notice."

"Ben, stop. Try to stop making jokes always. I know you are tired. I know you do not like to travel on coach. I also know that you are perhaps little bit scared of what we are doing, going away together when we only just met. And I think you use jokes as defence. I am scared as well; really quite scared by how fast this is happening. But I do not make jokes *all time, all day* until it is really making someone want to *throw me off coach onto road*! Okay? Now try to sleep, and let *me* sleep."

"Okay. I'll try. See, I'm shutting my eyes."

"Ben?"

"Mmmm?"

"I was not...how did you say...winding you up. I did kiss

girl at university. It was quite nice. Good night, Ben."

I opened my eyes, reached under my seat and pulled out my briefcase.

"What are you doing, Ben? You still cannot sleep? That is book about snowdrops? You always travel with…oh…*two* books about galanthus?"

"Yes, monographs of snowdrops in the wild and in cultivation."

"And what are papers? Also about galanthus? Yes, it says there: 'The Systematic Value of Nuclear DNA Content in *Galanthus* by B.M.J. Zonneveld' This is scientific paper?"

"Yes, it's very interesting. It's a study done in Holland using a technique called flow cytometry to work out the varying levels of cellular DNA content in different snowdrop species and garden hybrids. It's been quite useful to me for breeding new snowdrop varieties, helping to figure out which snowdrops might cross with other…Katka? Katka?"

Katka was snoring gently. Her head rocked with the motion of the coach and slid sideways onto my shoulder. Behind us the Czech kids were bumping around again and somehow managing to thud rhythmically against the back of my seat. It was going to be a long night. I sighed, looked down at Katka's sleeping face and couldn't help smiling. Later, when she started dribbling, I slid a sheet of Dr. Zonneveld's Systematic Value of Nuclear DNA Content in Galanthus study between my shoulder and her cheek to keep my shirt dry.

It was the end of a very long day as well as the start of a long sleepless night for me. Katka had woken me early that morning. The seasickness pills must have worn off during the night because she was up at six feeling queasy even though the water was calm, and had to spend the next hour in the toilet until a fresh pill kicked in. By which time there was so much noise on the boat, with everyone packing to leave on the last day of the book fair, that neither of us could get back to sleep.

In the breakfast room, the grumpy barman completely ignored me, while the beautiful blond Dutch barmaid came over and shared our table, chatting with Katka like they were long-lost sisters. When I checked out, she was waiting at the sliding door to the gangplank to give Katka a huge hug, a kiss goodbye and her address in Amsterdam.

The grass between the quay and the embankment up to the main road was white with frost and the morning air was colder than ever, turning our breath to steam as we walked through the city centre to the Messe halls. Yet again, Katka wouldn't let me get a taxi so it was lucky I only had a small suitcase and my briefcase to carry. But by the time we got to the book fair it still felt like my right arm had stretched a good six inches.

As it was the last day, Elena let Katka take the afternoon off so we could collect Katka's suitcase from *her* hotel, do some last-minute sightseeing together and have one last early dinner at the Italian restaurant, where Mrs proprietor cried and cuddled Katka before giving me a stern little lecture about treating her properly and looking after her. Interestingly, she didn't give Katka a lecture about treating *me* properly and looking after *me*. But when I pointed this out to her, and mentioned all the playful but painful finger-poking, arm-punching and whacking on the head with butter knives and hairbrushes, Mrs proprietor just laughed, pushed us out of the restaurant door and smacked me hard on the bum by way of farewell.

Then it was back to the book fair to help Elena and James pack up the stands. We put James and his luggage into a taxi to the airport before arguing loudly with Katka on the pavement about how far it was to the coach station, how many bags we had to carry, how little time we had before the night coach to Prague left, and (once again) how little damage to the environment one taxi ride would do - especially with three of us sharing. But Katka was adamant she wanted to walk through the city one last time and enjoy the frosty night air before spending eight hours on the coach.

And now here I was, at a quarter to midnight, not even half-way through the journey, horribly sleep deprived, with Katka snoring and gently dribbling onto my shoulder and a couple of strangers shagging just behind me. I couldn't even move to get more comfortable in case I woke Katka, and I could feel the coffee I'd drunk earlier starting to make a genuine visit to the coach's cramped toilet an imminent necessity.

What I *should* have been doing that day was checking to see how my various clumps of autumn-flowering snowdrops were getting on, and cross-pollinating the different forms and varieties if the weather back home was warm enough for the flowers to open wide and the pollen to run freely. Not many people know about the autumn snowdrops. Even amongst keen gardeners, they're not all that well known, and still fewer gardeners actually grow them. Of course real snowdrop enthusiasts will often have a few in their garden, but outside galanthophile circles they're quite a rarity. For a long time I had a particularly nice, large-flowered clump growing near my front gate where they could be seen from the street, and every October I'd get at least two or three people coming up the path to ring the doorbell and ask if I knew I had snowdrops flowering at the wrong time of year.

Once I even found a local television crew filming them over the garden wall after someone phoned the TV station to say they'd seen snowdrops flowering incredibly early due to global warming. The reporter wouldn't believe it was normal for them to flower in late October until I showed him photos and a write-up in one of my books. In the end they came back in January and did a short piece about my collection and Lady Cherrington's even bigger range of snowdrops down the road at Westcombe Manor. They went a bit heavy on the 'eccentric snowdrop collectors' angle, especially after meeting Lady C and the Colonel, but I suppose you can't blame them for that.

The week after the piece was broadcast, all the snowdrops disappeared from my front garden after someone sneaked in at night with a spade and nicked them. Luckily, I only had a small bit of ground at the front of the house so there weren't that many to steal. The vast bulk of the collection, including all the rarest ones and my own seedlings, was in the back garden and you couldn't get to them without going through the house because it was right in the middle of a terrace of cottages.

For Lady C, having rare snowdrops stolen was almost a regular occurrence. On her charity snowdrop open days she'd often catch people trying to dig up a prized bulb or two with trowels sneaked in under their coats. It infuriated the Colonel so much that one year he set up a security check at the gate, where Alfred the gardener was instructed to run a metal detector over everyone to make sure they didn't have any hidden digging implements. It was all a bit embarrassing and ultimately futile, since the following year Lady C discovered someone slyly hacking away at a snowdrop clump with a plastic kitchen spatula they've smuggle in past the metal detector.

More worrying for Lady C were the attentions of The Green Panther, as some people jokingly called him - usually people who hadn't had valuable snowdrops pinched by him. Or That Bloody Man as others referred to him - mostly those from whom he *had* nicked rare bulbs. No-one had ever seen his face or managed to identify him. The most anyone in snowdrop growing circles had ever seen of him was a glimpse of a mysterious male figure dressed from head to foot in black, slipping over a garden wall or fence in the dead of night with a bag full of treasured snowdrops over his shoulder. It wasn't known if he *only* nicked rare snowdrops or was also responsible for the high-profile thefts of other kinds of rare plants, from specialist gardens, nurseries and national collections, that occasionally hit the headlines in the British gardening press. Some people were convinced that he was. But he certainly had a taste for the very rarest and most expensive, or un-buyable, snowdrop varieties.

He'd struck a number of times at Lady C's garden, always choosing from amongst the very best of her snowdrops. Not surprising really, given that hers was one of the most extensive collections in the country with many incredibly rare varieties only to be found in a few select gardens. It drove her, the Colonel and Alfred the gardener crazy. During the snowdrop season they'd taken to setting all kinds of alarms and traps for That Bloody Man. So far without success, although Alfred swore that, on one of his night-time snowdrop patrols of the garden at Westcombe Manor, he did once catch a glimpse of The Green Panther out of the corner of his eye, flitting from tree to tree and bush to bush. For months afterwards, Alfred would regularly retell the tale to anyone who would listen, his eyes wide and his voice low with the drama of it all:

"But the moment I'd look straight at 'im, it was like he just melted into the shadows and turned invisible, like that there alien creature what was being hunted by whatsisname in the jungle in that film 'Predator'. And next mornin' our only clump of elwesii 'Rosemary Burnham' had been dug up! And it weren't no badger dug 'em up neither. There was *footprints*! And them there bulbs wasn't just ripped up and scattered…they was *gone*! Completely *vanished*!"

Anyway, the autumn-flowering snowdrops: Between us, Lady C and I had a lot of different forms, some long-established varieties and others new forms raised by me from seed. That autumn I was planning to cross-pollinate the best of them and I'd really been looking forward to returning home and getting to work transferring pollen with my trusty little sable-hair watercolour paint brush. Until Katka came along, that is.

"Ben? You are very thoughtful. What do you think about? Do you think about *us*?"

I looked down into Katka's sleepy eyes. She'd woken up and was watching me closely.

"Us? Yes, that's right. I was thinking about us."

"Not about snowdrops?"

"No."

Katka sat up, stretched her arms and yawned.

"Ben? Why do you stick piece of paper to my face? This is

joke?"

"Ah, I've been looking for that page. It's the one with the section on chromosomal polyploidy in Galanthus elwesii."

"You say you were thinking about *us,* Ben!"

"I was. *Some* of the time. Ouch! Now you're starting with *pinching*?"

When we finally got to Prague it was five thirty in the morning, still pitch black and even colder than Frankfurt. The small flat that Elena and Katka shared on the top floor of an old Soviet-era block was freezing and Katka and I had spread our coats on top of her duvet for added warmth.

"Ben? We are underneath your coat now. Ben? Wake up, Ben! If you wake up, I will tell you about kissing girl at university. Ben!"

It was the middle of the afternoon when I opened my eyes again. Katka and Elena were already up and clattering dishes in the tiny kitchen. The bedroom door opened and Katka came in wearing silky red pyjamas and carrying two mugs of black coffee.

"Here, some real Slovak coffee for you, Ben. This will wake you up. Heating is back on and there is hot water for shower."

"Thanks. Bloody hell, that *is* strong. It's not very hot, but it's certainly strong."

"Sorry. I was talking to Elena while I stir coffees. I should have brought sooner…"

"Eugh! Oh God, I've got a mouth full of coffee grounds. Don't you use a filter or a caffetiere or something?"

"No. This is Turecká káva. Here, spit into tissue. Turecká káva is Slovak for Turkish coffee. Is quite traditional way in Slovakia to make strong coffee. You put grinded coffee in cup then add boiled water and stir for long time until all of coffee goes to bottom of cup, then you drink. Never with milk, always black. But I put sugar to your cup because I know you like it. This way makes very strong coffee, very good to wake you properly in mornings. But you must be careful not to also drink grinded coffee at bottom of cup. I am sorry. I should warn you."

"No wonder it's strong if you keep stirring the coffee grounds around and around until they sink and then leave them in the cup to stew. How much do you put in a cup?"

"Three, four sometimes five spoons. Depends how strong you want coffee to be. I put four spoons in these cups. You do not like? It is too strong?"

"No, it's fine. Apart from the coffee grounds. Wow! Well I'm wide awake now."

"Good. Then you should get out of bed and dress. I will show you Praha. And today, specially for you, I will also put my hair into plaited pigtails. This is correct word, plaited? Yes? I have ribbons here. Now you will see how my sister and I looked as teenagers at village dances. You must also imagine I wear my teenage dancing clothes. Like in Dirty Dancing film. Very tight short-cut-off jeans trousers and tight shirt tied in knot at front under breasts. Okay? You can imagine this?"

"I'll try. Were the breasts this big when you were...yes? Okay, that helps."

I watched as Katka expertly plaited her hair into two pigtails tied with pink ribbons.

"Now I must have some sponky in my hair, Ben."

"Sorry? What did you say?"

"I said I need sponky in my hair."

Katka rummaged in her drawer and pulled out a plastic box of hair clips.

"Sponky. It is Slovak word for hair clips. Why? What did you think I say?"

"Nothing. Actually I thought you said...nothing, never mind."

"This is how my sister and I would often pin up our pigtails. I still like to do it sometimes now. You see? I wind plaits round and pin up with sponky like this. One of my old boyfriends tells me once that this makes me look little bit like Princess Leia in old Star Wars films."

Katka danced around the bedroom, wiggling her bottom and sticking out her boobs.

"Are you imagining also tight trousers and tight shirt tied up with bare stomach? You can imagine me as teenager, how I looked? Yes? Ben? What are you doing under duvet? Ben! Stop it!"

Katka whipped the duvet away, and of course Elena chose that exact moment to walk into the bedroom to tell us she'd made an omelette.

It was a fantastic omelette, stuffed with fresh wild mushrooms that Katka's father had sent her the week before, delicious earthy-tasting ceps which Katka said he'd collected himself in the forest around their village.

"My father loves to hunt for mushrooms. He knows all best places and always finds best kinds of huby; that is Slovak for mushrooms. These kind are called dubáky."

She shovelled a forkful of egg and mushrooms into her mouth and closed her eyes.

"You can *taste* forest when you eat them. You can smell damp forest floor. It is like you are *in* forest. I will take you to forest in Tatras to see if there are late mushrooms. We will dry some for you to take to England."

Katka spent what was left of the afternoon and the next few days showing me around Prague. She apologised constantly for the way it had become so touristy, saying I should have seen the city before all the Western tourists started coming. I thought it was still incredibly beautiful, the unspoilt old town and the bridges, and I was sorry to leave when Katka insisted we should catch a coach to the Tatras before the drunken British stag parties started arriving for the weekend.

At least I managed to dissuade her from taking a late-night coach again. She sulked a bit at the idea of wasting a whole day when we could travel by night. But Elena had confided to me that there was a very inexpensive Czech airlines flight from Prague to Poprad, the nearest big town to Katka's village, so I had a strong bargaining chip. We also had an interesting discussion about why Katka got seasick so easily but never got travel-sick on coaches. Car-sick? Yes, all the time apparently. Air-sick? She'd never flown but was sure she *would* be if she ever did.

We may not have been on a night coach but it still wasn't the most enjoyable trip of my life; ten-and-a-half hours, starting at 6.30 in the morning and calling at every little town on the God knows how many hundreds of kilometres journey. The countryside was pretty though, especially as we neared the Tatras. Katka was glued to the window when the western tip of the mountain range came into view.

"There! You see, Ben? The start of my beautiful Tatras. Ben, wake up! You are missing the first of the mountains. Are you *pretending* to be asleep?"

"Ouch! What did I tell you about the pinching? Is it much further?"

"Not far now. We will soon be there. Aren't they beautiful mountains?"

An hour later we arrived at the coach station in Poprad, a large town on the plain below the Tatras. A short trip on an electrified ski-train line took us up through the pine forests of the lower slopes to a quaint Alpine-style station in what Katka told me was Starý Smokovec. There were small electric tram-like trains sitting in the station waiting to leave, and she explained that these ran along the southern slopes of the mountains, taking skiers, tourists and locals to the various holiday resorts and ski villages.

"Starý means old, Ben, so this large village is Old Smokovec, and Nový Smokovec, New Smokovec, is along railway track to west; then some other villages further still along mountains. I love their names; Tatranská Polianka especially, and Štrbské Pleso, where railway line ends and there is very nice lake and ski centre. My father's restaurant is here in Starý Smokovec. But we must get train little way to the east, to Tatranská Lomnica and then find taxi to take us to my village."

97

She was pointing to the stations and villages on a colourful map fixed to a wall as I shivered and hugged myself against the bitterly cold air. Heavy dark clouds were rolling in over the mountain tops that rose up above the high-pitched ornate roof of the station building, and the ground under my shuffling feet was already turning white with frost as night closed in.

"I telephone my mother yesterday to say we are coming, but my father's car does not work, so we must take taxi for last part of journey. It is quite long walk to my village with heavy bags and it is almost dark. If we arrive earlier, it would be nice to walk through forest tracks but we cannot. I am sorry about this."

"I'll live with the disappointment, Katka. Dear God, is that really a place name? How did you pronounce that? That one there…"

"It is village resort Štrbské Pleso. This is quite difficult name for foreigners to say. It is, how you say in English, very tongue twisting. Some Slovak words have lot of consonants all together, but this name has probably more consonants together without vowels between than any other Slovak word. Similar tongue-twisting word, and also problem for non-Slovaks, is zmrzlina. This means ice-cream. Here, I write down for you. See?"

"Okay, well I guess I won't be buying many ice-creams then. Shame, I really fancy one right now."

"Really? But you are blue with cold…oh, I see, another Ben joke…quick, pick up bags! Here is train for Tatranská Lomnica. We must cross railway lines to platform over there. And we must find you warmer coat for mountains. You really *are* blue."

As the tram-train trundled through Starý Smokovec and slid into the dark mountain forest, I could see that much of the local architecture was Alpine-influenced like the railway station, with steep-roofed and ornately-gabled hotels, restaurants and chalet-style houses jostling shoulder-to-shoulder with more authentically Eastern European churches and long, low houses stretching back from the road into long, narrow gardens and orchards.

Twenty minutes on the little electric train and a short taxi-ride later, we were entering a pretty village tucked into a fold of the mountains amongst high trees. The taxi driver knew Katka and didn't need directions, taking us straight to a large, fairly modern balconied house set back a little from the road behind a much older traditional cottage. We'd barely climbed out of the car and started to heave our luggage from the boot when the front door of the larger house was flung open and people rushed down the steps and along the garden path past the cottage to greet us.

There was Katka's father, a big balding bear of a man with a large round stomach, huge hands and strong arms, squashing her in a massive rib-crushing hug before very formally shaking my hand and introducing himself in Slovak, Katka translating. Then her mother also shook my hand and introduced herself before planting kisses on both my cheeks. Katka's sister did the same, followed by her granny, a tiny little old woman in a long black dress and black headscarf, again shaking my hand before standing on tiptoe to kiss both my cheeks.

"It is very Slovak for women to greet by kissing on both cheeks when first being introduced," Katka breathlessly explained to me as her father crushed her in yet another bear-hug. "I hope it is not too embarrassing for you. Your face goes very pink. You English people do not do this greeting-kissing so much, I think. Only when you are really good friends, yes?"

"Yes. No, not so much. Sometimes. It depends. Not usually people you've only just met. Should I kiss them back or…"

"Would be nice if you do, but is not absolutely necessary. Especially with *this* one. Do not kiss *her*. She is just nosey neighbour who has certainly come to borrow something from my mother when she hears I am coming with foreign friend, so she has something to gossip about in village."

The neighbour gave me an appraising up-and-down look, shook my hand and kissed my cheeks. Then, last of all, a tall, bent old man with incredibly bushy eyebrows and a big droopy moustache shuffled down the steps in a dark suit, his thin bony hand held out in welcome.

"My granddad says he hopes you travelled safely and comfortably and that you must come to his house and drink his slivovica with him. He will tell you about when he fought with Slovak partisans in the mountains during Second World War."

"Really? That sounds interesting."

"Granny says he makes most of his war stories up."

"Oh."

"But he did fight against Germans with our partisans - our resistance fighters - and then with Russians when they liberate Slovakia. He was shot, but only once, in leg only. He will show you scar on side of head, but that was really accident with machine on collective farm. And ugly thing on chest near heart, but that is just birthmark. You can pretend to believe him if you like. Granny says it is easier than arguing."

In the kitchen, the two of us sat at the table as bottles, glasses, plates and cutlery were brought from the cupboards and Katka's father busied himself at the stove. I leaned over and whispered to Katka.

"Is it normal here to introduce yourself so formally when you shake hands? I mean the way they all shook hands and said their full names. In England you'd usually just tell someone your first name, like 'Hi, I'm Ben' rather than 'Good evening, I am Ben Brown'."

"When first meeting or introduced, yes, people will often do this. This is quite formal situation for them that I have brought you specially to meet them."

"Okay. It just seems a bit odd, introducing themselves so formally and shaking hands and then kissing…and when your father introduced himself and you translated, was his surname different to yours? Your mother said 'Krásnohorská' like you, but I'm sure your father said 'Krásnohorski' with 'ski' on the end, and you said the same thing when you translated. Or did I hear it wrong?"

"No, you hear correctly. It is normal in Slovakia to have different surname endings for men and women. My mother is Mária Krásnohorská with 'a' ending like me, but my father is Ján Krásnohorský with 'y' ending because he is man. Where male name ends in 'y', female version is 'a' and where male surname ends in consonant, without 'y', then female version will have 'ová' put onto end.

Even foreign names in Slovak are usually given male or female ending. For example, on covers of Harry Potter books published in Slovak language, J.K. Rowling is written as 'J.K. Rowlingová' with 'ová' ending to show she is woman. This is because surname 'Rowling' without such female ending would sound like she is man. In Slovak, all nouns, including surnames, have certain sex. Everything is feminine, masculine or neuter... "

"Like German."

"Yes, like German and some other languages. You have excellent grasp of linguistics."

"Really?"

"No, not really. As I say, all Slovak nouns are feminine, masculine or neuter. Usually feminine nouns will have 'a' ending, while masculine nouns mostly end with consonant. For example, klobása..."

Katka pointed to the plate of sausages that her sister had taken from the fridge.

"...sausage is klobása in Slovak, and it is feminine word so has 'a' ending."

Katka's mother put a huge jar of pickled gherkins on the table and Katka tapped the lid with her finger.

"Uhorka is cucumber. It has 'a' ending and so is also feminine word. Ben? Why do you laugh?"

"How can sausage and cucumber be *feminine*?"

"They just are."

"Next you'll be telling me 'banana' is a feminine word!"

"No, in Slovak it is 'banán', does not have 'a' ending and is masculine word"

"Thank God for that. But why would *anyone* decide that sausage and cucumber should be feminine, not masculine? I mean, just *look* at them, look at the *shape*."

Katka looked puzzled then sighed.

"Ah, I see. Yes, I suppose this would be funny for you. To me it seems normal. But yes, I suppose…by way, Ben, why do you whisper? No-one here speaks English; only me. My sister's children start to learn at school, and they try to teach her but up to now all she knows is hello and thank you."

"Okay, I didn't know that. But seriously…" I picked up a sausage and waggled it in front of Katka's face. "…how could anyone think 'sausage' should be feminine? *Everyone* knows a sausage looks like a willy."

"Willy? I am sorry, Ben, I do not know this word."

"A penis. Sausages are *famous* for looking like penises. There must be a million jokes where sausage means penis…what? What's wrong?"

Katka's grandparents, sitting at the other end of the table, and her mother and father were all staring at me as I waggled the sausage.

"Ben, we have same word in Slovak. They all know what *this* word 'penis' means. I think it is same in all languages. Please stop saying it and please put down sausage. Granny does not know where to look."

"Oh, right. Sorry."

"Ah! See? Now my father wants to tell you very rude joke about pickle slicer. He says I must translate. I am sorry, Ben. I have heard this before and it really is quite rude."

Katka's father chopped onions, grinning over his shoulder at me as Katka translated.

"This man who works in food factory tells his friend at bus-stop one day that he has started having urge to put his willy in pickle slicer at factory. His friend tells him he must fight this urge; he must think of his poor wife, how she will feel if he does this awful thing. This man agrees, but every day he tells his friend same thing, until one day he says 'I did it. I put my willy in pickle slicer, and now they have fired me from my job.' His friend says 'Who cares about your job?! Tell me about what happened with *pickle slicer*!' And this man says 'Oh, they fire her as well.' Ben, please do not laugh so much. You will encourage him to tell more, and he knows some *really* rude ones."

As Katka's father started another joke, her granny and granddad left, first making her promise we would visit them as soon as we'd finished eating. Her sister left soon after, to get a lift back to Poprad.

"My father makes for you some nice meaty food," said Katka as I laughed at her translation of yet another rude punch-line from her father's seemingly endless repertoire.

"I thought you said he always makes you potato dumplings and cheese sauce when you come home."

"Halušky, yes. He will make this for me, and some for you if you would like to try. I tell him you are not vegetarian, and he is very happy he can make for you some meaty dishes which he likes to eat. He would not have believed anyway if I had said you were vegetarian."

"I'm not."

"I know. But even if I tell him you are, he will not believe and will give you meat anyway. Slovak men are *never* vegetarian, and mostly Slovak women are also not. He will probably try to get *me* to eat some meat before this meal is finished. He always does. He says that first he makes for you his favourite snack for eating with vodka. It is bacon fat on bread with uncooked onions, special very hot ones from our garden."

Her father put chunks of white fat into what looked like a long-handled cast-iron bed-warmer that he'd taken off the stove. The fat sizzled in the pre-heated metal as he closed it and put it back into the fierce flame of a gas ring for a minute or two. Then he held it over thick-cut slices of bread and squeezed the tong-like arms so that melted fat poured out and dripped generously over the bread, onto which he piled chopped raw onions. Katka's mother poured vodka into small glasses for everyone and indicated for me to tuck in.

Katka pulled a disgusted face as I bit into the first grease-soaked slice, then she squeaked with delight as a plate of small dumplings in a white cheese sauce was plonked in front of her. I managed a couple of slices of the fatty bread and red-hot onions, washed down with vodka, and it really wasn't too bad, like a bacon sandwich without the bacon but with lots of grease and lashings of red-hot raw onions that turned your tongue numb. As I waved my hand in front of my mouth and fanned my tongue, Katka's mother grinned and poured more vodka, gesturing to me to knock it back quickly. I did, and it helped - a bit.

"You do not have to drink so fast, Ben," said Katka, her mouth full of dumplings. "If you have empty glass, they will just fill it again."

As if to prove her right, Katka's mother immediately gave me a refill and once again motioned to me to drink up.

"Ben, you must try some halušky. Dumplings are fresh home-made with flour and grated potato, then boiled. Sauce is made with Bryndza, special Slovak soft sheep's cheese. Here, eat."

Katka offered me a forkful of the small dumplings from her plate. After the fat-soaked bread and onions, the dumplings and cheese sauce were nice enough but seemed to lack something.

"Mmm. Cheesy. And...potatoey."

"You do not like Bryndzové halušky? It is really our national dish. You *must* like it!"

"It's okay. A little bit blan...oh, thank you."

With a big smile, Katka's father pushed a second plateful in front of me, but this time he'd poured melted bacon fat all over the dumplings and cheese sauce. He said something to Katka, who shook her head in disagreement.

"He says to tell you it is much better with bacon fat. I do not agree, but this is how most Slovaks will eat it; also with some…ah, he has made them for you…little pieces of crisp fried bacon meat, fat and skin on top. You really like it better this way, Ben? Nie! Nie! He always does this! Nie! He knows I do not want bacon but still he tries to make me eat it."

Katka's father had tipped a pile of what looked like crispy pork scratchings onto my dumplings and tried to do the same to Katka's. She pushed the frying pan aside and jabbed at him with her fork to make him take it away.

I was starting to feel a bit stuffed, but after this there was fried pork schnitzel with the best mashed potato I'd ever tasted.

"Katka, is this some kind of special Slovak potato variety? It's delicious, the most amazing mash I've ever eaten."

"No, my mother says it is not special potato, but my father always puts in lot of butter and also lot of cream. And I mean *lot*! This is how Slovaks always make it."

"Okay, and what's this in the breadcrumbs next to the schnitzel?"

"Fried cauliflower. It is a favourite with Slovaks. Nie! Nie! You see? My father tries to put schnitzel on my plate while I am not looking! I tell him I will just have potatoes and fried cauliflower but he will not listen."

"What's the death rate from heart-attacks like in Slovakia then? Pretty low, I expect, what with the incredibly healthy diet."

"Would you like some of my mother's pickled cucumbers, or my father's made-at-home sour cabbage? They are very good to eat with such greasy foods. Our sour cabbage is like German sauerkraut, but better of course. My father makes it in earthen jars in cellar. I will show you tomorrow. You shred white cabbage and put to special jars with salt, then leave to ferment. Jars have rim with water in, so lid floats and gas can bubble out. I can never eat too much of this. Here, try some."

"It does cut through the grease."

"Sometimes Slovaks will also fry this with onions, garlic

and caraway seeds to make hot sour cabbage for eating with meat and large bread dumplings. That is even more delicious."

At last the food stopped arriving, but only after I'd turned down a second helping of Slovak pancakes filled with sweet curd-cheese and smothered in dark chocolate - which Katka ate for me - and a plateful of smoked cheeses. I was alternately sipping at yet another shot of vodka and a glass of beer when Katka announced it was time to visit her granny and granddad. I stumbled down the path in the dark, hiccupping quietly and only tripping up a couple of times as we walked to the older cottage by the roadside, on the way passing through a large vegetable patch, now mostly bare earth except for rows of cabbages glistening with frost.

"It is quite common in Slovak villages," explained Katka, "for people to build houses in gardens of parents' houses. Village gardens are often very big with room for second house. Also village people often come and help each other with house building. It is quite nice communal thing to do, I think. And when someone else builds house, you go to help *them*. Most of people from village came and helped my father in some way or other to build our house when my sister and I were small children. Each had some skill that was needed, or just offered hard work with concrete blocks and cement."

Inside the cottage, Katka's granny and granddad sat waiting beside a huge built-in tiled wood-burning stove beneath a bare dangling light-bulb. The small kitchen table was covered with plates of food, glasses and bottles.

"I can't eat anything else, Katka! I really can't!"

"It is Slovak hospitality, Ben. They will keep offering until you have some. At least cut yourself bread and bacon so they will stop."

"That's not bacon. It's a slab of fat. There's no meat on it. Well, just tiny slivers."

"It is slanina, special Slovak kind of cold fatty bacon. You cut thin slice and eat with bread. Hold loaf in your arm like this and cut towards you. Here, use my granddad's hunting knife for bacon; it is always very sharp for thin slicing. And this is slivovica, plum brandy, made from my granddad's own plums from orchard behind house here. Be careful, it is strong. He always jokes you could make Molotov cocktails - petrol bombs - with it."

Katka patted me on the back.

"Coughing will stop soon, Ben. Breathe slowly and it will get better. Granddad says this is three years old and seventy-five per cent alcohol. He always asks for highest strength possible when he takes his fermented plum liquid to distillery in Poprad."

"Bloody hell! It's like drinking paint stripper! Seventy-five per cent? That's almost double normal spirit strength! Christ! My throat's gone numb!"

"Yes, it is quite common for villagers to pay local distillery to make slivovica for them in this way, and when distillers ask what strength they want, villagers almost always say 'strongest you can make, please.' When you finish this drink, we must go to my other granny and granddad's house at other end of village. Oh, you should not have put empty glass on table. Granddad will fill it again. See? Drink up, Ben, then we can go. But first Granny insists you have some cake, and you must take walnuts for the walk. They are from her own walnut tree. And some dried prunes. These are also her own, from their plums. And Granddad says take this small bottle of slivovica to keep you warm during walk. He thinks it will snow soon."

Outside, Katka, sniffed the air and agreed with her granddad that there might be snow on the way. As we walked, she explained that her other grandparents hardly ever came to her parents' house because of a long-running disagreement between the two granddads.

"Will there be more stories about fighting with the partisans in the mountains, living on wild berries and sleeping in bear caves? Was your other granddad in the resistance as well? I suppose a lot of the old men from around here would have been."

107

"My other granddad does not talk about war. He fought on other side, *with* Germans, *against* Russians. He was made to, even though he did not want to. Things were complicated here during Second World War. Things are always complicated in wars, I think. Especially when war is being fought in your forest, your fields, your own village, even on your doorstep."

"So that's why the granddads don't like each other?"

"Oh, no. War is long time ago, and my other granddad did not fight in these mountains. He was sent to separate part of country to fight against Russians. No, they argue many years ago about piglet my other granddad says this one did not pay him for. This granddad says he paid in bottles of slivovica, but my other granddad says this one's slivovica is so weak and awful-flavoured that he would never have accepted it as payment for one of his best piglets."

It was a long walk through the straggling village to an almost identical cottage on the far side, where Katka's other granny and granddad sat by another wood-fired stove and yet another kitchen table full of food and drink.

"Granddad says you must try *his* slivovica," said Katka the moment we sat down. "He says it is much better and stronger than my other granddad's; more than eighty per cent alcohol...Ben? Are you all right? Your face has gone very red."

An hour later, we were heading back to Katka's parents' house, our pockets bulging with yet more nuts, prunes, cakes and biscuits for the return journey, plus another bottle of slivovica to keep out the cold. On the way, we'd dropped in to say hello to Katka's aunty and share some of the slivovica with her, and as we left snowflakes had started drifting slowly down on the night air. I was trying to catch them on my tongue as we walked, and the last thing I remember was Katka shouting at me.

"Watch for ice, Ben! Be careful!"

The next morning Katka opened the bedroom curtains to let in a blinding blast of white light. I stuck my head under the duvet and groaned.

"Ohhh! Why is everything so sodding bright? Ouch, my head hurts!"

"You slipped and banged head on road. My father and I carried you into house. It was lucky we were just outside. And it is so bright because IT HAS SNOWED! Come and see, Ben! Please! It is so beautiful!"

"No, it's too bright! Is that juice and coffee?"

"Yes. And some bread, and eggs scrambled with fried onions. It will help your hangover. Eat."

"God, no! Take it away! I can't face any more greasy food. Ohhh, I think I'm going to be…"

"Eat your eggs and onions, or I will take you to my father's restaurant where he will make you eat and drink traditional Slovak hangover cures like pickled sausages, pickled herring fish and juice from sour cabbage."

"Pickled *sausages*?"

"Yes, they are small fatty sausages like bratwurst, pickled in vinegar, very traditional hangover remedy. Slovak name is utopenec. This means literally 'drowned man' because they look pale, fat and bloated floating in vinegar jar…Ben? Quick! Toilet is this way!"

Snow, Blue Skies and Fried Cheese

The next week was all about the snow. During the night almost thirty centimetres had fallen on the mountains and surrounding villages in what Katka gleefully described as the best early snowfall since her childhood. It was followed by clear skies, dazzling sunshine and temperatures barely above freezing by day and bone-chillingly sub-zero in the black, starry nights.

Above the village, the jagged peaks were beautiful with their dazzling white coats against the brilliant blue of the sky. Down below, the locals blithely took to the roads in their cars and trucks without waiting for the snow ploughs, flattening the snow and then driving frighteningly fast on the resulting ice.

It was certainly all about the snow for Katka, who couldn't get enough of the stuff; the walking through it, the rolling in it, the skiing and sledging on it, the snowball fights and the building snowmen with her sister's two young children - not to mention the stuffing it down my neck every time I turned my back. I'd almost forgotten what deep, crisp long-lasting snow was like after so many mild English winters with nothing but the odd short-lived, slushy global-warming sprinkling. Of course this was a couple of years before the very cold and snowy winter of 2008-09, which reminded everyone in the UK what a real freezing, snowy winter could be like after more than a decade of incredibly warm ones.

Not being a skier and so never having been on a snowy winter holiday before, I have to admit I had a lot of fun, even though I spent more time than I care to remember falling over and sliding down ski slopes on my bum.

For me, though, that week was probably as memorable for the food and the drink as for the snow. The days and nights were an endless procession of incredibly stomach-filling, cold-beating, artery-clogging food that Katka's family seemed to feel I needed in order to give my puny English body the slightest chance of coping with the rigours of a Slovak mountain winter. Not that they called it winter. Not yet. Apparently this 'not-so-deep' snowfall was just an appetiser for winter proper, which everyone assured me would be *much* snowier and *far* colder and for which I would need *proper* feeding-up. I would also need something warmer to wear than Katka's father's ancient ski-jacket which, like the borrowed snow-boots, was much too big for me and let in the cold wind - and snow down the neck - all too easily.

But oh, dear God, the food! Don't get me wrong, it was

mostly okay and often delicious in a thunkingly hearty meat and potato and dumpling, deep-fried, zillion-calories-a-portion sort of way. And being by birth a Lancashire lad, I wasn't completely un-used to stodgy food but this was in a completely new league. Since we mostly ate in Katka's father's restaurant or his kitchen at home, I also had to have every dish, and her father's particular version, its secret ingredients and techniques, lovingly explained to me, through Katka, over and over again. By the end of the week I could have written a Slovak cookbook.

For a start there were the dumplings, Katka's father's speciality: The cheesy Bryndzové halušky that I'd already tried; the pirohy, like half-moon-shaped ravioli with a filling of mashed potato, cheese and mint, smothered in fresh cream and/or bacon fat and crispy bacon bits; slices of large steamed bread dumplings that came with hot sauerkraut to accompany sausages, slow-cooked wild boar, beef and fried liver. And finally, the sweet pudding dumplings with whole plums and apricots inside, a Czech speciality rather than a Slovak one but very popular with the tourists at Katka's father's restaurant.

Then there were the potatoes: Chips, or hranolky, were on every menu, as were potatoes mashed and liberally laced with butter and cream, potatoes pan-fried in smoking-hot bacon fat, and fried potato pancakes filled with rich meat and sauce mixtures, of which my favourite was diabolská pochútka. This Katka translated as 'devil's tastybits'; not as hot as the name suggested, at least not compared to a British takeaway madras or vindaloo, but not bad and worth ordering for the name alone. The one thing I was almost never offered was plain boiled or steamed potatoes.

It seemed like nothing was boiled or baked if it could be fried. Even the bread and the cheese sometimes came deep-fried. I had Katka's sister to thank for the chronic day-long indigestion after she made me try lángoš from a roadside food stall; a thick pancake of deep-fried dough, like a crispy and very lumpy naan, oozing grease and rubbed with a watery raw-garlic paste. And I found the very idea of fried cheese hard to believe when we first had it for lunch, but Katka insisted I try it since it was yet another Slovak speciality and a good vegetarian stand-by for her when eating out. A thick wodge of Gruyère-type processed cheese, coated in bread crumbs and deep fried, came (always, apparently) with chips and a small jug of tartar sauce that you were supposed to pour over the crumb-coated cheese and chips before eating. They should call it 'Heart Attack on a Plate' or 'Death by Grease'.

As we walked to the train station, I looked back at her father's restaurant and rubbed at the heartburn in the centre of my chest, hoping it wasn't the start of a coronary.

"Katka, do your family have a problem with me?"

"No, Ben. They like you, and if they did not, they would still be nice to you because they know I am in love with you. Why?"

"I think they're trying to kill me - admittedly very slowly - with all this fatty food. I must have put on half-a-stone since we got here. And all the vodka and slivovica! By the time we leave I'm going to have a blood-cholesterol level that's through the roof and zero liver function. Did they stuff your other boyfriends like this? It could be their way of killing off unsuitable admirers."

"Yes, of course they feed my old boyfriends same way. But they were all Slovak, so did not complain like this. It is food for people who work hard in fields and forests, in freezing temperatures; this is how our food developed."

"Yeah, but I work behind a desk. Sometimes, if I'm coming up with cartoon ideas, I work lying on my back. I'm not sure I can afford to carry on playing coronary Russian roulette with zillion-calorie meals swimming in grease. God, I never thought I'd find myself begging for more greens, but don't they ever have veg with their food here? Some cabbage or Brussels sprouts?"

"Almost never. Cabbage here is really only for making into salted sour cabbage. Mostly, vegetables are preserved for winter, not eaten fresh. It is traditional, from before days of deep freezers. Once couple of years ago I remember my mother buying Brussels sprouts. It is first time she ever sees them. They are not usually grown in Slovakia and were sold here as great novelty. She did not know what to do with them, so she puts them in vinegar to pickle them. Yes, I know it is maybe funny to you, but it seemed sensible to her. Ben, it is really not so funny! Please stop laughing!"

"I'm sorry, it's just the thought of pickled Brussels…hey! You know I'm really getting tired of the snow down the back of the neck thing! It's cold enough already here without having snow shoved down your collar every five minutes! Hang on a minute…did you just say you were in love with me? Yes you did, I heard you! Katka, get away from me with that. Katka! Don't! Put that snow down! Bloody hell, you did it again!"

Actually, Katka had a bit of a row with a waiter over fried cheese in another café, in Štrbské Pleso, later in the week after we'd been skiing - or rather after Katka had been skiing and I'd been practising my falling over and sliding down on my bum looking like a prat.

Katka had exploded when she cut into her fried cheese to find that inside the crunchy breadcrumb crust was the traditional half-melted chunk of cheese plus a slice of ham. She had to kick up quite a fuss before the waiter reluctantly agreed to take her plate back to the kitchen and have a replacement made for her without the ham.

"This happens so many times," Katka grumbled. "They write 'fried cheese' on menu and do not say that they also put ham in it. Sometimes I even start to eat before I realise. It is really annoying, and every time when I complain and say I am vegetarian, they tell me 'It is only ham, is not *real* meat. Why you cannot eat ham?' It is same with chicken. Most Slovaks do not think these as *proper* meat and expect vegetarians will eat them. Even when I am at friends' houses, when they know for years I am vegetarian, still they will say to me 'We are eating meat tonight but we have some ham for you.' "

Not that Katka was always *totally* consistent in her vegetarianism, as I discovered one lunchtime after a long climb up snowy mountain tracks to a chalet café perched at the top of a scenic rocky pass. Katka ordered us two bowls of bean soup with chunks of bread, explaining that it was a very traditional mountain walking meal. It was a delicious soup, thick, savoury, spicy, dark brown and full of beans...and big chunks of smoked meat. I reached over and pulled Katka's bowl away from her as she slurped her first spoonful.

"Katka, stop! There's meat in it."

I held up a spoonful from my own bowl, with a large fatty piece of meat amongst the beans. Katka frowned and tried to pull her bowl away from me.

"It is okay, Ben. Thank you, but it is okay."

"No, really, yours has got meat in too. See? You can't eat it. Didn't it say on the menu there was meat in it?"

"This bean soup *always* has smoked pork in it. Give my bowl to me, Ben. I will eat it."

"You don't have to. I can eat yours. You get something vegetarian."

"Ben, give me my soup. It is traditional to have this soup in Slovak mountain chalets. It is usually only thing you can buy to eat in such small cafés at top of mountains, so I am quite used to have this when I am walking in Tatras. Give it to me."

"There's lots of other stuff on the menu here. Look, the waitress just gave that woman fried cheese and chips."

Katka leaned across the table and whispered threateningly.

"Ben, shut up and give my bean soup to me. I love this bean soup. I have loved it since I was child. It is my favourite soup. Give it to me now or I will never have sex with you again."

Although it might not always sound like it, generally Katka and I were getting on quite well. She never did admit to letting slip that she was falling in love with me, so of course I didn't tell *her* that I felt like I was falling in love too, but it was pretty obvious we both were. That's not to say we didn't have the occasional disagreement or difference of opinion. Like about whether it's funny to shove snow down someone's neck when you've already done it about a thousand times and they've asked you over and over again to pack it in. Or just how much it's generally considered acceptable to point and laugh like a hyena when someone falls and lands on their bum on the ski slopes for the hundredth time . Or whether someone was flirting outrageously with the hunky mountain rescue guys who gave us a lift in their huge four-wheel-drive.

"Ben, I know that guy from my school days. We were in same class."

"Well if he's an old friend, why'd he call you 'Kochka' instead of Katka. I heard him. If he's such an old friend why doesn't he know your name?"

"This was not *name* he calls me. He was telling me I *am* kočka. It is Czech for 'cat', and in Slovakia we use this as slang to mean woman who is very attractive, who is very 'hot'. What? When I was teenager at school, *all* boys thought I was kočka. This one thinks I still am. Do not look at me like that, I did *not* flirt with him. You *want* I should put more snow down your neck? Tell me you think I am still kočka or I will put so much snow down your neck you could build snowman with it."

Then there was the row about me falling over on the ice and not breaking my leg, or rather saying that I had when I hadn't. I mean, if you slip on ice and have a fall when you're running for a train, but you're okay, then you tell people you're okay when they rush to help, don't you? Well I knew the Slovak for 'yes' so when this woman was asking me stuff in Slovak and looking concerned, naturally I thought she was asking if I was okay. So I said yes. Perfectly reasonable, I thought. But then the woman got her mobile out and started shouting into it, and Katka knelt down and asked me which leg I'd broken.

"What do you mean, your leg is not broken, Ben? You tell

this woman it is. Yes you do. She asks if you break your leg and you say 'yes' to her. Why? Are you stupid? She is calling for ambulance."

"I thought she was asking if I was all right. That's what people would ask in England. 'Oh dear, that was a bad fall. Are you all right?' Why would anyone say 'Did you break your leg?' to someone? Why not ask if they're okay?"

"It is what we ask in Slovakia when someone looks like they might have been hurt. We ask if they have hurt themselves. If they slip badly on ice, it is quite normal to ask if you have broken leg because it is quite likely to happen. Perhaps it is because we have so much snow and ice in winter, because so many people *do* hurt themselves badly this way, *do* break legs. It is just how we ask, if you have hurt yourself, not if you are okay."

"Well it's a bloody stupid way of asking. Talk about being pessimistic. If you knew someone was ill, would you go to visit them in hospital, walk up to their bed and ask 'Are you dying?' Katka, what're you doing with that snow? Let go of my collar!"

She seemed pretty angry about the whole thing but I suspect she was just worried and upset that I might have *really* hurt myself. That didn't stop her stuffing yet more snow down my neck though, or sulking at me all the way home on the train.

The next day it was *my* turn to get pissed off with *her*. I mean, anyone would be wary and on edge if they'd just been told the sign by the forest track with a picture of a bear on it was a warning to *watch out* for bears. And it wasn't much reassurance to be told that only a *few* walkers got mauled by bears in the mountains every year; or that bears didn't normally come down this low and close to the villages unless an unusually heavy early snowfall forced them into the lower forest in search of food before their hibernation.

"Yes, yes this *is* unusually heavy early snowfall I suppose, Ben. But bears are only really dangerous when you disturb them unexpectedly and if there are cubs with them. Mostly they hear walkers coming and stay away. Just make lot of noise. Singing is good. I can teach you Slovak Pioneer marching songs if you like. No? Well if we do see some bear, then remember best thing is always to stand still and do not move. Even better is to lie down and pretend you are dead. No, you should never run. Bears can run fast as horses. No, climbing tree is also not good. Yes, I'm sure you *were* good tree climber when you were boy, but bears can climb too. Ben, put stick down. I really do not think anyone has ever managed to fight angry bear with pine branch. Just pretend to be dead. No Ben, you really could not run faster than bear and if you try to run or climb tree, I will make you unconscious so bear will think you are dead. Yes I *can* do it. No I will not need to use stick. Trust me, Ben, you will not have time to run away from bear *or* from me."

So I think anyone would be nervous if they had to nip behind a tree for a pee a few minutes later and re-emerged to find their companion had vanished. And I think anyone would have got annoyed if that 'friend' had suddenly leapt out behind them, growling and roaring like a bear, pushing them over and pinning them face-down on the ground as they screamed in abject terror. And I don't think any amount of sex that night could really be expected to make up for it.

The only other major upset I can recall came on our last day in the Tatras. Katka was obviously gearing up for a truly explosive and potentially relationship-destroying row when she whipped back the shower curtain to confront me with my mobile phone. She wanted to know who 'Prim' was and why she was texting me asking why I wasn't back from the book fair, and why 'Prim' was saying she'd been awake crying most of the night and desperately needed to talk to me.

"And take off my shower cap, Ben! I already tell you that you look stupid in it! Pink is not good colour on you. So who is 'Prim'? Your girlfriend in England? Your wife?"

I'd left my phone switched on with the text on the screen,

meaning to reply when I'd had my shower and talked to Katka about our travel plans, and she'd picked it up to take some photos for me of her sister's kids building an igloo. She was a bit suspicious when I tried to explain that Prim was short for Primula, aka Lady Cherrington, an eighty-nine-year-old fellow snowdrop enthusiast who was worried sick because she was about to lose her house and garden because of her idiotic husband's debts.

"Ben, this is stupid lie. Eighty-nine-year-old women do not know how to send text messages."

"Maybe not in Slovakia, Katka…actually, I suppose it's probably not that usual in England either…but Lady C isn't an ordinary eighty-nine-year-old. Look, here are some other texts from her. See? They're all about her garden and the snowdrops. And here's a photo of some autumn-flowering snowdrops she sent to me at the book fair."

"She uses lot of texting short words, like this 'How r u Ben?' and 'C u L…8…er'. She is really more than eighty years old? Her texting sounds like much younger person."

"She has a book of texting tips and hints. For her age, Lady C is surprisingly into new technology. During the snowdrop season she often uses her mobile to take photos of her snowdrops and send them to me. I do the same sometimes, especially if I have a new seedling flowering for the first time and I want a second opinion without dragging her down the road to my place."

"So you live near to each other?"

"Yes. Well, for the time being we do. I'm on the edge of town and her place is out in the countryside about a mile or so. It's an old manor house with a huge garden. Trouble is it's not going to be 'her place' much longer."

That's when I told Katka all about Lady C's problems. How her incompetent old fart of a husband, the Colonel, had lost vast sums of money with one stupid stock market investment and financial deal after another. And how as a result Lady C's family home, Westcombe Manor, was going to be grabbed by the bank, and the gardens she'd tended all her life, including her wonderful snowdrop woodland, sold off for building land. Her huge collection of rare snowdrops, one of the best in England, would have to make way for a development of 'executive homes', and there was nothing she could do about it. The snowdrops, thousands upon thousands of rare varieties and vast carpets of the more ordinary ones, would have to be dug up and most of them sold or given away to other enthusiasts before the bulldozers moved in. There was no way she and the Colonel could afford somewhere else with enough garden space for more than a tiny fraction of her collection. Worst of all, the stunning woodland setting in which she'd grown, cared for and shown visitors her snowdrops for so many years would disappear for ever beneath tarmac and bricks.

"That is so sad, Ben. Her garden sounds very nice. She has really lived there and looked after garden since she was child? Poor woman, to have this happen so close to end of her life, to see everything she has done in her garden destroyed. I would like to see this garden before it is gone. Would she let me see it if I come to England?"

"Of course she would. Look, I have to reply to her text anyway, to let her know when I'll be back. I'll ask her to take a couple of photos of the house and gardens and send them to us."

"You say she is 'Lady' Cherrington? She is aristocrat? And why do you call her 'Lady C'?"

"That's how I was first introduced to her by another snowdrop grower, and it's just stuck. Yes, I suppose she is an aristocrat, but not a typical one, and certainly not a rich one. Westcombe Manor's her ancestral home; been in the family for generations. She planted her first snowdrops in the woodland when she was ten. They were a present from a friend of her mother's who'd brought them down from his Scottish estate, from the grounds of his *castle* I think she said; only ordinary wild snowdrops, Galanthus nivalis, but a nice large-flowered, strong-growing form. She planted about fifty bulbs in small clumps and now, eighty years later, there must be hundreds of thousands. She just kept splitting the clumps and spreading them around. She also has a collection of nearly eight hundred different *named* snowdrops, and other growers give her more every year. Plus I've given her some of my better seedlings."

Later, as we were packing to leave, Lady C's answer arrived along with some photos. There was one of the front of the house, then various views of the formal gardens to the front, side and rear, one of them with Alfred the gardener's bum sticking up out of a border where he must have been cutting back and tidying plants and shrubs for the winter. And finally there was a snap of Lady C herself, probably taken by Alfred as she was resting one arm on his spade, plus a disturbing close-up of the Colonel leaning in close to the lens and leering obscenely, his face slightly distorted by its proximity to the camera phone.

"Here, have a look, Katka. I texted and told Lady C about you and she's sent a photo of herself and asked me to send her one of you. There are photos of the house and garden too."

"Oh, Ben, she is lovely. She reminds me a little of my great-granny, so small and with such nice eyes and beautiful smile...oh! My God! What is *that*?"

"Sorry, I should have warned you. She sent a photo of the Colonel as well. He does take a bit of getting used to, but he's basically harmless...well, unless you count using Lady C's house and garden as security with the bank for his catastrophic stock market gambles, his tendency towards outrageously sexist comments and of course his chronic flatulence...oh dear God, the farts...I get queasy just thinking about them."

"Ben, please delete this photograph of Lady Cherrington's Colonel. It frightens me, and if my sister's children see it they will have nightmares."

"Okay. Now which photo of *you* should I send her?"

"Well not *that* one. Ben, when did you take this? How did

you get your phone into shower without me noticing? Delete this one also, please; it makes my bottom look very big. Were you holding phone camera under shower curtain? There, I delete for you. Do not look at me like that. It was rude photograph and you took without permission. Ask next time, and try to use more flattering angle."

Katka was looking for a second time at the photo of Lady C and smiling, then staring at the one of the house with a look of wonder.

"Ben, this is really very beautiful house. It is built with stone? It is very big, and so is garden."

"That's not all of it. There's a massive vegetable plot as well, and a soft-fruit garden, plus the lean-too glasshouse and cold-frames. That's all to the side behind that yew hedge, and there's a small orchard beyond that; mostly apple trees, a couple of pears and a Victoria plum on the wall behind the glasshouse along with some free-standing plum trees, a damson and a medlar. The woodland is on the other side of the house. Some of the formal gardens will be sold with the house, but the rose garden, vegetable plot, fruit garden, orchard and woodland already have outline planning permission for new housing. It's the only way the bank could realise enough from the property to cover what the Colonel owes them, because the house itself needs a lot of renovation work done on it."

I took the phone from Katka and looked at the front of the house. It was undeniably a lovely old building, if a little neglected; not huge for a manor house but still quite impressive. And very pretty, built in an arts-and-crafts sort of style with stone mullioned windows, steep gables, tall chimney stacks and a mossy Cotswold stone tiled roof that sagged a little in places where there were problems with the timbers that Lady C had long meant to have put right - along with the ancient plumbing and the dodgy electrics - if she ever, through some unexpected miracle, had the money to spare. Ever the optimist, she regularly spent more than she could afford on lottery tickets and had for years kept a hundred pounds in premium bonds which she checked hopefully once a month to see if she'd won enough to make a start on all the things that needed doing.

"It's a bit run down but it is a lovely place. Some rich stock broker type will buy it after the developers have tarted it up and put in a heated pool and a new garage for the Range Rover and the Porche. The view from the terrace at the back is just stunning. It looks out over the garden and across the most beautiful little unspoilt side-valley, all green grass and trees and cows with a church spire in the distance. And there's a great little pub just down the road, where they do fantastic Sunday lunches."

Katka put her arms around my waist from behind and leaned her chin on my shoulder, looking at the photo on the small screen.

"The terrace faces south-west, so you can sit out on it watching the sunset and talking until really late on summer nights without any need for patio heaters or anything like that. The house walls and the terrace flagstones soak up so much warmth on a sunny day that they act like storage heaters well into the night. It's a lovely place to spend a summer's evening, provided you stay downwind of the Colonel. Or do I mean upwind? I can never remember. In winter when the snowdrops are out, the woodland is magical. On a warm sunny day, when the snowdrops lift their outer petals up high, there are so many of them that they fill the whole wood with their scent."

"Ben, you sound as if you love this garden too. You could not buy Lady Cherrington's house and save this garden and snowdrop wood? You are famous writer and cartoonist. It would cost too much for you?"

"I've already got a pretty big mortgage on my own house. To match what the bank are expecting to get for Lady C's house and land, I'd need to borrow close to a million on top of that and I wouldn't stand a snowball's chance in hell of ever getting a loan that big. Even if I did, just the interest payments would probably be more than I earn."

"You would need to borrow *million pounds*?"

"And that'd be on top of my existing mortgage. There's no way, and by the way I'm not exactly famous. My books sell okay, some of them, but not enough to ever make me rich, and certainly not rich enough to buy a house and garden like that. Although I *could* do with some extra space for my own snowdrops."

"Lady Cherrington's husband could really lose so much money on stock market? Without her knowing?"

"With the sort of daft deals he was doing? Easily. It started when she got her first computer three or four years ago. She wanted it to keep the records for her snowdrop collection, edit her garden photos, stuff like that. When the Colonel got his hands on it and discovered he could trade shares and do all kinds of other financial dealing and currency trading online, he was like Toad getting his hands on a new car. By the time she found out how much he'd lost, and that he'd been forging her signature and using the house as security for loans at the bank, it was too late. Oh, and he'd also discovered online casino sites, online poker and stuff like that, which didn't help."

"Toad? Yes, he does look little bit like toad, Ben. Also like...what is English name? Very slow creature with shell on back. Tortoise? Yes, like tortoise. Poor Lady Cherrington."

"I meant Toad in Wind In The Willows. Toad of Toad Hall? It's a children's book. No? Never mind. What time did you say the train leaves?"

"Yes, we must hurry, Ben. Everyone will be waiting to say goodbye. You know, I really would like to see Lady Cherrington's garden and smell all those snowdrops. I have never seen whole woodland filled with snowdrops, but it must be wonderful. My favourite flower scent is lime tree blossom. This is unofficial national tree of Slovakia. There are very old lime trees in grounds of Bratislava Castle which smell beautiful when flowering in summer. Also there is square in city centre which is small but with very big lime tree in middle, so when it flowers, scent is trapped and makes this warm sunny square just heaven to sit in, drinking coffee and breathing lime blossom perfume."

We carried our bags down the path to the front gate accompanied by Katka's father and mother, her sister and the kids. Her granny and granddad stood outside the cottage, waiting for us. They looked so sad as they hugged Katka goodbye, both of them bursting into tears, that I felt guilty about the times we'd sneaked past their door on our way home late at night.

It wasn't that we didn't want to see them, just that we knew they were sitting there waiting for our return every night with an open bottle of slivovica, bread, bacon, salami and cakes on the table. If they heard us coming up the garden path, they'd call out and we'd be in their kitchen for an hour or more having food and throat-numbing spirits forced on us even if we'd already spent the evening drinking and eating elsewhere. Then we'd have to face the same thing with Katka's parents, who were often sitting in their kitchen waiting for us as well, a fresh bottle of vodka ready to be opened, food on the table and a fresh selection of Katka's father's jokes waiting to be told. After the first couple of nights it was getting so exhausting that sometimes we just *had* to tiptoe quietly past the granny and granddad's door if we wanted to wake up feeling half-way human in the morning.

That didn't make me feel any less guilty, though, as they wiped tears from their cheeks and forced parting gifts onto us, including ridiculous amounts of food and drink for the journey; a bottle of slivovica and a bottle of wine from their own grapes, shelled walnuts, dried plums, sweet pastries filled with a sticky paste of ground poppy seeds and sugar, fatty bacon in grease-proof paper, fresh bread rolls from their oven, a jar of home-pickled cucumbers and another of home-made blackcurrant jam. Plus a bright red woollen hat and scarf that Katka's granny had knitted for her that week, a bag of dried beans for me to sow in my garden - the best kind of beans for making bean soup, apparently - and a handful of unshelled walnuts that they'd found for me when they'd heard I didn't have a walnut tree in my garden, so that I could plant them and grow myself one. The idea of a garden without a walnut tree seemed as crazy to them as the idea of growing one from seed seemed to me.

After more hugs and kisses from everyone, we jumped in the taxi and careered off along the icy road towards the railway station, the driver accelerating terrifyingly through the hairpin bends and turning round in his seat on the straight stretches to chat to Katka and eye the bottle of slivovica.

"He asks if this is my granddad's slivovica. He has heard it is very good and very strong. He would like to try some."

"While he's driving? Are you mad, Katka?"

"Of course not while he is driving. Well, I *hope* he does not mean while he is driving. Oh, look out! Pozor! Pozor!"

My head hit the back of the driver's headrest as he braked and skidded on the compacted snow, then bounced sideways against the window with a thud. As the car came to a stop, Katka pointed at the window.

"Ben! Behind you! There is *bear*!"

"Yes, very funny! Did we hit a snowdrift?"

"Seriously, Ben! Look behind you!"

"Oh, bloody hell! Fuck me!"

I'd turned round to find an enormous brown bear with its nose pressed against the car window inches from my head. It reared up onto its hind legs and pushed against the side of the car, making it rock wildly on its springs, before dropping back onto all fours, turning and ambling off into the forest.

"Ben, that was so amazing! I have never seen bear so close before, only from distance. It is lucky we did not hit him. He was crossing exactly in front of us. Ben, you will choke if you drink strong slivovica so fast as that. No, do not give to driver! My God, *men*! It was just some bear, not tyrannosaur!"

The Wrong Way to Peel a Banana

"Ouch! My elbow! That bloody hurt."

I sat on the floor of the sleeper compartment listening to the sound of the night train trundling through the Slovak countryside and rubbing my bruised elbow.

"You know, Katka, I've just realised why this train reminds me of when I was a kid. At first I thought it was just the way it goes so slowly and stops at every little town like our trains used to, so you can see things from the window instead of hurtling along between cities so fast everything's a blur. But it's the *sound* as well. Our trains used to make a sort of tiddly-dum, tiddly-dum, tiddly-dum noise but now they don't because they've welded all the tracks together so the wheels don't make any noise as they go over the joints. They just sort of whoosh along.

This train goes tiddly-dum, tiddly-dum. The rails must not be welded like ours, so they've still got gaps that make that lovely tiddly-dum sound. It so reminds me of going on trains when I was a kid. We used to go on holiday to…"

"Ben, this is very interesting but do you want to talk about trains all night or have sex?"

"Have sex. But can you come down to *my* bunk. I've fallen out of that top bunk twice now and this time I think I might have fractured my elbow."

Katka had won when it came to taking the night train, claiming, as usual, that it was a waste of a day's holiday time to spend it sitting on a train; better to travel while we slept. Except that I didn't sleep of course. I never have managed to sleep while travelling, in a plane, train, bus or car. Katka, on the other hand, got a good few hours' kip, snoring away on the top bunk as I rocked and rolled in the bottom one, nursing my elbow and occasionally sipping slivovica for the pain since we had no paracetamol or aspirin.

The sleeper coach attendant woke us just before Bratislava and minutes after I'd finally managed to drop off. A cold dawn greeted us as we stepped down from the train, the station speakers blaring loudly and a freezing wind blasting along the platform. As we were pulling in, we could see that so far they'd had nowhere near as much snow here as further north and east in the Tatras, but a few flakes were blowing in the wind and scurrying along the concrete as we left the station, and the leaden sky promised more. Katka inhaled the cold morning air deeply and smiled.

"I love Blava, Ben. I can't wait to show you the city. So much has changed since you were here before. Old Town now has lot of cafés and restaurants and new shops. Perhaps we can even go to opera."

"Excellent. But can I go to bed first?"

We found a good hotel and got a great room looking out across one of the biggest and most beautiful tree-lined squares in the Old Town with a view of the Slovak National Theatre, despite Katka's horrified protestations over the price. She'd asked the taxi driver to take us somewhere inexpensive - in Slovak, without my knowing of course - which I'd taken one look at and immediately rejected, insisting we find somewhere considerably less grotty. I must have looked very tired and grumpy because she didn't argue for more than two or three minutes before throwing her hands up and reluctantly allowing me to tell the driver in English that we wanted a better hotel.

"A *much* better hotel," I added, glaring sideways at Katka. "In the Old Town. With a good restaurant."

"Sure, no problem," said the driver, looking at Katka then grinning at me. "I know very good hotel. Very romantic."

Katka snorted and stared out of the car window at the traffic racing past outside.

"Ben, I could live for whole *month* on what this room costs for just one night," she grumbled as we went up in the elevator, but one look at the view, the huge marble bathroom and the size of the bed worked wonders on her.

"Ben, you can see our National Theatre! Look! It will be beautiful at night when it is lighted up. And have you seen bathroom? It is big as my mother's sitting room. Ben, this is really beautiful room. Thank you for insisting...Ben? Ben, wake up and look at view!"

I slept until four in the afternoon and it was already growing dark outside when Katka burst into the room waving tickets for the opera. She'd apparently undressed me and tucked me into bed while I slept, then gone off into the town on her own.

"Ben, I managed to get tickets for tonight's opera at Slovak National Theatre. It is one of my favourites, Puccini's Madame Butterfly. Sometimes you can get quite cheaply tickets that people have booked but then cancelled at last minute if you wait in booking office. I often do this when I am student, sometimes waiting whole afternoon for tickets to some opera, play or music concert. This time I only wait two hours.

Tickets used to be *very* cheap under communist regime and before there were so many tourists; cheap enough even for poor student like me. Now it is much more expensive. As Slovak, I can manage to get tickets for less than tourists by talking to right people, but still costs a lot more now. As my father says, only thing which has become cheaper since communist regime is membership of Communist Party.

I am having very, very hot bath now. You should have bath too, then we can have early dinner before opera starts. I will call you when I am in bath. It is big enough for *both* of us at same time."

I have to say I was impressed to discover that Katka had been a devotee of the theatre, opera and classical music concerts and recitals since her student days. Even more impressed that under the communist regime a student could have afforded seats at the National Theatre on a regular basis, even by hanging around for last minute bargains. According to Katka, books - another of her passions, which I guess is why she ended up working for a publisher - were a lot cheaper under the communist regime as well. The ones that weren't banned, that is.

Impressed as I was, I can't say I was looking forward to the opera. I'd never been to one but I understood it to be an acquired taste. As it turned out, the evening would probably have gone better if I could have figured out what was going on, or if Katka had been a little less absorbed in the opera and a little more prepared to explain things to me. That was also the evening when I found out about the Slovak 'pssst'.

"Katka, you said there'd be subtitles."

"There are. I showed you. Actually we call them *surtitles* because they are *above* stage."

"But you didn't say they'd be in *Slovak*. I thought you meant English subtitles."

It was okay for Katka. An opera in Italian was no problem for her since she spoke the language. I, on the other hand, didn't get a word of it. I might have recognised the odd word or two if they'd been talking, but I didn't stand a chance with Italian *singing*.

"I am sorry, Ben. I am used to coming to opera with Slovak friends. They do not usually understand Italian but can read Slovak surtitles above stage. I forgot that of course Slovak surtitles will be no use for *you*. Now stop talking. This is very beautiful part of opera."

"So what's happening now? Is she…"

"Ben! Pssst!"

"What?"

"Pssst!"

"What?"

"Ben! Why do you keep saying 'what' when I tell you to be quiet?"

"You were trying to get my attention. You were saying 'pssst'."

"No, in Slovak 'pssst' means 'be quiet'."

"No, Katka, 'pssst' means 'Hey, you! I'm trying to get your

attention'. You say 'shush' to get someone to be quiet. That or 'shut up', or 'shut the f…'"

"Ben, 'pssst' in Slovakia means 'be quiet'. Now pssst!"

"You're joking. That's just ridiculous. No-one says 'pssst' when they mean…"

That's when the well-dressed elderly woman in the row behind poked me hard in the back with her umbrella and said very loudly: "Pssst!"

Walking round the Old Town later with Katka, I was struck by how much it had changed. When I was there all those years before, it wasn't long after the end of the communist regime and a lot of the buildings were pretty tatty, new cafes and restaurants were only just starting to open up and I didn't hear a single British or American voice the whole time I was there. Things were much more basic then. Not much choice in the restaurants for a start. I remember one small cellar restaurant where fish fingers were one of the specialities, served with chips and pickled cucumber. Another café served fish fingers as a side dish with pizzas. The kids from the university had explained to me that in the old days fish fingers had been unknown in Slovakia, and that when they first arrived they were considered a Western delicacy. What really tickled me was when the young waiter came over and hovered by my chair, looking at my fish fingers and asking me very earnestly in heavily accented English: "Is everything okay, sir? Are you enjoying your meal?" Then he picked up the Heinz ketchup bottle and, with a flourish, poured a fresh dollop onto my plate for me.

Now there were crowded cafés everywhere, people sitting out at pavement tables even in the freezing night air, their coat collars turned up against the cold and the snow flurries, talking, laughing, drinking and eating like it was a warm summer's evening. Almost every street boasted brightly lit shops and restaurants. The beautiful old buildings and squares had been renovated, expensive cars drove slowly over the cobbles and I distinctly heard one or two English accents as we walked, along with American and Japanese. Bratislava still didn't seem as touristy as Prague, but it was obviously starting to feature on the tourism map.

I felt sad that I'd missed the chance to see it with Katka all those years ago, when the city was more run down but somehow also more interesting and dramatic, freshly emerged from the isolation and mystery of the Cold War and the Iron Curtain era.

It felt exciting visiting the place then. Arriving in Bratislava from Vienna in those days seemed a little edgy, almost thrilling, a bit like stepping into a Le Carré spy novel. The barrel of the sub-machine gun hanging from the border guard's shoulder had nudged my arm as I sat in the coach at the Petržalka border crossing on the outskirts of the city, surrounded by tired Slovak workers returning from their new jobs in the Austrian capital. The border guard had sucked his teeth disapprovingly at the sight of my British passport before taking it, along with everyone else's, to be examined in a rusting corrugated iron shack while more armed guards stood around under the glare of the floodlights, managing to look bored and threatening at the same time.

The city itself also felt a little threatening then, the centre dark and gloomy by night, grey, colourless and dusty by day, the Old Town neglected and quite shabby, with paint peeling from the walls. Now it felt much more prosperous, brighter and prettier, better cared for and more Western, but also somehow more ordinary, less mysterious and much safer.

I felt it would have been incredibly romantic to have fallen in love with Katka on that first visit, as Katka's friend Zuzana had tried to arrange; to have met her along with those other earnest students in the smoke-filled bars and cafés, where they talked about whether their new freedoms were here to stay or if a new strong-arm nationalist president, aligned more with Moscow than the West, was going to drag them back into their repressive past. It would have fitted perfectly with the mood of that first visit to have had a whirlwind romance with a beautiful young Slovak woman. Instead I'd gone home to England to finish tying up the loose ends of a failed relationship, divide up the CD collection and throw myself into my work.

Still, I was with Katka *now* and, though it might seem less romantic than meeting in the more dramatic setting of immediate post-revolution Bratislava, it still felt pretty damn brilliant. Or it would if she'd just stop hitting me on the sodding arm.

"Ouch! What was that for this time?"

"That was for making so much noise at opera. We were almost thrown out."

"I thought we talked about the arm hitting. You said you'd stop it. And anyway, I still say it's ridiculous to tell someone to be quiet by saying…"

"Ben, why do you think we argue about so many things? Always about such stupid little unimportant things?"

"Because you're very argumentative?"

"No. I have been thinking about it. You tell me that your brother in New Zealand is younger than you. I also have just one younger sister. So, we are both oldest children. It is obvious this is why we argue and disagree so much. We are both used to having our own way, saying what is right and what is wrong."

"Well, you certainly seem to be."

"What? Never mind. I am in love with you, Ben, and I do not want to disagree or argue with you so much. This should be happy time for us."

"It is a happy time."

"More happy, Ben. More happy. We must try not to argue and disagree so much about silly little things. Do you agree?"

"Yes, of course. Let's do that. Where are you going?"

Katka had spotted a stall selling street food; sausages, deep-fried lángoš, hot wine, heart-shaped honeybreads and a small selection of fruit. She returned and handed me a honeybread heart, kissed me and started to peel a banana for herself.

"Thanks…Katka, what're you doing?"

"I am peeling banana, Ben. I am hungry. I was too excited about opera to eat very much at dinner. Do you want one? I bought whole bunch."

"You peeled it from the wrong end. You're supposed to peel a banana…look, I'll show you."

I took a banana, broke the skin by bending the stalk and peeled back the skin from the stalk end.

"No, Ben, in Slovakia we always hold banana by stalk, so you use it like handle to hold banana while you eat, and we peel skin down from other end, not from stalk end."

"Don't be daft. No-one does it that way."

"Slovaks do, Ben. Here, I will show you. I will buy more bananas and will give to Slovaks here in street. You will see how they peel, and it will not be from stalk end. They will hold stalk end. It is sensible way to eat banana. Otherwise you do not have stalk to use as handle."

"And I'm going to find some English people and show *you* that we do it the other way around. It's just stupid to hold the stalk."

That's how Katka and I ended up on our first night out in Bratislava stopping people in the street and getting them to peel bananas for us; each of us getting in turns rattier and more triumphant as it turned out that Slovaks *do* hold the stalk and peel from the other end while the two nice, but puzzled, English couples we accosted both did it the other way round and confirmed that as far as they could recall, so did most other English people. Hah!

To this day neither of us has got around to finding some way, possibly on the internet, of carrying out a more wide-ranging survey to find out if Slovaks are the only ones who hold the stalk end or English people are the only ones who don't. But I'm sure it's pretty high on both of our 'things to do before I die' lists.

As I climbed into bed back at the hotel, Katka stood at the window looking out at the square and the National Theatre.

"Ben, you know all this evening as we walk through the Old Town, I have been thinking…"

"What? 'Why do I hit Ben on the arm so much'?"

"No, I keep thinking how sad it is that we did not meet and become lovers here in Blava all those years ago when Zuzana tried to make me come back from the Tatras so she could put us together. We would not have lost all those years between then and now.

And I wish I had been here to show you Blava as it was then. It is good that it has been made to look prettier, the buildings and streets repaired, lots of shops and cafés, nicer for the tourists and nicer for those people who live here and can afford to come to the Old Town. But in some ways I liked more how it was before; less improved and smartened-up for tourists.

I expect you like it better how it is now, Ben. What were you thinking when we walk in Old Town tonight? How pretty the young Slovak girls look in the cafés these days? How stupid it is not to peel banana from end with stalk?"

The next day we went to meet a couple of Katka's university friends who were still living in Bratislava. Outside the café, Katka clutched my arm tightly, a huge grin on her face.

"Ben, this will be nice surprise for you. Can you guess? One of these friends is Zuzana, my best friend from university who you met all those years ago."

"Katka, why are you telling me if it's supposed to be a surprise? The whole point of a surprise is that it's *a surprise*. Now I know."

"Because it will be even bigger surprise for Zuzana and I want to make some fun with her. It will be big laugh. I tell her on telephone that I will bring my new boyfriend, but I do not say who. I want to warn you that I will pretend not to know who you are."

"What? You mean like when you thought I was Steve Watkins the famous penguin cartoonist?"

"Ben, I thought you would forget about that by now. No, I will pretend not to know you are man who Zuzana wanted me to come and meet all those years ago."

Inside, I immediately recognised the blond woman standing at the bar with a shorter, dark-haired companion. Even after ten years, she'd changed very little. I hoped she'd remember *me*. Katka rushed over to hug her and it was a good ten or fifteen seconds before Zuzana spotted me over Katka's shoulder. It took a few more seconds to register, then her eyes opened wide and her jaw dropped.

"Katka! This is your new boyfriend? Do you remember me, Ben? Katka, do you *know* who this is? My God, Katka! This is Ben! Yes, I know you know his name. I mean this is that English man from our end of university time, the one I wrote to you about, the one I wanted you to come back to Blava for. How did you find each other after all this time? You really did not know he is…"

"Hi, Zuzana. Nice to see you again. Katka knows. She's just winding you up."

"Winding me? I am sorry, I do not…Katka, why do you hit him like that? You are still doing this to your boyfriends? I told you so many times, you think it is funny to hit on the arm like that but sometimes boys just think it hurts. Some of them told me. Others stopped being your boyfriends because of it."

"*Thank* you, Zuzana! I've been trying to tell her that ever since we first met."

"Oh shut up, Ben. You are wimp. Zuzana, I am so happy to see you. And Kristina, let me hug you. I met Ben at book fair in Frankfurt. Yes, sorry Ben, *the* book fair. Ben has been trying to help me improve my English, especially to remember to use *the* and *a*. He has been reminding me *a lot* this morning. For that alone he deserves a hit on his arm.

Also, he goes home to England in couple of days but he has not yet said if he will come back to see me. For *that* he deserves *more* than hit on arm."

"Of course I'll come back to see you. I thought that was

135

obvious. Do I have to *say* it?"

All three women looked at me and answered as one.

"*Yes*! *Of course*!"

"Oh. Well I was going to talk to you about it before I left, Katka. I just thought it was pretty much a given. And you never *asked* me if I was coming back. But I am, if you want me to. Only not on a long-distance coach, not between London and Prague. Sorry, but I…"

"Eco-terrorist! Ben, how many times we have talked about this flying business and global warming? How many?!"

"Sorry, Katka, but I looked at that coach timetable you got this morning and it's almost *twenty-four hours* to London from Prague. I can't go twenty-four hours without sleep. Will you stop hitting me?!"

"If you will be flying here and there and causing global warming every time you come to see me, Ben, then I do not *want* you to come back!"

Zuzana sighed, shook her head and waved to the barman.

"I will get us all some vodkas. We will need them. You do not change much, Katka, you know this?"

Eventually, we agreed on a compromise. There was no way I was doing twenty-four-hour sleepless coach journeys between London and Prague, so I'd be taking the plane when I came to see Katka. And there was no way Katka would fly, so she'd catch the coach when she came to see *me*, which she'd try to do as much as possible, so I wouldn't have to fly to visit *her*. It sounds easy saying it now, but it took us over an hour, two double vodkas each and a lot of peacekeeping and diplomacy by Zuzana and Kristina to get there. It might not have taken quite so long if, when we all ordered curd-cheese-filled pancakes, Katka hadn't chosen chocolate sauce and sliced bananas to go with hers, then asked a puzzled waiter to bring her the banana so she could peel and slice it herself at the table. I sometimes wonder if she ever did explain to her friends exactly why she made such a performance of so very slowly and so very deliberately peeling that banana while holding it by the stalk end and smiling sweetly at me across the table the whole time.

By the following morning, we'd made up and went seeing sights that I'd missed on my first visit, when I'd spent most of my time around the city centre and the Old Town, mainly in bars and cafés, visiting only the obvious attractions like Bratislava Castle. This time, Katka took me to places like the Slavín monument, pointing to the sky high on a hill above Bratislava and visible for miles around, where nearly seven thousand Soviet soldiers who died liberating the city and surrounding region at the end of the war were buried; and on a freezing boat trip up the Danube to see the ruins of the medieval Devín Castle, which we survived by huddling together for warmth and sharing large glasses of fiery pear brandy, hruškovica, from the bar then gulping down boiling-hot fish soup in the riverside café below the castle.

We caught the train to Prague the following afternoon, Katka agreeing to go during the day since it was only a four hour journey, so we had the evening and night together before the horrendously expensive flight I'd managed to book to Heathrow Airport at short notice.

We walked from Katka and Elena's flat into the centre, across Karl's Bridge and up towards the castle, stopping at a Hungarian restaurant that Katka really liked where they served a range of authentic Czech, Slovak and Hungarian dishes at candlelit tables as a gypsy band played in the corner. The proprietor obviously knew Katka well. He brought us a complimentary bottle of sparkling Hungarian wine and, as we waited for our fruit dumplings at the end of the meal, pleaded with her until she got up and sang Slovak and Hungarian folk songs with the band, who also seemed to know her - especially the old violinist, who hugged and kissed her like a long-lost granddaughter.

She was still humming happily when we walked back down to the Bridge and stood watching the lights reflected in the dark swirling waters just like we'd done in Frankfurt. As we crossed over and headed for the jazz bar where Elena was playing that night, suddenly out of nowhere it started snowing heavily and Katka leaned over and whispered in my ear.

"Ben, it will feel very cold here now…"

"Oh I don't know. It was bloody freezing earlier but the wind's dropped and when it starts snowing heavily like this doesn't the temperature usually rise a bit? Mind you, if the sky clears again tonight when there's snow on the ground, it's going to get pretty icy. I hope my flight's going to be okay in the morning."

"Actually, Ben, I was trying to say, it will feel very cold here now…*without you*."

"Oh, right. Sorry. That would have been very romantic. Probably the most romantic thing anyone's ever said to me. Sorry! I mean *definitely* the most romantic thing anyone's ever…you're going to hit me on the arm again, aren't you?"

Katka put her arm round my waist and squeezed me tight as we walked on.

"Probably, but you won't know when. It will be at moment when you are least expecting it. Now, relax and enjoy rest of our last evening together until Christmas."

A Very Slovak Christmas

That first Christmas spent with Katka at her mother and father's house in the mountains was really something special. It was the kind of beautiful, snowy winter-wonderland Christmas we long for in England and almost never see. But that wasn't the only difference. For a start, I discovered that in Slovakia the big day, with Christmas dinner and the presents, was actually on Christmas Eve. Which Katka forgot to tell me until I arrived in Prague on December 22nd.

It was late evening when I got to the flat and I was looking forward to a hot shower and an early night after the pre-holiday bedlam at Heathrow. Instead, I was rushed to the station to catch a night train to the Tatras as Katka explained that we had to be there early the next day or we'd miss the end of the Christmas preparations.

Because this was one of the last trains before the holidays, it was crammed to bursting point with skiers and people heading home for Christmas, and of course all the sleeper compartments had been taken. So we had to spend three hours sitting on our luggage in a crowded corridor being poked and whacked by passing skis, ski sticks and rucksacks before a couple of seats finally came free in a nearby compartment and Katka could fall asleep and dribble romantically on my shoulder.

When we arrived in the Tatras mid-morning the day before Christmas Eve, the snow was already much deeper than when we were there in November - almost a metre in places, with head-high drifts here and there along the roads - and more was falling. Long icicles hung from the eaves of the buildings, and the taxi driver told Katka they'd had minus thirty centigrade three nights before, but that it had since warmed up again. The car's heater was on full blast. I knew because I'd checked as soon as we got in. But I was still shivering as I asked Katka what the hell 'warmed up again' was supposed to mean, only to be told that they'd gone down to just minus eighteen the last couple of nights and no lower than minus four or five during the day. Which she insisted, exchanging amused looks with the driver as I continued to hug myself tight and shiver, wasn't really all that unusual for late December in the mountains.

As we walked up the garden path, Katka's father and her sister's children were leaving the house with a saw and a sledge for a trip into the forest in search of the perfect Christmas tree. Inside, the kitchen was warm and full of people, baking smells and the sound of Slovak Christmas carols coming from the CD player.

As apparently happened every year, Katka's entire family was already crowded into the house, helping prepare for the big day. Her mother, sister and one granny were busy around the large kitchen table, which you could barely see for mixing bowls, baking ingredients, greased trays and floury towels. Katka's aunt was sitting in a corner by the wood-burning stove, while the other granny perched on a high-backed wooden bench against the wall on the other side of the stove, separating the two granddads, who were seemingly prepared to forgive and forget their differences for this one special time of year - though, Katka explained, they would still argue noisily throughout the holiday as they constantly sipped and compared each other's plum brandy, having each brought a selection of their best bottles with them for just that purpose. Only Katka's sister's husband was missing, stuck covering the holiday period as duty electrical engineer at a power station construction site just over the Czech border in Germany.

Katka barely had her coat off before she was helping in the kitchen. She told me her mother would have been baking special Christmas cakes and biscuits all week but that there was always plenty still to do at the last minute. Right now they were starting the mix for the traditional honeybreads, so I should hurry up, take the bags upstairs where a hot bath was apparently run and waiting for me, then get back down to the kitchen to help cut out honeybread shapes for the Christmas tree.

"They already have the honeybread cutters out, Ben. See? Holly leaf shapes, star shapes, Christmas tree shapes, mushroom shapes…no, I don't know *why* mushroom shapes for Christmas, Ben…just go! Quick! Or you'll be too late to help."

Katka shook the bunch of metal biscuit cutters, gathered like keys on a big ring, and pointed to the door. I could really, *really* have done with some sleep, but the glass of slivovica one of the granddads had forced me to knock back the moment we entered the kitchen was putting new life into me, so I dropped the bags in our room and looked longingly at the bed only for a moment before heading for the bathroom. I was just about to step into the ready-filled bath when I spotted the fish. Two of them. Two great big sodding fish swimming around in the bath.

"What the fuck?! Katka!"

At first I thought I was hallucinating, maybe from sleep deprivation coupled with the stupidly strong slivovica, then I heard Katka and her sister giggling outside the door.

"Katka? There's fucking fish in the bath!"

"Sorry, Ben, fish are doing *what* in bath?"

There was more giggling from the landing as Katka whispered to her sister.

"No, I don't mean they're fu...I mean there are *fish* in the bath...*just swimming*. You know what I mean."

Katka opened the door, slipped inside and turned on the shower, a huge grin on her face, as I stood staring into the bath.

"I am sorry Ben. It was just for some laughs. They are carp. It is traditional to have this fish for Slovak Christmas dinner. It is also traditional to buy this fish alive few days before Christmas and keep in bath, running fresh water in every day, before killing and cooking. If killed straight from carp pond and sold dead, carp can taste muddy. Keeping in bath cleans them through with fresh water, makes them taste not so muddy. My mother hates to have them in bathroom but my father insists to put them here for better flavour. When we were children, we would feed them and they would be like pets for us, for few days anyway. You can stroke them if you like, Ben. No? Okay. Stop staring at bath and have shower. We are going to roll out honeybread dough ready for cutting soon."

When I got downstairs, Katka and her granny were rolling brown dough on the table to the sound of the Christmas carols. Katka stopped, wiped her floury hands and changed the CD.

"Good shower, Ben? Come on, let's pick this up."

She turned the volume high as loud, funky electronic dance music burst from the speakers. We shouted to each other over the music as she and her sister danced on the spot and bumped their hips together.

"What's this, Katka?"

"Chemical Brothers! You do not know them? They are English! I *love* hard techno dance music! Don't you? I love to dance! We should go dancing in Poprad some night!"

"Mmmm. I'll look forward to that!"

At that moment the children burst through the front door, heaving a large and bushy Christmas tree base-first along the hallway past the open kitchen door, followed by Katka's father, grimacing at the loud music and shoving his fingers in his ears. The aunty, the two granddads and one of the grannies all got up and left for the sitting room as well, shaking their heads at the booming speakers - and at the second granny, who was bopping along with the two younger women, bumping hips with them and waving her rolling pin in time to the music.

We spent the next hour baking trays of cut-out dough shapes and cooling them on racks until we had two massive piles of biscuits on plates, smelling of warm honey and cinnamon; one pile for eating now and the other to be threaded with needles and hung on the tree for later. Then Katka's mother and sister started to clear the table for lunch while we went into the sitting room to see how the children were getting on with the tree decorations.

I have to admit it was quite charming and tastefully done, even if my own taste in Christmas tree decorating leans more towards the garish, with lots of coloured lights, gaudy baubles and lashings of sparkly tinsel. These tree decorations were apparently very traditional; stars, bells, angels and suchlike skilfully hand-crafted from straw and tiny ribbons, some made by the grannies and others bought by Katka from folk-art shops in Bratislava and Prague, while the lights were small white imitation candles. Later, when we'd threaded the honeybreads and hung them on the branches, the whole room smelled of pine needles, honey and cinnamon, mixed with the scent of wood smoke from the open log fire.

After a late lunch, Katka and I sat on the floor with the children, looking through family photo albums by the light of the fire and the tree while it grew dark outside. As Katka flicked through the third book, I stopped her at a photograph of her and her sister as teenagers in the garden.

"Yes, Ben. I thought you might like this one."

"You both look very nice...especially with the pigtails. Why do you have black hands?"

I looked at the next photo, where Katka's mother and one of the grannies also had black hands.

"And so do they. Was there some sort of craze for sticking fingers in electric sockets back in those days? I suppose village life might have been a bit dull, but there must have been other stuff you could do for excitement, surely?"

"Ben, are you mad? Why would we stick our fingers...oh, it is another one of your jokes. Black hands are from peeling walnuts from our tree. You can see there, buckets with nuts and peeled green nut cases. Juice from outside casings of walnuts always stains hands. In Slovak villages in late summer when walnuts ripen, you will see many women with black hands from peeling walnuts."

"Why don't they wear rubber gloves?"

"Have you ever tried to peel walnuts wearing gloves, Ben? Anyway, staining washes off after couple of weeks. Slovak village women do not worry about something so small as black hands. Look, there is photograph of us with our biggest ever pig. I forget how many kilos he weighed, but there were *lot* of smoked sausages in our attic that year. We called him Trotsky. It was joke. I was learning English at school and found out English for pig's foot is trotter."

The children had lost interest in the album and were heading for the door, asking Katka something in Slovak to which she smiled and nodded.

"Ben, listen quickly - I must tell you something before

children return…"

"Okay. If you could just explain to me exactly how I'm supposed to *listen quickly…*"

"Shut up, Ben. Just listen. I forgot to say that children cleaned one of your shoes and one of my shoes and put them out for Mikuláš. You do this in England? No? Well, on night of December fifth, children in Slovakia clean one of their shoes and put it outside front door of house for Mikuláš, who is our version of your Saint Nicholas or Santa Claus. He comes during night and if children have been good during year and have cleaned shoe very well, then he leaves some chocolate or sweets in shoe for them. If they have been bad, or have not cleaned shoe nicely, he will leave piece of coal or small brush for sweeping doorstep as punishment.

Next morning, children look to find what he has left for them. Of course we miss this because we are not here then, so they put out our shoes because they hope Mikuláš will make special visit for us. I think they put out their own shoes as well, hoping for second lot of chocolate or sweets for them also."

There were yelps of excitement from the hallway.

"Don't people steal the shoes? And anyway we're not children so why would we get any chocolate?"

"Ben, why would people steal just one left shoe or one right shoe? Well, maybe in cities or in flats children might put shoes by bedroom doors these days. I don't know. I am from village, and in villages people often do not even lock doors. No-one would steal shoes from doorways. And sometimes Mikuláš will come for grown-up people also, if they have been very, very good and children put out a shoe for them. Now look surprised when they come. I put chocolate in shoes when I went to kitchen for more coffee."

The children ran into the room, their arms full of shoes. In Katka's shoe and in their shoes were little net bags full of chocolate coins, chocolate snowmen and chocolate Santas. In *my* shoe there was a lump of coal and what looked like a small pastry brush from the kitchen.

"Oh, poor Ben! Children say you must have been *very* naughty to get coal *and* a brush to sweep the doorstep. Perhaps if you phoned me from England more often, then Mikuláš would bring you chocolate. But children say they will share with you."

After dinner, while Katka and her sister gave the children a bath, I looked through the photo albums again, alone on the sitting room floor. Katka's father, mother, aunt and grandparents were in the kitchen drinking borovička, a vaguely gin-like spirit made with juniper berries, and nibbling on plates of savoury delicacies like pagáč, a small bun baked with a sprinkling of pork scratchings, and little glazed puff-pastries made with cheese and caraway seeds. As much as anything else, I was getting away from the constant pressure to eat more and drink more even though we'd all just polished off a huge meal with lots of beer and vodka.

As I listened to the children's laughter from upstairs, the Christmas tree started to shake. I leaned over and reached under the dense, bushy branches to check if the trunk was loose in the stand, only to whip my hand back out as something deep in the bowels of the tree scratched me. I yelped in pain and surprise as the house cat, a big ginger tom called, imaginatively, Ryško - the Slovak for Ginger - leaped out of the tree with a honeybread in his mouth and raced out of the room.

"Bad Ryško!" shouted Katka as she almost tripped over him in the doorway. "I am sorry, Ben, I should have warned you that we try to keep this door closed when Christmas tree has honeybreads on it. Every year Ryško tries to get them, so it is competition to see who will eat most, us or him. One year he manages to take fourteen. It is his best record. Come on, I will wash your scratch and tell my mother Ryško made his first score. She will start score-paper on kitchen notice board to see how many he catches from tree *this* year. Usually he must hide in hallway behind coats and boots, waiting to creep in past feet when someone opens door, but if you keep leaving door open, maybe he will beat his record."

When I came downstairs late on Christmas Eve morning, the kitchen was already steamy and busy with last-minute preparations for Christmas dinner. Katka and her sister were peeling potatoes and carrots, their mother was stirring a huge pot on the stove, the aunty was cleaning and filleting the fish from the bathroom and their father was preparing a large bird for the oven. I offered to help but was told everything was in hand and I should join the children and the grandparents in the sitting room, where they were about to watch a video of an old Slovak children's TV series.

"It was on television when I was child," explained Katka as she pushed me out of the kitchen. "It was one of my favourite television series. You will like it. I will bring you coffee and breakfast when vegetables for Christmas potato salad are cooking."

"Why didn't you wake me earlier? Have you already done the presents? And did you say *Christmas potato salad*?"

"You were very tired, Ben. I could not wake you. No, we have presents after dinner. And yes, Christmas potato salad. Go on, you will miss beginning of video, which is very important part. Without beginning, you will not know what is happening."

I caught the start of the first episode, and ten minutes in I still had very little idea what was going on. A lorry and a crane had arrived at a middle-aged man's house in the suburbs of what was obviously a Slovak town, where uniformed officials had overseen the lifting of a huge parcel from the lorry into his garden and left, after giving the bemused man some paperwork. He'd then unwrapped the parcel to find a very pretty little girl inside, who he took into the house, fed soup to and put to bed. At that point, Katka came in with coffee and ham and eggs for me and explained.

"You see, Ben, this series is called 'Bambulka's Adventures'…Ben? Did you let cat into room when you come in? I think I see something move in tree. He is very quick and sneaky. Ah-hah! I see you, Ryško! Get out of tree!"

Katka grabbed a branch and shook the tree. The cat fell out, another honeybread in its mouth, and shot behind the settee.

"That is two honeybreads to Ryško. We must catch up with him. Pass honeybreads to children, please. Now, this little girl is called Bambulka. She has been sent in parcel from country called Bambulkovo. You saw postmen deliver parcel? She is sent to this man, Uncle Jozef - although he is not really her uncle and does not know her at all, and she does not know him. There is letter asking him to help her learn proper ways to behave, to ask politely for things, say 'thank you', not be rude to grownups, eat nicely, go to bed on time, help with chores and so on.

It is difficult for him because she is very wilful and does not like to be told what to do, and he has never had his own children, is really quite lonely and little bit grumpy man, so he must learn new ways to behave as well. They have big fights, but after time she learns to be well behaved, he learns some important things about children and about himself, and they both come to care very much about each other. Then, they get letter from land of Bambulkovo saying she is ready to go back there now…"

Katka made a soft half-gulping, half-choking noise in her throat and turned away.

"Are you okay, Katka? Have you got something in your eye?"

"No, I am fine, Ben. Stop staring at my eyes. I only rub them because I am tired and they are itchy. We did not all sleep most of morning as you did."

"Were you cryi…"

"Ben, do you want I should have to hit you on arm at Christmas, *do you*? In front of children and grannies and granddads? Okay then. But Bambulka does not want to go back. She wants to stay with Uncle Jozef and he wants to keep her, so she stays and lives with him like daughter and they are happy ever after. It is very moving…"

"I see. Right. Okay. You do realise you've given away the ending. And I wonder what the TV people would say if you went to them with an idea like that *these* days? You'd never get it made, with all the worries about…Katka? Do you want a tissue?"

When the video finished, nearly two hours later, Katka and I took the children out for an hour or so of sledging, snowman building and snowballing, returning frozen through and starving as the others were finishing setting the table. We just had time for a hot bath to warm up, the bath now being fish-free and, Katka assured me, thoroughly cleaned.

"No, Ben, for second time that is *not* fish…how did you say…fish *pooh*? No it really is not. It is just little pieces of dirt or grit. Hurry up, everyone will be waiting for us."

When we sat down at the kitchen table, now extended with wooden add-ons at each end and covered with festive tablecloths hand-embroidered with Christmas motifs by the grannies, I discovered just how bizarre a Slovak Christmas dinner can appear to someone more used to turkey, roast potatoes, sprouts and gravy. First, there was the traditional Slovak Christmas soup, more of a thick stew made with pearl barley, dried mushrooms, sour cabbage and stock - definitely an acquired taste.

"So barley, mushroom and *sauerkraut* soup?"

"Yes, Ben. Try it. You will like it."

"I wouldn't bet on it."

"What was that, Ben?"

"Nothing. Mmmm. Very nice."

Next there were carp fillets baked in sour-cream sauce, and Slovak Christmas potato salad, made with potatoes, sliced hard-boiled eggs, diced carrots, peas, chopped raw onions, diced pickled cucumbers and mayonnaise, the generous lacing of chopped gherkins making the mix much more vinegary and astringent than typical English potato salad.

That - sauerkraut soup, muddy fish in sour-cream, and

potato salad - was, according to Katka, the true traditional Slovak Christmas dinner, on which she would be quite happy to gorge herself, with no other embellishments. Luckily for *me*, Katka's family, like most Slovaks, enjoy having a little meat with their Christmas meal too, so there was also a large platter piled high with pan-fried breaded pork schnitzels, made from local wild boar shot in the forest by a friend of the family, a huge roast goose almost as big as a turkey and plates and plates of smoked sausages.

Katka's father had roasted some potatoes in goose fat for me, and her mother proudly brought out a large jar of pickled Brussels sprouts that she'd had at the back of the store cupboard for years. It seems Katka had told her they were an English Christmas dinner speciality and that they would make me feel really at home. Katka and her sister had trouble suppressing their giggles as their mother spooned the vinegary sprouts onto my plate alongside the roast potatoes, thick juicy slices of goose meat, schnitzels, potato salad and sour-cream-sauce-smothered carp.

After the main course an incredible array of different cakes was brought out and spread on the table. My favourites were the rum-baba-like little balls made from chocolate cake crumbs soaked in rum, filled with plum jam and rolled in desiccated coconut.

As Katka's father opened bottles of sparkling wine to help the adults wash down second, third and fourth helpings of cake, the children rushed off to fetch armfuls of presents from under the Christmas tree and hand them out to everyone.

Katka looked a little disappointed by her first present from me, a signed copy of 'Snowdrops, A Monograph of Cultivated Galanthus', the best book to date on snowdrops, illustrated with close-up photographs that I thought might help her to appreciate the differences between the many named forms. Luckily her second present from me went down a lot better.

"French Lime Blossom Cologne? Ben, where did you find this? It smells wonderful, just like sitting under lime trees at flowering time. Thank you."

"Well, you told me the smell of lime tree blossom was your favourite flower scent, so I did an internet search and found a shop in London that specialises in French flower essences and perfumes, and they had this. It is nice, isn't it? Now what did you get me? Oh…it's a web cam."

"Yes, Ben. I bought one for each of us. Now we can talk and see each other through computers when we are apart instead of just on telephones. You can download internet programme to do it very easily. You do not think this is good idea?"

"Yes. Actually, yes I do. It's a great idea. I can call you at bedtime and we can have a nice long chat with the web cams. Brilliant idea, Katka. I wish I'd thought of it."

"I know what you are thinking, Ben and answer is no. I give you web cam and first thing you think about is web cam sex. This is so we can see each other when we are *talking*, see expressions, not…give web cam back to me! I change my mind!"

"Sorry. I want it, I really do. It's a lovely idea, Katka. Thank you."

"And there will be no stupid sex suggestions from you when we use web cams? No 'Please, please put hair in pigtails and take off pyjamas, Katka' nonsense? Anyone on internet could see!"

"I really don't think they could, Katka…could they?"

"You know you should feel lucky we have such technology now to keep in touch when apart. We had no mobiles and computers when I was at university; most houses did not even have telephones, thanks to communist regime. When my boyfriend wanted to speak to me, he had to wait in long queue in entrance of hall of residence at his university in Brno to use only telephone in building, which was on desk of caretaker. I had to wait in entrance of *my* hall of residence in Bratislava for him to call and ask *our* caretaker, who also had only telephone on his desk, to be allowed to talk to me. And if I wanted to telephone *him*, I had to do same.

Sometimes I would wait for hours for call from him if there was long queue for telephone in his hall of residence, or if line was busy at my end. And, of course, caretakers were sitting right by telephone at both ends, hearing everything we say to each other. It was very difficult to keep in communication in those days and was probably one of reasons our relationship did not survive…plus of course fact that he was having lots of sex with other girls in Brno while I was in Blava."

"Okay. Well don't worry, *I'm* not having sex with other women when we're apart. In fact I'm not having sex with *any* women when we're apart - not even you apparently. Although if I *was* having sex with another woman, I suppose you wouldn't be able to see her on the web cam if she was under the desk. That was a joke! Leave my arm alone, it's still sore from this morning. Y'know a *really* useful Christmas present would have been some sort of protective arm pads. Hey, let go! That was another joke. Give me the web cam back, it's a lovely present."

After everyone had opened their presents, and the children had gone off to play with theirs, the adults carried on talking, drinking and nibbling at cakes, nuts and fruit while the afternoon turned to evening. Katka was getting cheerfully tiddly and started cuddling up to me. Her father, on the other hand, seemed to be growing increasingly serious, thoughtful and introverted the more he drank. Looking at the clock, he solemnly raised his glass and waited for everyone to stop talking.

"Tomáš!"

Everyone raised their glasses and toasted, Katka whispering in my ear to join in and that she'd explain after.

"Tomáš!"

After that, Katka's father cheered up and started telling jokes. As he made the aunty and the grandparents roar with laughter, Katka told me that they always drank a toast to Tomáš at seven o'clock on Christmas Eve.

"He was my father's older brother. During national service with Army as young man, he was stationed very near West German border. This was during communist era of course, when border between Czechoslovakia and West Germany was guarded and we were not allowed across. Place where Tomáš was stationed was in what we called 'leaky' part of border with lots of very dangerous marshes, where not so many fences could be built and where people would often try to cross to West. Some people would even come from East Germany to try to cross there. Many drowned in marshes and many were killed or caught by border guards.

Tomáš and some friends from his unit decided to escape across marshes in dark on Christmas Eve. It was very cold and there was thick ice on marshes, which they thought would be safer, and they hoped border guards were more likely to stay in barracks and guard-towers because of extreme cold and Christmas Eve celebrations. Two were caught, one fell through ice running away from guards and drowned, and Tomáš was shot and killed while trying to save his drowning friend. Guards shouted for him to put up hands and walk back to them but instead he ran to hole in ice to look for his friend, so they fired at him. Official report said he died at seven o'clock."

Katka's father paused to top up his drink, raised his glass in another toast, boomed "Socializmus!" and clinked glasses with Katka and the aunty before starting yet another joke.

"What was that, Katka? It sounded like 'socialism'. Or did I hear wrong?"

"It was toast to socialism. Why?"

"Well, y'know, with everything that happened to your father under the communist regime, losing his job for not toeing the line and his brother shot by the border guards, why would he want to toast socialism?"

"Because he is socialist. He always has been. You must remember, Ben, we never did have real socialism or even real communism here. We had Stalinism, and when we tried to change, tried to move towards less totalitarian, less repressive communism or 'communism with friendly face', Russia sent in tanks. But my father would never let them take away his belief in principles of true socialism, his belief in people working together for good of everyone, helping each other, not just caring about yourself alone; like when everyone from village comes together and helps to build this house, and many times that my father helped to build houses for other people in village. Not everything about those days was bad, you know."

"It's just ironic that he was a socialist all that time but he was persecuted and…"

"Well, he was not only one. And he is also very stubborn man, so…"

"Katka! Spievaj! Spievaj!"

Her father was gesturing for Katka to stand up.

"I am sorry, Ben, but I must do this. It is Christmas tradition. I think this also will be quite confusing for you, but I must sing Russian National Anthem in Russian. It has been my, how do you say in English…my party trick, since I was small child."

"The Russian National Anthem?"

"Yes. All children in Slovakia were taught Russian as compulsory subject when I was at school, and learning Russian National Anthem was included in those studies. I suppose it was part of Russian colonialist strategy towards us, but it is actually very beautiful song, all about how Mother Russia has united all peoples in what you in West called USSR, to help each other and build a better, fairer world for everyone, with freedom for everyone…yes, Ben, I know there is lot of irony in this. But it just happened I was good at languages and was only one in my class who could sing whole of this anthem in Russian at age of nine.

My father was very proud of my achievement, and also liked sentiments in this song, despite irony of it. Also, Russian is really very beautiful language, especially for poetry and songs. Later I can recite for you some poetry of Pushkin in

Russian. It is very moving. Now be quiet. I must try to remember words to anthem."

She was right, Russian is a beautiful-sounding language, certainly when sung. And the poetry she read for me later sounded equally beautiful. There were indeed some ironic smiles around the table for the Russian anthem, but Katka sang it earnestly and rousingly, standing and saluting just as they were taught in school, and everyone applauded loudly at the end just as they would have done when she was nine. It was surprisingly touching, and both grannies wiped away a tear afterwards.

Katka asked me if I had a party trick I could do for everyone, and I told her there was a spoof ventriloquism act that I came up with at a New Year's Eve party in England but that it involved my willy, a pair of glasses, a cigarette and a glass of beer. People had seemed to find it pretty funny then, but admittedly everyone was incredibly drunk, including me.

"Really, people thought it was hilarious, Katka. Especially when I pretended to drink the beer while making my willy talk, and then made it sound like my willy was saying 'He always drinks too much. Where's the toilet?' I've got a video someone made of it. No? A bit too rude?"

Katka gave me one of her looks, shook her head sadly and never asked me about party tricks ever again.

That night we were the last ones to go to bed, lying on the settee by the Christmas tree, chatting and looking through the snowdrop book.

"Ben, I am still not sure if I really like these double-flowered snowdrops. Some are quite pretty, but also some are bit messy and even ugly, especially the…how do you call them…*spiky* doubles, those just do not really look like snowdrops at all, more like little white and green *brushes*.

Poculi…poculifo…how do you say this…poculiform? Yes? Poculiform ones with inside petals as long as outside petals are very nice, but I still like most of all snowdrops which are proper snowdrop shape, with long outside petals and shorter inside petals. Green marks on outside petals I like, and snowdrops with yellow marks instead of green are very pretty. You know, there are beautiful photographs in this book, Ben. But it makes me think of your friend Lady Cherrington and her sad garden problems. Must she still sell her house and garden? Does bank not decide to let her keep it? No? That is shame. I promise I will come to England to see you at snowdrop time and also meet Lady Cherrington and see her snowdrop woodland if she will allow me, okay?"

"Of course she'll let you. Maybe you could come in time for her snowdrop lunch."

"Snowdrop *lunch*? She cannot eat snowdrops, Ben! They are poisonous. Are you idiot? Do you try to kill her? Is this some kind of crazy assisted suicide plan because bank is taking her house and garden away? She does not want to live, and you will help her by cooking and feeding *snowdrops* to her? You are mad!"

"Whoa! Steady on! I know you've had a few drinks and you're a teensy bit sloshed...yes you are...don't hit my arm...look, it's not a lunch *of* snowdrops, it's a lunch she arranges every year in the middle of the snowdrop season for her best snowdrop-growing friends. We gather at her house, about twenty or so of us, to look at the snowdrops, and her hellebore flowers and anything else there is to see, and have a bit of lunch together. It's a chance for us all to view her newest snowdrops, bring our own new ones to show, do some swaps, talk about snowdrops generally and what's happening in the snowdrop world, who's discovered a new snowdrop, who's flowered a particularly good seedling, that sort of thing. And no, we don't eat the snowdrops. Lady C usually has a side of smoked salmon, roast beef and all the trimmings to follow, and a traditional hot pud like apple crumble and custard. It's always a great day. You'll enjoy meeting some of the other snowdrop people. They're interesting...well, most of them are.

It'll be her last proper snowdrop lunch, where we can all see the snowdrops in the garden and the woodland. After that she'll have to start digging them up, and her other special plants, ready for moving out. She's planning one last special lunch at the end of the snowdrop season where she'll be giving away the best of her collection, and then some nurserymen will be coming round to dig up what's left, the less rare snowdrops and plants, before the bulldozers arrive.

If you're going to be in England in February, you could come to the Snowdrop Gala with me as well, and there are some other snowdrops gardens I try to visit at least once during the season. You might like to see those too."

"Snowdrop Gala? What is this? Some kind of snowdrop festival?"

"Sort of. It's a gathering of usually about three hundred very keen snowdrop enthusiasts from all over England, Scotland, Wales, Holland, Belgium, Germany, Austria, even the U.S. and Japan. They choose a different part of England every year, always close to some large snowdrop garden or estate that can be visited. There are lectures, slide shows, nurseries selling rare snowdrops, a lunch, then the garden visits."

"Lectures? About snowdrops? That sounds like lot of fun, Ben."

"Okay, you don't have to sit through the lectures."

"You promise?"

"Yes."

Katka put down the book and snuggled up close. I was looking at the Christmas tree, doing what I do with Christmas trees every year, and have done since I was a child - half-closing my eyes so that the lights look like twinkling stars through my lashes.

"Don't fall asleep, Ben! I have one other present for you."

"I'm not going to sleep, I'm just...never mind. Another present? Where? Why didn't you give it to me earlier when you gave me the web cam?"

"Because this is *special* present, Ben. I only want *you* to see. Give me five minutes to go to bedroom and put it on, then you can come upstairs."

Ten minutes later, Katka and I were in bed. She was whispering sexily in Russian and wearing the special present, which was *very* nice *indeed*, when there was a crashing thud and a loud miaow from downstairs.

"Ben, did you leave sitting room door open again? I think Ryško knocks Christmas tree down."

"Leave it. They're only honeybreads. We can bake more. Can you whisper to me in Russian again? Katka? That was *so* sexy."

"Ben! What is that *smell*?!"

"Oh. Sorry! It must be those pickled Brussels sprouts."

Apart from Katka constantly telling me off for forgetting to shut the sitting room door - by the time we left for Prague, the cat's score had risen to an all-time record of twenty-three snaffled honeybreads - we had surprisingly few rows during that first Christmas and New Year. Though admittedly there *was* the occasional hiccup, like the time Katka lost her temper with me because I wouldn't wear a hat and nearly died. Okay, maybe I didn't nearly die, but it felt like it and I still think she could have been a bit more sympathetic about the whole episode.

We'd been to a party in Starý Smokovec on New Year's Eve, or Silvester as Slovaks call it, and were leaving about quarter to one in the morning. We'd got a lift there from Katka's village but hadn't managed to find anyone at the party who was going back that way. The trains weren't running and there were no taxis, so we decided to start walking and try to thumb a lift. But the roads were deserted, except for one incredibly drunken driver who said he could take us part of the way; an offer that we politely refused. The roads, though recently gritted, were sheet ice and dangerous enough without putting our lives in the hands of someone steering with one hand while holding a bottle of vodka in the other.

After a few minutes, I stopped and pulled out my mobile.

"Who do you try to telephone, Ben? It is one in morning."

"I want to send a 'Happy New Year' text to my friends and family. I meant to do it at the party but forgot, and I want to do it before the road gets right in amongst the trees and I lose the signal. What's the Slovak for 'Happy New Year'?"

Katka clutched the hood of her coat with both hands to stop the freezing wind blowing it back, huddled in close to me and spelled out the Slovak words.

"Hurry up, Ben. It is very cold. We must keep walking. Yes that is right, 'Šťastný Nový Rok', but you will have to explain that it means Happy New Year, and also if you want to wish everyone Happy New Year for *whole* of this next year, for *all* of year two thousand and seven, you must not put capitals but write 'nový rok' with all small letters. Otherwise, if you write 'Nový Rok' with capital letters, it will mean Happy New Year for just New Year's Day."

"Well first of all, they won't know the difference, and second of all what the hell are you talking about? That's nuts. Why would you want to wish someone Happy New Year just for *one day* and not the whole year? Unless you didn't like them. Is that it?"

"No, Ben. It is too complicated to explain right now. Just different kinds of greeting for different situations. You see, 'Nový Rok' means New Year's Day, but 'nový rok' means new year. Oh, never mind. Come *on*, we must walk. And I *tell* you to bring hat, but you won't do it, will you? Sprostý, sprostý chlap!"

"Okay, I'm finished. And I do know what 'Sprostý chlap' means. I've heard it often enough."

"Then come on, you stupid man. You will freeze to death without hat. I told you and I told you that you will need hat in this cold. Stupid bloody man."

Okay, so I hadn't taken a hat with me, but we were going to a party and I hate the way hats flatten my hair down, I also have a general sartorial aversion to woolly hats, and anyway we had a lift there and were supposed to get one back as well. Katka had argued that I'd at least need a hat for the midnight fireworks display, but I'm not the kind of wuss who has to put on a woolly bobble hat to spend twenty minutes outside in someone's garden.

"Ben, forecast was for below minus twenty centigrade tonight, and with wind chill this means more like minus twenty five or minus thirty. I told you this, but you still do not bring hat! You are not used to conditions we get in mountains in winter."

"I'll be fine. The slivovica's keeping me warm. Hey, look at the stars. I've never seen so many. I suppose it's the lack of street lights around here and the clear air."

"Yes, is clear air. Is from Russia and is also very bloody cold air! Now *walk*, Ben!"

With hindsight, yes I probably should have taken a hat. They say you lose more heat through your head than anywhere else, as Katka kept reminding me every few minutes - probably losing more heat through her mouth than anywhere else - as we trudged along the road on our eight kilometre trek back to the village. Halfway there, the warming and cheering effect of the vodka and slivovica I'd drunk at the party started to wear off. Three quarters of the way home, I wanted to lie down in the snow by the roadside and go to sleep. I'd heard of that happening to people in extreme cold, but never expected to have it happen to me.

"Get up, Ben! No, you must not sleep! Not even for few minutes. You must keep moving. Get up or I will kick you. I mean it."

"Ouch!"

I don't remember very much about the last kilometre, but apparently Katka had to drag and practically carry me all the way, shouting and yelling at me to keep me moving my legs. Actually, yes, I remember the shouting, and I'm not convinced it was always completely necessary for her to shout quite that much, quite so loudly and with quite so much swearing.

The next day, she stomped down the garden path with a toolbox to where her father's car had been sitting immobilised for the last three months and fixed it so we wouldn't be stuck for a lift again. Not just like that, of course; it took three hours in the freezing cold, four mugs of steaming coffee, a couple of largish glasses of vodka and a lot of swearing, but eventually she had it running as smoothly as you could expect an old car to in those conditions. As I shivered by her side, handing her the wrong tools and letting her grumble at me and call me 'sprostý' a bit more to make up for the previous night, she explained that her father had passed on some of his pre-restaurant-era engineering skills to her.

"From when I was very small, he would always let me watch and help when he had to mend things - his car, our washing machine, boiler, whatever was broken - and he would show me how he was fixing those problems, explain how things worked. I always loved mechanical things and I became as good as him at making them work properly. Problem now is that he will leave such things, put off making repairs because he knows eventually I will do it. He says I always make better job of it than him, but that is just excuse. Now please hand me adjustable spanner…no, that is torque spanner!"

The only other slight upset was a minor tiff when we were back in Prague, about me not getting a present for Katka's name's day on the fifth of January. I know! Exactly! What the hell is a *name's day*? And why should I have bought her a present? It wasn't her birthday. But it turns out that each day of the year in Slovakia is permanently allocated to one (or sometimes two or three) of the most common Slovak forenames. Their calendars always have written alongside each date the name or names for that particular day, so everyone knows what they are. And on the date in the calendar that your forename appears, you have a name's day and everyone is supposed to wish you 'Happy Name's Day' and give you presents. As I explained to her, how *the hell* was I supposed to know that? Didn't stop Katka sulking until after lunchtime, though. She only cheered up when we'd had lunch in our favourite café and I'd bought her the amber bracelet she made a great show of admiring in a nearby jewellery shop.

"Thank you, Ben! It is so beautiful. I love amber. You do know that I have *two* name's days? You will not spoil my next name's day by forgetting it?"

"I didn't forget *this* one! I didn't even *know* about it until today when you started sulking. And why do you have *two*?"

"Because I have two forenames, Katarina and Andrea. Today is name's day for people called Andrea, which is my *second* forename, my middle name. I never told you this? Hmm. I thought I did. Anyway, as you *do* know, my first name is Katarina and name's day for women called Katarina is twenty fifth of November. You will remember? Promise?"

"Yes, but I thought *today* must be your name's day for being Katarina. You said it was your name's day but you didn't specify the name. So I have to remember *two* name's days, *and* your birthday?"

"Yes, of course. And *your* name's day is thirty first of March, name's day for men called Benjamin in Slovakia. Ben is short for Benjamin, yes? I checked on calendar so I will not forget, like you did."

"For the last time, I didn't *forget*, I just didn't *know*!"

"Okay. Ben, when is my birthday?"

"Bloody hell, it's cold today. Can we hurry up and get back to the flat?"

"You forget when my birthday is as well, don't you, Ben?"

"Not *as well*. Just…yes, sorry. Tell me it again when we're back at the flat and I'll put it in my diary. And your name's days."

"Do you have middle name, Ben?"

"No, just Ben."

"So just one name's day. That is easy for me. You really did not know about name's days? I did not explain to you why we call New Year's Eve 'Silvester' in Slovakia?"

"No, you were probably too busy telling me off for not wearing a hat."

"Thirty-first of December is name's day for men called

Silvester. It is name always written on calendar for that day, so people just came to call that occasion Silvester. I really did not tell you this? Perhaps I told you and you forget this also?"

"Katka! For the last sodding time, I did not forget! I didn't *know* about…"

"Okay, never mind. What date is my other name's day? One for my first name, Katarina?"

"Bloody hell! I said I'd write it down in my diary when we get back, okay?"

"You forget already? I just tell you this."

"Ouch! Stop hitting my arm!"

"You don't forget which date I come to England to see you, Ben?"

"No. You're arriving on Friday the second of February so we can go to Lady C's snowdrop lunch on the Sunday."

"And I must travel back to Praha on Monday fifth of February for important meeting about opening new office in Blava. I am sorry I cannot stay until Snowdrop Gala. You will meet me in London at coach station? You will not *forget*?"

"No! No! No! And if you hit me on the arm again, I'm going to tell a policeman."

"Really? Good luck with that, Ben."

The Snowdrop Lunch

Katka's coach from Prague was late arriving in London due to bad weather delaying the ferry sailing, and the choppy crossing had made her horribly seasick; so she wasn't in the best of moods when she finally turned up at Victoria Coach Station, and on top of that she was coming down with a stinking cold.

Yet she still insisted on a guided tour so, ignoring the

sniffly protestations that she'd rather walk, I shoved her into a black cab that took us via Buckingham Palace to Trafalgar Square. From there I lugged her bags against a blustery headwind down the Embankment to an even windier Westminster Bridge to see the steely-grey Thames, the Houses of Parliament and Big Ben in all their overcast and drizzly glory. Then I put her into a cab to Paddington Station, against yet another background of wheezing objections and sniffling protests that she'd prefer walking, to get the authentic feel of the city. I told her I wasn't sure she ought to get the authentic feel of London on a cold, windy February afternoon with a bad cold - not unless she wanted to get pneumonia.

The train was barely out of the station before Katka was asleep with her head on my shoulder, breathing noisily through her mouth. I tried not to inhale her germs as the couple opposite went 'aww' and 'how romantic' when I told them she'd just done a twenty-seven-hour coach journey from the Czech Republic to see me and explained how we'd met, and how we'd discovered we nearly met years before. I was starting to feel quite soppy and emotional myself as I recounted the story. Looking down at Katka, I thought how beautiful she looked, even tired out and full of cold, and that I really was incredibly lucky to have met her at last. Then she sneezed loudly, jerked awake and look around, startled and still half asleep, with a thin dribble of snot running from one nostril.

"Uh? Ben? Are we there?"

"No. Do you have a tissue?"

"Why has train stopped? We are not at station."

"Dunno. Wrong kind of drizzle on the tracks probably."

"What?"

"Nothing. Will you for God's sake wipe your nose."

I'd left my car in the railway station car park, and the first thing Katka did when we arrived was glare disapprovingly and complain about how big it was. Driving through the town, I tried to explain that it was a diesel and reasonably economical but she wasn't having any of it.

"It may be diesel engine, Ben, but must be big one. Two litres? Three litres? You should have smaller car. This is your house, Ben? Really? It is beautiful. Real English cottage, built with stone like Lady Cherrington's house. Do you even have rose growing by door?"

"It's Cotswold stone, but it's only a terraced cottage, just two bedrooms. I hope you weren't expecting something more impressive. And I have a daphne by the door, not a rose. Daphne bholua, from the Himalayas; one of the best forms, called Jacqueline Postill. It's flowering now. Can you smell it? Or are you too bunged up to smell anything?"

"Oh! Yes! I can smell even from street, and even with this horrible cold. It is wonderful. I like this scent almost as much as lime tree blossom. Bože môj! It is so strong when you are closer. Like woman's perfume."

"I often get people knocking on the door to ask what it is when they've smelled it from the pavement. It can start flowering in December in a mild winter, and we've had nothing *but* mild winters the last few years. I planted it against the wall by the door so I can smell it every time I come in and out. But it's getting a bit big now."

"And, oh! Snowdrops…everywhere! You *do* have lot of snowdrops, Ben."

"This is nothing. Wait till you see the *back* garden. It's a bit narrow but it's long, and it's *really* full of snowdrops. There are some early hellebores flowering as well, and more Daphne bholua, winter box, early crocus and primroses, and the Rhododendron dauricum Midwinter is looking good. Come on through and I'll show you; there's still just about enough light to have a look round, though the snowdrop flowers have all pretty much closed up for the night."

"Ben, can I have bath and go to bed? I am really tired. I will see garden tomorrow."

"Of course. I'll run you a bath and make something to eat. I can take a look round later with a torch."

"You will look at garden in dark with *torch*? Why? Are you crazy?"

"I just need to check the cats haven't been digging in my snowdrop seedling beds again, and I have to do a quick slug hunt. I keep finding tiny little baby slugs in the frames with this year's seed pots. And a lot of the snowdrop flowers in the garden are being eaten by small black slugs too. I've been plagued by them these last few mild winters. I don't like using slug pellets 'cos of the birds and frogs and toads, so I catch the little buggers when they're climbing up to eat the petals after dark, and I squish them.

While I'm at it, I might dig up a few new seedlings that started flowering recently and put them in pots to bring inside so I can get a closer look at them. Katka? Are you asleep? Come on, you can't go to sleep sitting on your bags in the hall!"

"Ben, please stop talking about snowdrops and carry me up to bed."

"*Carry* you? Y'know these stairs are quite steep. I'm not sure it'd be safe…"

"Ben! I carry you for almost whole kilometre to my village so you do not die of freezing cold when you want to sleep in snow, and you will not carry me up one set of steps to bedroom?"

"We call them *stairs,* not *steps.* And I'm just worried about dropping you. I mean, they really are steep and you're quite heavy…ouch! That's right, hit my lifting arm. That'll help."

The next morning the wind had dropped, the sun was out and the snowdrops were opening wide, so I let Katka sleep while I went out to do some pollinating. It was nearly noon when she appeared at the back door in my dressing gown. I was kneeling on a small cushion, hunched over a bed of snowdrops, a jeweller's eyeglass clamped in my eye, a small sable watercolour paint brush in one hand and an upturned snowdrop flower in the other. I was busy transferring pollen from a matchbox to the delicate stigma of the flower, so I didn't see Katka straight away - not until she bellowed across the garden, making me jump and accidentally pull the flower off its stalk.

"Ben! Where do you keep coffee? I cannot find it!"

"Thanks, Katka! That was the only flower of this snowdrop that I had this year and I wanted to cross it with…"

"Ben, why do you kneel down in front of snowdrops? You *worship* them? You really are mad English gardener! Please tell me where is coffee…oh my God! Ben, you really do have *lot* of snowdrops!"

I glanced over my shoulder, making a mental note to use the pollen from the decapitated flower in my hand for a different cross, and saw Katka looking past me up the garden. She was staring at the endless clumps and drifts of snowdrops amongst the shrubs and hellebores, and then at the rows of snowdrop-filled pots cluttering the patio behind the house and lining the garden paths, bursting out of the frames and the small greenhouse and generally taking up every inch of spare space.

"Ben, this garden is *full* with snowdrops and even paths are half full with snowdrops in pots! How do you even *walk* here?"

"Very carefully. No! Don't try to come out until I've moved a few pots. I know where to put my feet, but you'll…just stay there. The coffee's in the fridge. I read somewhere that it keeps better that way. I got some good Italian stuff for you, extra dark roast, high strength. I'll be in soon."

"What do you do? Not *really* worshiping snowdrops I hope."

"I'm pollinating, doing crosses between snowdrops to make new ones."

"You want *more* snowdrops? Why? You do not have enough already? You must have thousands here."

"Not just *more*, different ones with new flower shapes, new markings, bigger flowers, stronger stems, and more disease resistant. That's especially important, disease resistance, because…"

"Coffee is in fridge? Okay. I will make for you also. Ben? What is this smell out here?"

"Oh, the drains? I've been meaning to…"

"No, this perfume. It is different from daphne at front door, but also very nice and very strong."

"That'll be the winter box, those small shrubs on your right with the little white flowers. I'll pick some shoots and bring them in. No, don't try to get to them yourself! Mind the pots! You'll…"

"Sorry, Ben. Was that special pot of snowdrops? I will make coffee. Sorry."

In the kitchen, I put my kneeling cushion on the table, pushed the sprigs of winter box into a small jug and took a mug of coffee from Katka.

"So, Ben, that is why all cushions on your settee and chairs are muddy? You should take off covers and wash. Perhaps also stop taking cushions to garden. These are very tiny little flowers for such strong perfume. Winter box? Mmmm, beautiful smell. I am amazed I can smell them even with this cold. You have such wonderful smelly winter flowers in England."

"Wait till you get close to Lady C's wintersweet. She has it growing up against the wall of the house and the scent is just amazing. The flowers have no stems, so you have to pick them off the twigs like berries and float them in a bowl of water. Just a few in a bowl with fill an entire room with their perfume. Oh, you made toast…*lots* of toast."

"Yes, Ben. I find electric toasting machine so I cook toast for us both. I *love* toast. It is very English, yes? Tea and toast? In Slovakia and Czech Republic, cooking toast is not really something we do until very recently. Only just now some people start to buy electric toasting machines in Slovakia. My sister has just bought one and she tells my mother she must as well, for when you visit."

There was almost a whole loaf's worth of toast piled on a plate and Katka was already munching on a slice thickly smeared with a bright yellow paste.

"What's that, Katka? It looks like…"

"Is mustard. I find in refrigerator. I especially love to eat mustard on toast. This English mustard is very good, nice and hot. Also garlic rubbed on toast is very good. Do you have garlic? You should try."

"I'm just going to have some marmalade, thanks. Do you have marmalade in Slovakia? This is Lady C's home-made stuff. Have a bite."

"We do not make this in Slovakia but I know it is great English tradition to eat with toast. Oh, is delicious! Here, you finish my toast with mustard. I *love* Lady Cherrington's marmalade."

Katka chewed on the toast and marmalade, rolling her eyes with delight.

"She puts whisky in it, probably quite a lot; certainly picks you up in the morning. Can I do you another slice, Katka?"

She took a second slice and looked around the kitchen, her eyes settling on the calendar on the wall.

"Rooms in this cottage are quite small, Ben. Nice, but small. You work here also, on your books? In room upstairs with computer and artist's drawing desk? I see it when I look around. Is this work calendar? You have lot of appointments."

"No, those are snowdrop events that I'm hoping to go to. Well, not all of them, but some."

"There is one almost every day this month, Ben. Sometimes two on one day. Nettetaler Schneeglockentage?"

"That's a snowdrop gala in Germany. I probably won't make it to that one. But I try to get to as many snowdrop events as I can in the UK. There are so many these days, though; dozens of snowdrop gardens open to the public every year now, and of course there are the snowdrop galas, snowdrop tours, snowdrop lecture days, loads of organised stuff like that, plus private invitations to snowdrop lunches and to see collections that aren't open to the public. Most are in England, but there are quite a few events in Scotland now as well, and Northern Ireland, the Netherlands, Germany…a lot of German and Dutch collectors come over here for the English events, whole coach-loads of them. We even get the odd one or two from places like America and Japan.

Then there are the early Royal Horticultural Society shows. Always a good range of snowdrop nurseries putting on displays at those, showing their new varieties and putting them up for awards, and lots of galanthophiles wandering around, meeting up, chatting and swapping snowdrop gossip."

"Snowdrop *gossip*? You *gossip* about *snowdrops*?"

"Well, yes, and about snowdrop people; rumours about who's found a new snowdrop, how much the latest rare varieties are likely to sell for on ebay, who's had snowdrops stolen from their garden this year…"

"People *steal* snowdrops?"

"There's quite a lot of nicking goes on, people visiting snowdrop gardens with trowels in their pockets, whipping a few special bulbs out of the ground when no-one's looking. Some growers don't put labels with names by their snowdrops any more in case that makes it easier for people to spot the rarest ones when their gardens are open to the public. They'll just have labels with numbers that they can look up in a record book with all the names in it.

Lady C's husband, The Colonel, doesn't stop there. He always has to take things that little bit too far - metal detectors to find hidden trowels in people's pockets on Lady C's garden open days, trip wires and pressure pads in the soil that set off alarms if people step into the borders where the rarest snowdrops are, hidden CCTV cameras…one year he wanted to put some old anti-personnel mines that he'd kept from his Army days into the ground around Lady C's most valuable snowdrops, so they'd go off if anyone tried digging up the bulbs or even standing too close. He said he'd get Alfred the gardener to reduce the charge so the mines weren't lethal, just powerful enough to blow someone off their feet. Alfred didn't look too happy about that, and Lady C wasn't too chuffed about the possibility of having her favourite snowdrops blown sky-high, so she vetoed it. Mind you, she probably wouldn't mind blowing up the Green Panther."

"*Green* Panther? I have heard of *Pink* Panther, Ben, but…"

"That's what some people call this bloke who's been stealing a lot of special snowdrops from people's gardens, sometimes in broad daylight during garden open days but mostly in the middle of the night, sneaking in under cover of dark. He's been at it for years now and we're pretty sure it's always the same person. He only goes for the rarest snowdrops, always seems to know exactly where to find them even if they're not labelled, and always the same size footprints left in the beds and borders.

He's managed to nick some of Lady C's best snowdrops despite the Colonel's lunatic security measures and I'll bet he has his eye on some of her latest additions. He'll have to get past Alfred first though; the Colonel has the poor old bugger on night-time patrol right the way through the snowdrop season, and I happen to know he's bought Alfred a set of ex-Army night-vision goggles this year. From the hints he's been dropping, I think the Colonel may have got his hands on an illicit supply of flash-bang stun grenades too, so the Panther may be in for a shock if he does turn up."

"Mmmm. Ben, try this."

"What is it? Oh bloody hell! That's revolting!"

"It is toast spread with mustard and then with marmalade. I like it."

That night I showed Katka some of the snowdrops being auctioned on ebay. There was an especially rare one coming to the end of bidding, with just a few minutes left.

"Fifty-six pounds for *one* snowdrop bulb, Ben!? I cannot believe this. Who would pay…"

"Wait. I've been watching this one. People have been holding back, trying not to push the price too high early on and hoping to whack a winning bid in at the last minute. Look what happens when I put in a bid. There, sixty pounds."

"Ben, you are not paying sixty pounds for one snowdrop! You are crazy!"

"See? Someone else already put in a maximum bid above that so I've been outbid. I'll keep clicking the refresh button so we can see how the bidding goes now."

"Not all named snowdrops are this expensive to buy I hope?"

"No, of course not. In the catalogues they start as little as two or three pounds a bulb for old favourites like 'Atkinsii', 'Magnet' and 'S. Arnott' that have been around a long time, then on a sliding scale depending on rarity, up to maybe thirty, forty or fifty pounds. But it's in the auctions for the very rarest ones, like these on ebay, that the prices people will pay gets really silly. See?"

"Seventy pounds! Eighty-five pounds! Ben, this is mad!"

"They haven't finished yet. This is a *really* rare new snowdrop. There'll be collectors who'd give their right arm for it…ninety-five pounds…and a hundred…just ten seconds to go…hundred-and-twenty pounds…five seconds…bloody hell someone got that in right at the very last second!"

"Ben, I cannot believe this! *Hundred-and-fifty pounds* for just *one* snowdrop bulb!"

"I know! Over the next few years professional growers will chip bulbs of that snowdrop variety over and over again until there are enough to sell it at just thirty or forty pounds, but because it's *the* latest thing, some people just can't wait and will pay daft money to have it *now*."

"Okay, first, what do you mean, '*chip*' snowdrops?"

"It's not what you think, Katka. We don't put salt and vinegar on them or anything like that."

"That is joke? It is terrible, Ben. Please do not ever tell that joke again to anyone. Promise me. It is really, really very bad joke."

"What if I change it to ketchup?"

"I am too tired and ill with this cold to hit you on arm now, Ben, but I will get better."

"Fair enough."

"And second, Ben, why do you say *only* thirty or forty pounds? You think thirty or forty pounds for one bulb is *only*? How much do you *spend* on snowdrops, Ben? Oh, wait! I remember that I see you write 'chip' on some labels in pots of snowdrops you bring into kitchen. To chip is some kind of propagating technique?"

I was glad Katka had changed the subject away from how much I spend on new snowdrops as I suspected that would only lead to trouble. So I was quick to explain about the chipping, not that I ever need an excuse to bore people about snowdrop stuff like that.

"It's cutting the bulbs into small segments, down through the base, so a new little bulb grows on each segment. If you give them the right treatment, put them in damp vermiculite in plastic bags and…"

"So you will chip all these snowdrops in kitchen to make more of them?"

"Yes. They're seedlings I've selected from the seed beds and potted up because I think they might be worth chipping, so I bring them in to have a closer look. If I chip a single bulb this year when the leaves die down, in two or three years I'll have a clump of maybe a dozen bulbs instead of just one. It depends how big the first bulb is and how many chips I can cut it into. Sometimes, with a big bulb, I can increase it to…"

"Ben? How many snowdrops do you think you have in garden?"

"What? I don't know. Thousands."

"And how fast do they increase just growing in ground without chipping?"

"It varies, but they generally double every two to four years, depending on how vigorous the variety is."

"And every year you get how many new ones from seed sowing?"

"I sow a few hundred seeds a year. Maybe five or six hundred. So probably four or five hundred seedlings a year."

"And you chip how many seedlings a year?"

"It depends. Some years there are more worth chipping, some years less. On average I select out something like fifty to a hundred seedlings to chip and grow on as clumps for further assessment in the garden. I also chip some of the best old varieties every year, the ones I really like, to make new clumps. Altogether I probably chip two or three hundred bulbs a year. Why?"

"Have you done math on this, Ben? Should I get you calculator? Your garden is already full with snowdrops. Frames and greenhouse are full with snowdrops. Paths are full with snowdrops. Right now kitchen is also full with snowdrops. Where will you put all these new ones you raise from seed and make from chips?"

"I know, I know, I need a bigger garden. I'll have to start looking…"

"Hapchee! Hapchee! Oh, this cold is getting worse, Ben! I must go to bed early if we are going to Lady Cherrington's snowdrop lunch in morning. But seriously, Ben, find calculator and do math. Seems to me you will need *much* bigger garden. Hapchee! Hapchee!"

Sneezing loudly in Slovak, Katka headed for the kitchen while I had a quick look at how some of the other snowdrop auctions were going on ebay.

"You go on up to bed, Katka. I just have to go out with the torch and do a quick check around the snowdrops after I've finished here."

In the hall I met Katka returning from the kitchen. She was clutching a hot water bottle and a glass of hot milk and honey and sniffing loudly.

"I have locked back door and hidden key, Ben. I have also hidden your torch, in case you think of climbing out through window to look at snowdrops. Come to bed. I need to warm my feet on you."

It was late morning when we arrived at Lady C's. Katka had been tossing and turning half the night and woke up absolutely streaming, so I'd put her back to bed for a couple more hours. We pulled into the drive just as everyone else was trooping inside for pre-lunch drinks, having already done a tour of the snowdrops in the main garden. The usual timetable was looking at the beds and borders around the house in the morning, followed by lunch then a walk through the snowdrop woodland in the afternoon. Lady C waited for us by the front door, looking concerned as Katka climbed out of the car, blowing her nose loudly.

"This must be Katka. Hello dear. You poor thing. Are you sure you feel up to looking at silly snowdrops? Yes? Well, I'll take you two for a *very* quick spin around the garden to see the highlights then whizz you both inside for a drink and something to eat by a warm fire. Come on, this way."

I have to say, Lady C and I were both surprised and impressed by how many of the snowdrops Katka recognised and was able to put names to. Not all of them by any means, but she got a hell of a lot right, even if she did have to get down on her hands and knees a lot of the time to get a closer look. But then snowdrop enthusiasts spend half their time on their knees, turning the flowers up to get a good look, so that just made her seem even more of an expert.

"Have you been reading the snowdrop book?"

"Of course I have, Ben. It was Christmas present, so of course I read it, and I do search on internet and find web sites with very nice photographs of many different snowdrop varieties; English websites, and Irish and German too.

By way, I also discover, through web search, internet forum where snowdrop growers and collectors discuss snowdrops and show photographs. I could not believe this when I first find it - *chat room* for snowdrop collectors!"

Lady C smiled at this.

"We *are* all a bit bonkers, Katka, especially the men. You know what *they* can get like when it comes to collecting things."

"Yes, I do, Lady Cherrington. Ben, you know you really write lot of times on this internet forum. From forum statistics, I see you spend sometimes as much as two hours every day on forum during snowdrop season, talking to other collectors and growers. Between this and looking at snowdrop auctions on ebay, when do you ever get work done? And let me remember, what was your forum nickname? Oh yes, 'Big Ben'. I can assure you *that* is something we will be discussing later."

Lady C chuckled and led us to another part of the garden. We didn't look at every clump of snowdrops. That would have taken hours. Instead, Lady C showed us just the best and the newest. Actually she was showing them mainly to Katka, as I'd already seen most of them over the previous days and weeks.

There were some stunning recent additions to Lady C's collection. She'd been given various beautiful new virescent and green-tipped snowdrops, nivalis and elwesii selections with lots of green shading and striping on the outside petals to compliment the green marks on the inners. She also had some very good new yellow-marked snowdrops, including a very special yellow nivalis with the usual bright yellow inner mark plus pretty yellow tips to the outer petals, discovered in a French woodland. Then there were two handsome new poculiform nivalis, also found very recently in woodland populations of ordinary snowdrops. But I knew what Lady C would save for last - this year's pièce de résistance, her brand new pride and joy, given to her only a few days ago. I hoped Katka would appreciate just how special it was, and I could tell Lady C was hoping the same. She kept glancing expectantly at Katka as we approached the small bed tucked into a sheltered niche below the breakfast room window. Alfred the gardener was sitting, stiffly alert, on a wooden chair with a flask of tea and a container of sandwiches, guarding a single snowdrop planted by the trunk of the wintersweet growing against the wall, the shrub's small yellow flowers scenting the mild air all around. I picked a flower and held it under Katka's bunged-up, red nose.

"No, Ben. I already told you I cannot smell *anything* today. I could not smell daphne at your front door. I could not even smell *coffee*! I could not smell if elephant made enormous stink with bottom right under my nose…oh, I am sorry Lady Cherrington, that was rude! I am feeling really ill today and Ben can be bit annoying sometimes."

"That's quite all right, dear. Speaking of stinky farts, wait till you meet my husband, Oliver. He'll clear your sinuses for you. Eh, Ben? Now this is something very new and *very special*, Katka. It was discovered at Myddleton House, E.A. Bowles' old garden near London. I don't suppose you'll know about Mister Bowles?"

"Yes, he was famous gardener and snowdrop collector. I read in snowdrop book which Ben gives to me. And this is poculiform snowdrop, with all six petals equal length. It is beautiful! Also large flower and tall stem for poculiform I think, and leaves are plicate, turned back at edges, so it is not nivalis but plicatus? Most poculiform snowdrops are nivalis, no? There was no plicatus poculiform snowdrop in book or on websites. Is really *very* lovely!"

Lady C smiled as Katka dropped onto her knees to admire the flower close up.

"Yes, dear, it's either a plicatus or a plicatus hybrid. Only three or four people in the country have bulbs at the moment. Most snowdrop growers don't even know about it yet. I just hope that bloody man, the Green sodding Panther, doesn't get wind of it or he'll be round here like a shot, sneaking in through the woodland at night like he did the time he got my only clump of 'Rosemary Burnham'! The bastard!"

I'd joined Katka on my knees by the flower bed, taken an empty matchbox from my coat pocket and started tapping the snowdrop flower while holding it over the open box. Katka stared at me.

"What are you doing, Ben?"

"Trying to collect some pollen to use in crosses with other poculiforms. I already pollinated this flower earlier in the week. No, the pollen's not running, Lady C. I'll try again this afternoon when the air's warmer."

As I helped Katka back up to her feet, she started sneezing violently.

"Hapchee! Hapchee!"

"She means 'Atchoo'," I explained to Lady C, then dodged Katka's fist, which missed my arm by a good six inches. Luckily for me, the illness was slowing down her swing quite a lot. Unfortunately Lady C twigged that I was having a dig at Katka and elbowed me in the ribs as she stepped past me to take Katka's arm and lead her away.

"Oh dear! You poor thing, Katka. Let's get you inside and find you a nice glass of whisky. If Oliver hasn't drunk it all."

As we turned to head back the way we'd come, Alfred bit into a thick cheese and onion sandwich and munched noisily while staring suspiciously across the lawn at a startled blackbird flying out of the shrubbery.

I followed Katka and Lady C back to the front door, where I supported Lady C as she struggled to take off her wellies, and where Katka stared worriedly at some of the cars in the driveway.

"There are very upper-class people here, Ben," she whispered. "I see when we arrive. Very upper-class-looking people wearing very upper-class-looking clothes and with very expensive cars. Perhaps you should take me to your cottage and then you can come back here without me."

"Don't be silly, Katka."

"That is *Rolls Royce* car parked over there, no? And that is…I don't know, but looks like very expensive antique car."

"And that's a Honda, and that one's a Citroen 2CV, and that's…a Bentley…okay, yes, one or two of them might be a bit posh, but Lady C invites all sorts of people to her snowdrop lunches and most aren't the slightest bit upper-class. Come on, they're all nice people. You'll like them. Except perhaps for....Lady C? You didn't invite that bloody idiot Humphrey Whimpleton-Pughe again did you? Oh God, you did! *Why*?"

Lady C smiled apologetically as she waved us into the stone-flagged entrance hall.

"I know, Ben, but it would be rude not to. Sorry it's not very warm in here, Katka. The heating's on the blink again and I can't afford to keep getting the repair man out to look at it. He just goes on and on about our old boiler being a dinosaur of a machine and never manages to get it running again for more than a few days. There's oil in the tank but the boiler just won't fire up. Now follow me, along this passage, Katka. Mind the step."

In the kitchen, Lady C took a silver tray of smoked salmon on brown bread from the table, handed another one to Katka and a plate of lemon wedges to me, then led us through to what her husband, The Colonel, refers to rather grandly as the dining hall. I suppose it is a lot bigger than the average dining room, with high windows, a huge refectory table and a massive stone fireplace, but I always think dining *hall* is pushing it a bit. That's the Colonel for you, though - Lady C always talks about the garden while the Colonel says the *grounds*; she says 'my gardener, Alfred' but the Colonel calls him 'my *man*, Alfred'. I really can't think *why* I like Lady C so much more than The Colonel.

There were thirty or more people standing around chatting with glasses in their hands. The breadcrumbs on a couple of empty trays indicated that they'd already started eating and we were bringing fresh supplies. Katka was hanging back by the kitchen door, obviously delaying the moment when she'd have to properly enter the room and mix with everyone. I could see she was eyeing the assembled waxed country jackets, tweeds, elbow pads, cord trousers, Fair Isle jumpers, cashmere cardigans, sensible shoes and suchlike displays of middle-class fashion sense with a mixture of trepidation and continental amusement. A log fire was burning in the grate, but the room was still chilly and Katka had shivered as we walked in.

"Ben," she whispered, clutching her tray to her, "on internet snowdrop discussion forum, this man Jeremy who you talk to lot of times, he is your friend? You seem *very* friendly. You send each other really lot of personal messages through forum."

"Yes, he's my best friend...hang on, Katka, how do you know what personal messages I send and get on the forum? That's private. No-one could know that unless they..."

"Okay, yes, I hack into your membership account and read messages. It was too easy, Ben. You really should use stronger passwords. Birthday dates and names of colours are not good to use. So, this Jeremy, he looks really *gorgeous* in his forum photograph."

"Gorgeous and *gay*, so you can stop licking your lips."

"You are sure Jeremy is gay? He does not look gay. He looks hunky, reminds me of young George Clooney."

"Yes, I'm sure. He has a boyfriend. Actually he's had several since I've known him. Also, he waggled his willy at me in the toilets the first time we met at a snowdrop gala. It was after the gala dinner. We were both having a wee and chatting about snowdrops, and he shook his willy then turned away from the urinal and just stood there talking to me with it still in his hand for a moment before putting it away. I think it was his way of checking if I was interested. It was quite impressive actually."

"Really? How impressive, Ben?"

"You have no shame, Katka. And put your tongue back in your mouth."

"You were not tempted, even little bit? You are quite pretty-looking for man, Ben. You do not *ever* have some gay feelings for another man?"

"No, but I do get hit on by gay men quite a lot."

"That is because you look little bit like you could be gay. You have certain kind of softness and gentleness about you which could be mistaken for gayness. I can see how they might pick you up on their...I forget, how do they say it in

English...gaydar? Yes?"

"You think I look quite *pretty*?"

"For man, yes."

"But not as good-looking as Jeremy? Not *hunky*?"

"Oh my God, no! He is..."

"Gorgeous and hunky. Yes, I think we've established that. So I'm really not hunky at all?"

"More cute and cuddly. Will Jeremy be here today?"

"He's usually invited. I expect he's around somewhere. That bloke over there has an empty plate and he's looking at your tray of sandwiches. You'd better offer him some. Yes, the podgy bloke with the yellow waistcoat and the walrus moustache. Go on."

Even as I pushed Katka towards Humphrey, I felt sorry. It was an evil thing to do and she didn't really deserve it, despite all the stuff about how hunky Jeremy was and how hunky I wasn't. Of course I didn't know then just how bad it was going to be. I thought Humphrey would be his usual obnoxious self, not put on an extra-special display of sexist xenophobia and unashamed racism.

"About time, girl! Saw you slacking by the door. Tried to catch your eye. Can't you see my plate's empty?"

Humphrey grabbed a handful of smoked salmon sandwiches, then another, greedily piling his plate high and barking at Katka.

"Don't *sniff* when you're serving, girl! Don't they teach you anything in catering college? What did you say? I can't understand you. It's the accent. Are you *Polish*? Bloody Poles! Coming over here taking jobs from English workers! I've a good mind to get Primula to complain to your employer. What was that? What did you say? Stupid fat *what*? Primula!"

Lady C, having overheard all this - along with everyone else in the room - rounded angrily on Humphrey, her small fists clenched tightly and her face white with rage.

"*Humphrey*! Katka is a guest, not catering staff! She's Ben's friend and she's here to see the snowdrops just like you, so please mind your manners!"

Humphrey puffed himself up and rolled his eyes, speaking loudly to the room.

"Oh dear, Primula! What *are* we coming to? Poles at snowdrop lunches? Eastern Europeans? Ex-commies? Next thing we'll be letting bloody Pakis in! Get a grip old girl!"

I really don't think I'd ever seen either Lady C or Katka so angry before. They both exploded together.

"I told you, I am not Polish, I am Slovak! And I said you are stupid fat…"

"Humphrey! Please leave! *Now*! Put your plate down and go. I won't ask you twice."

"Primula old girl, don't be silly. You can't boot me out just for ticking off the help."

"She is *not* the *help*, Humphrey. I do not *have* 'help' and Katka is my *guest*. Now piss off and never come back!"

That's the moment Jeremy chose to walk into the room. Sizing up the situation in an instant, he prised Humphrey's plate from his fat fingers and handed it to Katka before taking Humphrey by the arm and marching him out of the door and into the hall.

"About time too, Lady C. Come on Humphrey, I've always wanted to do this. I think I speak for just about everyone here when I say that you really are undoubtedly the rudest, most arrogant, greedy, annoying, boring, self-important, know-all little twat I've ever had the displeasure to meet. If I was Lady C, I'd have given you your marching orders years ago."

Everyone in the room had frozen, watching open-mouthed as Jeremy - all six-foot, broad-shouldered, rugby-playing, gym-toned hunk of him - almost picked the podgy little Billy Bunter-shaped Humphrey up by the elbow and carried him out. There were smiles as Humphrey's indignant squeals of protest carried through from the hallway.

"Put me down! Get your filthy queer hands off me, Jeremy! I'll have you for sexual assault, you poof! Ouch! Ouch! Ouch!"

As Jeremy strode back into the room, Lady C looked concerned.

"You didn't hurt him, did you? I know he's a horrible, horrible man but…"

"No, of course not. I just helped him out with my foot. He might have a sore backside for a few days but nothing serious. You really should have banned him from these lunches years ago, Lady C. All he ever does is show off, put people down and make out that he's *the* expert on snowdrops when we all know he hasn't been growing them for a *fraction* of the time you have. Good riddance to him."

Jeremy turned to Katka and flashed her a smile that I just knew was turning her knees to jelly.

"Hello, you must be Katka. Ben's told me all about you. Let me take that tray and plate and get you a drink. You look frozen. Whisky? Double? Where've you hidden the good stuff, Colonel? Never mind, I'll find it. Hi, Ben. She's every bit as lovely as you said."

I thought Katka was going to swoon. Luckily Lady C clapped her hands and announced lunch, ordering everyone into the kitchen to open up the countless ovens of her ancient and massive Aga range and help themselves from the various dishes keeping warm therein.

"Jeremy is very nice, Ben," whispered Katka.

"Yes. And gay, remember, *very* gay. Now put your eyeballs back in your head and make sure you grab lots of Lady C's roast potatoes; they're legendary for their crispiness and fluffiness. Her gravy's to die for too. I'm having the beef, but there's always something for non-meat eaters as well."

Katka hardly ate anything and after lunch was looking so poorly that Lady C insisted she was in no fit state to tramp round the woodland looking at more snowdrops. Instead, a large and rather threadbare high-backed armchair was placed by the dining hall fire for her.

"You stay here, dear," said Lady C, giving Katka a very large glass of the Colonel's best malt whisky and tucking a red tartan rug around her knees. "I'm sorry it's so cold but, as I said, the boiler's conked out again. Third time this month. It's been out of commission for a week now, but it costs so much to have the man come. Now if you get bored, do feel free to have a look around the house. Go anywhere - we don't have any secrets. Well, Oliver might have. Probably best to stay out of his study. You never know what might be lying around. I once found an unwashed pair of his underpants being used as a bookmark. Not a pretty sight, I can tell you!"

"Thank you, Lady Cherrington. I will be okay."

"Call me Primula, Katka. We won't be long. Right, outdoor shoes and boots back on, everyone; the woodland walk is especially muddy this year after all the rain we've had."

When we got back an hour-and-a-half later and looked into the dining hall, the chair by the fire was empty. Lady C had already seen everyone else off in the driveway, so it was just her, me and Jeremy. The Colonel was outside, making sure Alfred was still on guard duty and hadn't nipped off for a pee. Apparently the Colonel had provided him with an empty bottle to use in an emergency. Suddenly there were loud clanging noises from upstairs and the heating pipes and radiator in the entrance hall rattled. Lady C reached out and touched the radiator.

"It's getting hot! I *thought* it felt warmer in here."

At that moment Katka appeared on the stairs, a hammer in one hand and a tool box in the other.

"I found boiler and tools in basement when I look round house. This, by way, is *really* beautiful house, Lady Cherrington. Also *very big*. Ben, did you know this house has *two* stairs, this big one and smaller one up from passage behind kitchen? So many rooms, stairs and passages; I get lost, which is how I find boiler room and tools. I fix boiler, by way. I think will be okay for now but there are some parts which are very worn. I adapt them with wire, screws and tools to make them work better for time being, but they should be replaced in longer term. I have also freed and greased sticking valves on radiators which were not becoming hot. I hope you do not mind, Lady Cherrington?"

"Not at all, and it's Primula, dear. You're a miracle worker, Katka. Now come and wash your hands and we'll talk more while I make some tea. I've never been to Slovakia, so you must tell me all about it. You boys can help yourselves to more of the good whisky if Oliver hasn't hidden it again. If he has, try looking in the cistern of the downstairs loo. He spends an inordinate amount of time in there with his newspaper and always seems much more cheerful when he comes out than when he goes in. Of course, given his prolonged bouts of constipation, there may be a more innocent explanation for that, but I still have my suspicions."

It was dark by the time we left, Lady C and Jeremy walking us out to the car, where Katka suddenly threw her arms around a very surprised Lady C, nearly knocking her off her feet before hugging her tightly.

"I am so sorry about your lovely house and garden, Lady Cherrington!"

"*Primula*, dear."

"Yes...Primula. I am so sorry you will lose all this. It is beautiful garden and beautiful house. If I was living here as many years as you, I would be very sad to leave. Banks are real bastards!"

"Please don't cry, dear. This big old house was becoming too much for me and Oliver to manage anyway. It'll be hard work lifting and giving away all the snowdrops before the builders come, but we'll manage somehow, and Oliver and I will be fine."

"But I can never visit you here again. I will never see this garden again. I must go back to Praha in morning, but I did not see woodland garden, and when I come again, it will all be over! You will have gone and builders will be here!"

By now Katka and Lady C were clinging onto each other equally tightly and it became difficult to tell who was consoling who, but finally we managed to prise them apart and edge Katka towards the open passenger door. On the drive home she finally stopped sobbing, turned to me and asked:

"Ben, you are *sure* Jeremy is gay? He pinched my bottom as I get into car."

"He was probably being ironic, or messing around or something. Yes, he's definitely one hundred per cent gay."

"Perhaps he is little bit bisexual."

"I really don't think so. I've never seen or heard him show the slightest sexual interest in a woman. I mean, he's very friendly with women, but not, y'know…*interested*."

"Perhaps he just appreciates a nice bottom."

"What?!"

"Don't look at me like that, Ben! You know what I mean! Just drive car. And hurry up. We must leave for London very early and I still need to pack. So you are *very* good friends, you and Jeremy?"

"Don't start that again, Katka. We're friends. We chat a lot through the online snowdrop forum because we're both snowdrop growers and collectors, just like all the other people on the forum, and we meet up at snowdrop events like today's. The rest of the year we get together for a drink or a meal maybe once a month, and even then we still mostly talk about snowdrops."

"He does not look like someone who would be interested in snowdrops and gardening. He looks more like professional sportsman. Is he?"

"No. Well he does play rugby, but he works at GCHQ in Cheltenham, about fifteen miles from here. That's the Government Communications Headquarters; it's a big ultra-modern doughnut-shaped state-of-the-art building on the edge of Cheltenham covered in satellite disks and antennae, where they listen in to foreign communications - radio, satellite, phones, really any kind of electronic communications by foreign governments and agencies that they're interested in monitoring. It used to be mostly the Russians and the Warsaw Pact countries like Poland and Czechoslovakia they eavesdropped on. Probably still the Russians, but I should think now it's also the Middle East, Iran, terrorist organisations, stuff like that."

"So he is a *spy*, your friend Jeremy?"

"A spy? No! Well, sort of. Not a James Bond type spy though. Maybe a techno-spy. I don't really know. They're not supposed to talk about what they do, but I think Jeremy *might* be involved in the same sort of thing that Lady C's husband, the Colonel, used to be in - encryption and decryption, code breaking, that kind of thing. The Colonel worked at GCHQ too, a long time ago, during the Cold War, but I've heard him talking to Jeremy about it sometimes and Jeremy always seems very interested and knowledgeable."

"So Jeremy is *code genius*, like in film with Russell Crowe, 'Beautiful Mind'? And how do you know so much about government communications spying headquarters? You will not get into trouble for knowing this? It is not secret?"

"Not *very* secret these days, no, and I think it's mostly done with computers now, though Jeremy *is* brilliant at crosswords. He can do the most mind-bending cryptic crossword in a few minutes, and he can solve Sudoku quizzes in not time at all. Maybe he *is* some kind of a genius."

"By way, Ben, I know of course that you deliberately send me to give sandwiches to horrible Humphrey man."

"Oh. Sorry but you *were* going on rather a lot about how *gorgeous and hunky* Jeremy is, and I had no idea Humphrey was going to be so...I mean he's usually just averagely obnoxious, not the way he was today. No-one really likes him but they've all put up with him for years. I don't know why. He seems to think he should be the King of the snowdrop world; that everyone should just give him the latest and rarest snowdrops, and if he isn't given them willingly then he tries to bully people into giving them to him or selling them to him. He's a nasty piece of work."

"Well, thank you for making me take him sandwiches, Ben. That was real treat for me. Just don't expect sex tonight."

"Oh please, Katka! I was so looking forward to it, what with you being so snotty and bunged-up and full of germs."

"Then we *are* having sex, whether you want to or not!"

"How do you know that's not what I really wanted all the time?"

"Then there will *not* be any sex!"

"And how do you know *that* isn't what I wanted...ouch! Don't hit my arm when I'm driving!"

The next morning, as we queued for Katka's coach in London, she watched a CCTV camera slowly panning across the crowded platforms.

"You know, Ben, your government does not just spy on other countries. They spy on their *own* country too. I have never seen so many cameras watching people. They are everywhere - on streets, at railway stations, here at coach station.

I read in your newspaper that UK has more CCTV cameras than anywhere else in world. It was story about threat to civil liberties here from increasing surveillance. Always *more* cameras and *better* cameras, *more* powers for police and authorities, *more* listening to telephone calls, reading emails and keeping records of what people do on internet. And also new identity cards which you never had before, plus database of all children in UK, which will of course become database of all *adults* when children grow up."

We both watched the camera pan back across the coach station as our queue shuffled forward.

"I read it too, Katka. It's been in the news a lot lately. And it *is* starting to feel a little like being in The Village."

"What? Ben, please tell me you do not have cameras watching people even in little villages."

"No. Well, one or two bigger villages might. I think I read something...no, I mean *The Village*. It was a place in this old TV series called 'The Prisoner', where they had total surveillance everywhere all the time, watching people non-stop. And no-one could escape."

I pushed Katka's bags into the luggage hold and she continued to watch, fascinated, as the camera began yet another sweep over the platforms and coaches.

"You know, Ben, even under repressive regime in Czechoslovakia during communist times, I think we were not watched so closely as you are now in UK. It is strange that in Eastern Europe we have been moving towards more freedom and less surveillance, while you are going in other direction."

With that cheery thought, we kissed and Katka climbed on board the coach. I watched her settle into a window seat and, just before the coach pulled away, press a hastily-scribbled note against the glass for me to read: "I love you, Ben! Call me on Valentine's Day! And clean your toilet!"

I really didn't need reminding about the toilet thing. She'd been on at me about it for days and had already made me promise to get something really strong - and probably very bad for the environment - to shift the limescale. I'd also promised to clean the fridge, which apparently smelled funny, wash the covers of the cushions I'd been using for kneeling in the garden, and give Lady C a big hug from Katka when I went to start helping dig up the snowdrops.

When I got home, I found similar reminders on Post-it notes stuck to the toilet, the fridge and every cushion in the place, plus one on my pillow which reminded me again that Katka loved me and another that read: "Yes, you *do* snore! I will bring tape recorder and prove it!"

I'd told Katka that I was really sorry but I couldn't go to Prague to see her on Valentine's Day because of work commitments and, although I think she suspected that 'work commitments' might actually mean snowdrop events, she was surprisingly laid back about it, only asking that I call her in the evening so we could have a cosy Valentines Day chat via our computer web cams. I'd asked if she'd be putting her hair in pigtails and wearing my 'special Christmas present', to which she'd replied that perhaps we could light candles to make it romantic. I'd queried whether the web cams would work by candle-light and, more importantly, whether I'd be able to see the special Christmas present underwear. That was when she hit me with one of the dirty cushions.

The Maybe Ring

What Katka didn't know was that I'd already booked a flight to Prague on Valentine's Day to surprise her. So at six in the evening on February 14th, instead of being at home I was just round the corner from Katka and Elena's flat, carrying my overnight bag, a bottle of wine and a bunch of red roses.

I was expecting Katka to be home since we'd arranged to talk on the web cams at six thirty. What I wasn't expecting as I turned the corner was to see Katka standing under a street lamp on the pavement beside a bright red Ferrari. She was being handed a huge heart-shaped box of chocolates by a very flashy-looking guy with long blond hair tied back in a pony tail and wearing silk suit, open-neck shirt and white trainers. I watched him put his arm around her waist and leaned in to kiss her, then I turned on my heel, my heart sinking. At the corner I bumped into Elena coming the other way and tried to push past her, but she grabbed my arm and stopped me,

"Ben? What are you...oh, I see. Ben, wait! I know this looks very bad, but it is okay, I promise...look!"

Elena turned me around so I could see Katka hitting the blond guy around the head with the box of chocolates, shouting angrily at him in Slovak. Elena let go of my arm and ran across the road towards them, also shouting loudly and angrily. Together, she and Katka hit, pushed and shoved the guy back into his car and stood there, hands on hips, watching him speed off into the dark. As I walked up, Elena nudged Katka, whispered to her and then bent down to pick up the battered chocolate box. Katka whipped around and saw me standing on the other side of the road, feeling as close to tears as I'd been for years. I turned to walk away again, but Katka shouted after me.

"Ben! Where are you going? I thought you were in England!"

"So I see. I wanted to surprise you. I didn't think you'd already have a date."

"Do not be so stupid, Ben! If that is what you think of me, then I do not want you here. Go on, go back to England!"

Elena walked past Katka, carrying the chocolates with one hand and clipping her around the ear with the other before waving for me to cross over to them.

"Katka, shut up! It is not Ben you are angry with. It is Radko, remember? Do not blame Ben because he sees you having what really looks to him like lovers' argument. Ben, come inside. I will make coffee and Katka will explain. These are very good chocolates. Belgian. Excellent!"

Turns out the guy with the Ferrari was an old boyfriend of Katka's from her university days. Apparently he'd tracked her down to the flat in Prague a couple of years before through mutual friends and kept turning up every few months with expensive gifts for Katka, trying to restart the relationship.

When Katka went to change for dinner, Elena gave me the *real* dirt on Radko. According to her, he was half Slovak, half Bulgarian; the son of a Bulgarian gangster, sent to study in Bratislava, his mother's home city, so he could stay with his grandparents. Katka had gone out with him a couple of times but then called it a day because he was, in Elena's words "Complete dick head, always showing off, always partying and drinking, never studying and always boasting how rich and important his father is."

A friend told Katka the rumours about Radko's father being some kind of gangster godfather in Bulgaria and that was the last straw. When she dumped him, they had a huge row and Radko got drunk and started slapping her around outside a bar.

She got a black eye and a split lip and he ended up in accident and emergency with two broken fingers, a cracked rib and concussion. Elena said Katka visited Radko in hospital afterwards but refused to ever go out with him again. She hadn't seen him since those university days, until he turned up in Prague out of the blue looking for her and wanting to cry on her shoulder about how his wife had divorced him 'for no reason at all'.

We left Elena in front of the TV with the bottle of wine and box of chocolates while we went out to our favourite restaurant across the river near the castle. As we stepped out of the building, Katka was greeted by yet another man, this one tall, broad-shouldered and very handsome in a dashing and swarthy Heathcliff on the moor, Wuthering Heights, curly-black-haired and flashing-dark-eyed sort of way. He grabbed her, hugged her tight and kissed her on both cheeks as I stood in the doorway watching incredulously.

"Oh for crying out loud! This is ridiculous! Can't you people leave her alone?! She's *my* girlfriend now! I've made a dinner reservation! I've come all the way from London! I love her and if you don't put her down *right now* I'm going to hit you so fucking hard…"

"Ben, this is my brother-in-law, Zoltan. My sister's husband. Luckily for you he does not speak English. Smile nicely and shake hands."

I continued shouting almost as loudly but with a huge smile on my face and my hand held out, trying to switch seamlessly from loud, angry and aggressive to loud, what-a-nice-surprise and happy-to-meet-you. It wasn't easy, but I think I pulled it off because Zoltan smiled back and politely shook the hand I'd offered instead of crushing my neck in his mighty fist.

It seems he was on his way to see his wife and kids for the first time in nearly a month and had called round to say hello on his way to the railway station to get a train back home. So we found a taxi, saw him off on the platform and got to the restaurant almost an hour late. Amazingly they were still holding the table for us, even though the place was full of couples having candle-lit Valentine dinners and they could probably have given our table away three times over. They really seemed to like Katka there.

"So, Zoltan is very good looking in a dark, romantic hero sort of way, Katka. Where did your sister find him? In a novel?"

"His father is Slovak but his mother is beautiful Hungarian Gypsy from very good, quite rich Roma family. She was really quite famous singer in Hungary when she was younger. Now, because it is Valentine Day I will demonstrate my love for you by ordering for you something disgustingly meaty to eat and in return you will gaze lovingly at me in candle-light and tell me how beautiful I am, and how much you adore me, while you eat it."

Walking back from the restaurant, we stopped in the middle of Karl's Bridge, holding hands and watching the dark water. I hadn't planned what happened next. In fact I hadn't even thought about it until that moment, so it surprised me just as much as it did Katka.

"Katka? Will you marry me?"

"What?"

"Will you marry me? I love you and I want to marry you."

"Oh, Ben...maybe."

"Is that the Slovak 'maybe', the one that really means yes?"

"No, it is English maybe, one that means maybe. I am sorry, Ben, but we only know each other for quite short time. I really cannot say now that I will marry you. But I *can* say maybe. Yes, I think maybe. Can we leave it like this for now? Please?"

We walked on across the bridge in silence. An old woman was selling cheap jewellery for tourists under the shelter of the bridge's tower and as we passed her stand I took out my wallet.

"Katka, hang on a second. I want to get something."

"What are you doing, Ben? You are giving her equivalent

of around twenty pounds for *wooden ring*, Ben! Are you crazy? It is very nice polished wooden ring but price ticket is only couple of pounds. Why do you not take some money back? She is trying to give to you."

"It's okay. Tell her to keep it. Here, put it on. It's a 'maybe' ring."

"*Maybe* ring?"

"Yes. A maybe ring. Are you going to put it on?"

"Ben, that is lovely. There, I put it on. This is nicest thing anyone ever gave me. I love it."

"So you should. It cost me twenty quid."

"You know she will probably spend it on vodka."

"D'you think it's too late to go back for the change? Ouch! I thought you'd stopped with the arm hitting. Elena told me you put Radko in hospital when he tried to beat you up. Is that true? Because I have to say it's got me a bit worried. Maybe I should take that ring back. Ouch! Again, with the arm hitting!"

When we got back to the flat, Elena had already gone to bed, having eaten more than half the chocolates and polished off the bottle of wine. While Katka showered, I used her computer to check my emails.

"Ben? You want shower? I am finished. You are still doing emails? Hurry up and come to bed. It is Valentine Day and I think I will wear special Christmas present."

"I'll be there in a minute. There's a snowdrop on ebay that I'd really like to have and the auction's going to end in a couple of minutes but there don't seem to be many people bidding. I might get it."

"Did you hear, Ben? I said I will wear your *special Christmas present*. Hurry up. I am tired. I think I drink too much champagne at restaurant."

"Here we go. Just a minute left. No-one's bidding. I'm still the top bidder at twenty-five pounds. That's not a bad price for a bulb of...no! You bastard! Thirty pounds? Okay, I'll go to thirty-five but that's my limit. You sod! Forty! Should I try...now someone else is bidding! Fifty-five? Seventy?

Eighty? Oh for crying out loud! It went for eighty-five pounds! Look at this, Katka. It's not worth half that. Katka?"

In the bedroom Katka was snoring softly, her hand on the pillow by her face with the wooden maybe ring on her engagement finger. As I climbed in beside her I peeked under the duvet. She *was* wearing my special Christmas present. Stupid bloody ebay.

Before I left, Katka said she'd visit me for another weekend as early as possible in March and could she "please, please" come to stay with me for a week at Easter. At first I thought she was desperate to see as much of me as possible, but it turned out she just wanted a good excuse not to have to go home to her parents' village for the Easter holidays. Apparently Katka's mother expected her to go home to see the family every Christmas and Easter and would nag her interminably if it looked like Katka was staying away. This year, however, I was Katka's trump card, the ace in the hole that would beat any emotional blackmail her mother could possibly come up with.

"I will tell her you invited me to England for Easter and I already agreed because you asked me to marry you and I only said 'maybe' instead of 'yes', and it would make you very, very unhappy if I also did not agree to be with you at Easter holidays, which are a favourite holiday for you because...come on, Ben, help me...because..."

"It's your excuse, not mine. And I have no idea why I might like Easter so much that I'd be distraught if you didn't spend it with me. I mean, I like chocolate eggs but I can quite happily eat them on my own if I have to."

"No, I cannot say I told you 'maybe' because then she will nag me for not saying 'yes'. She likes you, and so does my father and my sister. My brother-in-law thinks you may be little bit unhinged because you smile and shout at same time. I will just say that you will be very lonely, unhappy and miserable if I am not with you. She will believe that. She knows effect I have on men."

194

"Is she also aware of just how modest and self-effacing you are? Anyway, why are you desperate not to be at home over Easter?"

According to Katka, it was the traditional Slovak village Easter fertility rites that drove her crazy, and always had done. She explained how on Easter Monday unmarried village girls of all ages were supposed to dress in their best clothes and wait demurely for groups of village boys of their own age, who went around the houses in groups of four, five or six, to call on them. The girls would have to stay at home, available for visits, all day and when a group of boys called, the mothers would invite them in so that they could recite an Easter poem and throw water and/or cheap perfume on the girls and then ritually hit them - gently, but even so! - with small whips made from platted willow shoots intertwined with coloured ribbons. In the old days, she said, before the whole thing was toned down a bit, the girls would actually be dragged out to the household well or water pump and have whole buckets of cold water poured over them before being 'whipped'.

The girls would have to thank the boys and give them, traditionally, hard-boiled eggs that the girls had hand-painted; these days, more commonly chocolate or some money. Older boys, teenagers for example, would also be invited to stay and eat and drink after the ritual cleansing and whipping, while the older girls were supposed to entertain them with lively conversation as they drip-dried.

"It is ridiculous circus and humiliating," fumed Katka. "It is treated as just bit of fun, but all that symbolism is horrible and with older boys and girls it still has some element of match-making about it; boys coming to check out what is available in village, what is on market stall for them to choose!"

"My sister and I hated it. We would refuse to dress up, but our mother would insist it was expected. When boys came and threw perfume on us and tried to hit us, sometimes we could not stop ourselves and we would hit them back. Once there was such big fight in our sitting room that chair and coffee table were broken. Other time we pushed especially horrid boy who hit us too hard into our well. My father had to use ladder to get him out."

"How old were you?"

"When chair and table were broken? Fourteen or fifteen, I think. Tradition is that village boys and girls must take part in this stupid carnival until they are married."

"But surely you wouldn't still be expected to; not at your age. Don't look at me like that. You know what I mean. You're not a…"

"Be careful, Ben. Be *very* careful."

"I mean you're not married but you're not a teenager either. Who would come round to…y'know with the cheap perfume and whips?"

"Probably no-one. Boys and girls generally stop doing it when they are in early twenties because that is when most get married. But I still have to watch boys going around to other houses, and I know they are doing this to other girls. I don't like it. And you never know, even with some older woman, teenage boys might knock on door for joke because they know she is not married yet. Some older men will also still see it as chance to call and make romantic overtures to unmarried women."

Katka stopped and burst out laughing.

"My father tells me once about time I did not go home for Easter despite my mother nagging me. Older single man from our village, quite ugly with huge moustache and little bit stupid, knocked on door in his best suit to ask if he could see both daughters because it was Easter. My father tells him one is now married and other lives in Praha. He replies 'That is pity. I was hoping to have a choice. When will the unmarried daughter come home?' My father gets him drunk with vodka and sends him away."

As I climbed into the taxi for the airport, I suddenly realised that with all the drama about Katka's old boyfriend, the brother-in-law and the maybe ring, I'd completely forgotten to tell her the news about Lady C.

"Hang on. I didn't tell you. Lady C's had a stay of execution on leaving Westcombe Manor. The builder the bank was selling the house and land to went bust, so the deal's off. They have to start looking for a new buyer, and that might take some time. The bank has told Lady C she can stay put for now. They've even hinted that they might be open to an offer if she can come up with something close to what they were negotiating with the builders. I think they're getting a bit desperate for some kind of a result. She can't possibly raise that sort of money, but she thinks she can stall them and may even get to spend another snowdrop season there if she plays it right."

"Ben, that is wonderful! Why did you not tell me this before? Give my love to Primula and tell her I will see her at Easter. Tell her also about maybe ring. She will think it is funny."

"You mean romantic."

"Yes, that too."

It Never Rains but It Pours

At Easter we bought a load of very dark chocolate eggs that were on special offer and scoffed them together. The weather was fantastic, an amazing unseasonal heat wave, and the news was full of stories about spring arriving early. The winter just ended had been declared the warmest in England for three hundred and fifty years and that April turned out to be the hottest ever recorded, so global warming was firmly on the agenda and Katka's favourite topic for conversation - when she could find time between mouthfuls of dark chocolate and chocolate-allergy sneezing bouts.

We spent a lot of time at Lady C's. The snowdrops were long over of course, but there were plenty of spring flowers to see and Jeremy came over from Cheltenham to join us for lunch on the terrace on Easter Day. The sun was so hot that it felt like mid-summer, the bees were buzzing and the Colonel was mercifully almost flatulence-free for a change. All in all, it was a wonderful time.

I wish I could say the same for all the other times Katka came over on the coach from Prague that year. As soon as the real summer was due to start, it began raining and just didn't stop, eventually turning into our wettest summer ever, with widespread flooding. The waterworks at Tewkesbury that served us was knocked out by floods and most of the town, including my house and Lady C's place, was without mains water for a fortnight, along with nearby Cheltenham and Gloucester.

For the time being, Katka had banned me from flying to Prague to see her and contributing even more to global warming. She said she'd rather get the coach to come and see me, but every time she did it was still pouring down. On one visit she joked that, never mind wind and wave power; the UK should put money into developing *rain power* as an alternative energy source.

"Seriously, Ben, does it never stop raining here? If you could just harness the power of all this stupid rain, you would not need all those new nuclear power stations your government wants to build. My God! I have never been anywhere so *wet*!"

It was indeed wet. Wet is what England was that summer. Except for one glorious week in August when the sun came out. Of course Katka wasn't here for that but I did manage to get some weeding done in the garden.

One of the biggest surprises for me that summer - apart from how fast the weeds were growing and how many snails one small garden could hold - came when I answered the door one morning to find Katka's ex-boyfriend Radko on the doorstep looking for her. Somehow he'd found out she was over here and got hold of my address. They had yet another blazing row and she sent him packing, but not before I saw what I'm sure was the butt of a handgun in a shoulder holster as his Armani jacket flapped in the wind. Katka said that was ridiculous. How could he bring a gun through airport security? I didn't have an answer to that, but I know what I saw and it wasn't an iPod.

The other big surprise that summer was when Katka phoned to say she was pregnant. She'd taken a test and it was positive. On the phone she sounded like she was excited but trying not to be, as if she wasn't sure how I'd take the news.

"It must have been at Easter, Ben. We were not very careful. So are you happy about this? You can tell me the truth."

"I'm very happy. Just because it was an accident doesn't mean I'm not happy. But what about you? Are *you* happy? That's more important. After all, you're the one who's pregnant."

"I am happy, Ben, and I am very happy that you are happy. I was worried that you might be…I don't know…that you would be…"

"Let me take a wild guess…not happy?"

"I was going to say 'typical man'. But okay, not happy."

"So does this mean we need to upgrade the maybe ring? I assume you want to get married now, and if you tell me 'maybe' again, I'm hanging up."

"We do not *have* to, but I think my mother and father would like it if we get married, and especially if we could have wedding in Slovakia."

My family were all on the other side of the world, and Katka was worried about the village gossip if she was too obviously pregnant at the ceremony, so we agreed on a quick wedding in the Tatras with me only needing to take along Jeremy as my best man.

The week before the wedding, Katka phoned again to say

she'd had a scan and it was twins. This time she sounded even more concerned about my reaction.

"You are still happy, Ben?"

"Twice as happy."

"Really?"

"No, that was a joke. I mean I'm still happy, but 'twice as happy' was a…twins? You're sure?"

"Yes, I am sure. They showed me on monitor screen and I *can* count to two. I think I am twice as *scared* now, Ben."

"Scared? They give you drugs if it hurts too much, and with twins I expect you'll get twice as much."

"No, Ben, I am scared this pregnancy will be bad thing for *us*, for our relationship; that it was not what you wanted. Now, with twins, it could be twice as much not what you wanted. Do you hate me, Ben? Have I trapped you?"

"Katka, don't be daft! I love you!"

"…or have *you* trapped *me*? Have we trapped each other? Are we trapped, Ben?"

"Okay, now *I'm* scared too. Look, I think we weren't being very careful because we both sort of wanted this. I know it wasn't actually planned, but I think we knew it might happen. I mean *twins* is a bit of a surprise, but it'll be fine. Unless they're identical. I mean how do you tell them apart? If one's been naughty, how do you know which one it was? You could end up shouting at the wrong one. Maybe we could give them labels. Or I've got some indelible markers…"

"Ben, why would you want to shout at our babies? Also, they are not snowdrops you know, so they will not need labels, and you are *not* marking them with indelible pens!"

"Just until we learn to tell them apart? Somewhere not very obvious? Maybe just a little tick on one and a cross on the other? Katka? Are you there? Katka? I was joking. Katka? You've hung up, haven't you?"

The wedding turned out to be a Gypsy-style knees-up organised by Katka's brother-in-law, with a Gypsy band, mountains of food prepared by Katka's dad, smashing plates, drinking and dancing till dawn, and a knife fight between two of Zoltan's more disreputable cousins. Okay, not really. That's what I tell people, but it actually finished before midnight and there was just a bit of a drunken scuffle in the car park over a rather pretty waitress.

Katka wanted to keep working as long as possible before leaving her job in Prague. I think she felt we'd need the money. She also, I think, was very reluctant to give up the independence that her job gave her, even though I'd assured her she should have no problems getting work in publishing in England, especially as I had contacts in the business. So she was well into her third trimester when I went to bring her back to the UK in early November. I'd booked flights, since there was no way I was letting her do a twenty-four-hour coach journey at seven-and-a-half months pregnant.

She'd argued of course but I'd won, so she was supposed to have a letter from her doctor telling the airline she was okay to fly. It was just routine, but she happened to have a bloody minded male doctor who thought she was taking a stupid risk flying so late in a multiple pregnancy. He'd only give her a letter for the airline if she agreed to have a couple of stitches put in to "help prevent premature birth" during the flight. Katka had told him where he could put his stitches and stormed out. That's why we ended up at the back of a check-in queue with Katka wrapped in a very baggy old raincoat of Elena's, trying to hide her heavily pregnant tummy until we were on the plane and in the air.

"He really wanted to put stitches in your…"

"Yes. He is a stupid barbaric man. Can we please not talk about this when there are people around?"

"Okay. You'll have to take your coat off when we go through security but make sure you put it back on at the gate before we board, and try not to look so nervous or they'll suspect something. They probably won't turn us away if we explain everything, but just in case."

"Ben, I *am* nervous. I have never flown before."

201

"Never?"

"No. Not even *without* twins inside me."

We got aboard okay. The stewardess who helped Katka with her seat belt looked a little surprised at the size of her tummy, but she said nothing even though she obviously hadn't been notified that there'd be a heavily pregnant woman on the flight. Katka held my hand tight as we taxied but burst into a broad smile as the plane revved up and roared down the runway for takeoff, lifting into the air and banking sharply so we could see the city and the river below the wing tip.

"That was *fun*, Ben. Will landing be just as exciting?"

"Probably, if it's as windy at Heathrow as it was when I left yesterday. We're still getting nothing but wind and rain over there, and landing in strong cross-winds at Heathrow can be a bit hairy."

The wind was even stronger when we arrived than when I flew out, making the wings dip and lift wildly on our approach, the engines whining as the pilot tried to keep us level. I was clutching the arms of my seat, my knuckles white, while Katka gazed calmly out of the window at the ground hurtling towards us.

"Look, Ben…fire trucks! Ben? You look very pale. Oh no! The babies are coming out of me!"

"*What*?!"

"I am joking! Do the wings always go up and down this much? It is like fairground ride! Is lot of fun, no?"

It was a good half-hour later in baggage claim before I spoke to Katka again.

"There, Ben, that is my bag. Please get it, and stop this stupid sulking. I did not know you were really scared. I thought you just pretended as joke. But I was fine. Turns out I really *like* flying. That is big surprise!"

"These bags weigh a ton. Did you really have to bring so many books?"

Katka had been fetching books on the coach with her all summer. They'd taken over all my spare shelf space and were piled high on both sides of the sofa and heaped in every corner. Visitors were impressed to find Tolstoy, Dostoyevsky and Pushkin in the original Russian lying around the bathroom, but it was starting to get so I couldn't move for Slovak and Russian editions of the classics and a whole slew of modern writers from Richard Dawkins and Germaine Greer to Philip Pullman and J.K. Rowling.

"It is easy to get books in Slovak and Russian in England, Ben? No, I thought not. You take that handle and I will take this. Now, one two three, lift."

Everything was okay for the first couple of weeks. Well, as okay as things could be given that the pregnancy - the backache, the tiredness, the giving up coffee, etc - was making Katka more irritable and *much* more argumentative than normal. Oh yes, I didn't mention the coffee, did I? Katka had decided to give up her five or six cups of incredibly strong black Turkish coffee a day, because it made the twins restless and might not be good for them. I pointed out a number of times that Katka not being able to drink coffee wasn't good for *her* or *me* - but especially for *me* - and that maybe we should risk the kids coming out as ready-to-go caffeine addicts. But I was shouted down. And when I say shouted down...well, you get the picture. Sometimes there was quite a lot of shouting and grumbling, especially in the mornings and particularly if I was stupid enough to offer Katka a nice cup of Earl Grey tea with her toast and marmalade instead of her usual industrial-strength caffeine hit.

Things got worse towards the end of November as the days grew shorter, the rain continued and Katka developed winter blues with a vengeance.

"I can't help it, Ben. I am used to blue skies and a lot of white snow in winter. In Praha it was not as snowy as in Tatras but I could go home at weekends for deep snow and clear skies in mountains. These gray cloudy English skies all the time drive me crazy. We have not seen any sun for weeks. And the rain! The endless fucking rain!"

It was just my luck that the winter of 2007-08 turned out to be almost as mild, wet and dull as the last one, like a never-ending autumn that went on into December and January with barely a night-time frost, let alone any snow to cheer Katka up - apart from one solitary short-lived snowfall in January that lasted all of one night and half the next day.

I didn't make things any better by forgetting her name's day. Yes, I know she went on about it enough back in January, when I messed up because I didn't know about the Slovak tradition of names' days. And yes, I did put her Katarina first-name's day, November twenty fifth, in my diary. There was just a lot of other stuff in there for that week. It didn't help that the sodding pony-tail-wearing ex-boyfriend remembered and sent her flowers and a card with his mobile number on it. I mean, what was with this guy? Katka was married and heavily pregnant but he was *still* pursuing her.

I tried to make amends by cooking Katka's favourite Slovak meal for dinner. Waitrose had packets of potato dumplings, larger and rounder than the traditional Slovak ones and of course not home-made with all fresh ingredients, but not bad, and I could break them up smaller to make them look a bit more hand-prepared. The cheese sauce was the real problem. The nearest I could think of to the Bryndza sheep's cheese they used in Slovakia was a mixture of crème fraiche and crumbly Wensleydale, which I melted down and mixed with a little mashed potato as I'd seen Katka's father do.

Katka ate it. By that stage of the pregnancy she'd eat anything, especially if it had marmalade or mustard on it, and preferably both. But I could tell my attempt at halušky was a disappointment, so that's when I decided to start The Great Bryndza Hunt.

The next day I spent all morning phoning round the delis and specialist food shops in Gloucestershire, then in the surrounding counties, followed by an afternoon on the internet searching for a mail-order cheese outfit or specialist Eastern European food business anywhere in the country who could supply packets of Bryndza - all without any luck. So, with the help of one of Katka's dictionaries, I sent her sister a badly written and very ungrammatical email in Slovak begging for help. I got an answer back saying simply "Okay." Two days later a FedEx driver turned up at the door with a packet from Slovakia. I didn't have time to open or hide it before Katka walked into the kitchen and started sniffing.

"Ben! I can smell something...like Bryndza cheese...what is that parcel? It smells like...it is *Bryndza!* And also...dried mushrooms! Oh my God!"

She was holding the packet to her nose, a look of pure joy on her face. I handed her a knife and she sliced the parcel open to reveal six packs of soft Bryndza, a large plastic bag of her father's dried mushrooms, a bottle of her grandfather's slivovica and a note from her mother.

"Did you ask them to send this, Ben? This is wonderful! Now we can make *proper* halušky! And my father has also sent us dried mushrooms for our Christmas soup!"

"Oh goody. Slovak Christmas soup."

"Come on, Ben, get some potatoes and flour. We are making halušky!"

"It's nine o-clock in the morning. You wouldn't rather have some toast or a crumpet? Okay...I'll get the potatoes."

Half an hour later we'd grated potatoes - and the tips of two of my fingers - mixed them with flour (the potatoes, not the tips of my fingers), chopped and boiled the dough for the dumplings, made the Bryndza sauce, and were eating Bryndzové halušky for breakfast. Katka was so happy she didn't even object when I chopped and fried a couple of slices of bacon in olive oil to pour over my dumplings and sauce. Back in the summer she'd have been running for the toilet if I'd tried that, but thankfully the morning sickness was now long past and I could have sworn she watched me eating the bacon almost enviously. When I sat back down after putting the kettle on - Katka wanted a coffee to celebrate and make her morning perfect - I could have sworn a couple of forkfuls of my bacony dumplings had gone, but she hotly denied swiping any while my back was turned.

Katka did her best to keep busy to counteract the winter blues, constantly going for long walks in the woods and on the hills, and spending many hours at Lady C's getting the boiler going again and again, fixing leaks, replacing roof tiles blown off in the gales…oh yes, she was up on the roof when I called to pick her up one drizzly day in December; Lady C said she'd mentioned the water coming in through the ceiling in the main bedroom and couldn't stop Katka squeezing out through a skylight to fix it with a bucket of cement and a garden trowel. When I drove up to the front of the house, the first thing I saw was Lady C leaning out of the skylight, clutching the end of an outstretched umbrella while Katka held onto the handle with one hand and tapped a large stone tile into place with the other.

We had a few words about *that* when we got home. Also about how Katka kept fixing Lady C's oil-guzzling old boiler but insisted on constantly turning off *our* heating. I was getting fed up with turning it on only to find she'd switched it off again minutes later. I'd put it back on, but the radiators would stay cold because, just to be sure, she'd gone around and turned off the thermostatic valves on those too. If I tried turning them back on, she'd follow me around turning them off again. It was like an endless game of musical radiators. Eventually she'd re-programmed the heating to come on for just an hour in the morning and had hidden the instruction manual. I tried simply switching the boiler on manually, as I always did when it felt chilly, but she'd somehow managed to disable that function and I had no idea how to even begin undoing whatever it was that she'd done to the electrics.

"Primula and Colonel are old, Ben. They feel the cold much more than us. We have talked about this. Weather is very warm for December, so it is wasteful and bad for global warming to have heating on all the time. Put on some thicker jersey or light the stove in sitting room if you are cold."

"But my desk isn't in the sitting room. You're in there reading all the time, and you always say you're not cold enough for the stove until after dark."

"That is because I wear thick jerseys. And the stove is nice for the evenings. More romantic than putting on central heating, I think. You do not like it?"

"Yes of course I do. I'd just like to know where the instructions for the boiler are. In case of an emergency. It's not safe having them hidden. The boiler could blow up if there's a fault and I can't…"

"Good try, Ben. I know where the instructions are, your boiler is not going to blow up and you would not know what to do if it did, even with instruction manual. Now put on a jersey and go back to work. I am trying to read Kafka here."

To be honest, before Katka arrived I'd lit a few offcuts of wood in the sitting room stove maybe two or three times a year, mostly at Christmas. Then Katka started returning from her walks in the woods around the town with bundles of scavenged firewood in her rucksack. Soon she'd bought a small saw to take with her and we had a growing woodpile by the front door, which I kept tripping over but which did mean we could sit and cuddle in front of a real fire every night.

Talking of changes, there was also the little matter of the car. Katka had found the paperwork for my car, taken it to the garage and arranged a trade-in for a smaller, more fuel efficient one, all without my knowledge.

"But it's *pink!* You've traded my car in for a *pink* one! And what about when the twins are born and we have to cart baby stuff around with us. Did you think about *that*, Katka?"

"Ben, there is enough room for two baby seats and for a twin-size baby buggy plus our luggage and babies' luggage. I check all this. Also, it is not pink. It is Misty Rose. The salesman said you do not see many of this car in that colour, so it is quite unique."

"First, you can't say '*quite* unique', second *it's bloody pink* and third I'm not surprised you don't see many in that colour because *it's bloody pink*!"

"Get in, Ben. I will drive you down to sign paperwork and arrange the loan. Details of the deal are on passenger seat. I persuaded them to reduce price because of some small faults I find when I look it over. They put it up on ramp in the garage workshop and mechanics let me use their tools to check everything thoroughly. I make a big fuss about some problems that I can fix easily and they take quite a lot of money off the price for us. It is also very low mileage for year."

"Are you even okay to drive at this stage, with the seat belt and everything? How did you fit behind the wheel? Okay, I'm getting in; there's no need to shove. You got that much for the trade-in? That's not bad. But it's still *pink*. Look! Even the seats are pink!"

"Misty Rose, Ben, and I like it."

The Christmas tree was another sore point. For a start, Katka thought it was ridiculous to buy one in mid-December, so long before Christmas. I pointed out that we didn't have the option of nipping out into a pine forest just behind our house the day before Christmas Eve to choose one. If you wanted a good tree, you needed to get down to the garden centre before the bushiest ones were gone and you ended up with a thin, straggly left-over.

Katka huffed and puffed, but I put the tree in the stand anyway, arguing that now we had it there was no point leaving it outside. That afternoon, when she went for a walk, I got out my usual box of coloured lights (three sets), coloured baubles, red, blue, purple and silver tinsel ropes, packets of silver and red draping tinsel and the fairy with the pink tutu, and put them all on as a surprise for when she got back. It was getting dark when Katka returned with yet another bundle of wood, and I'd put the tree in its usual position in the sitting room window where it could be seen from the street. As she walked up the path, I switched on the lights and looked out to see her reaction. Katka was standing in the front garden staring at the lit-up tree in amazement, then she burst out laughing.

"Oh my God, Ben! Your Christmas tree looks like a prostitute!" she shouted.

A little old lady walking past in the street gave her a funny look but Katka just smiled, pointed to the tree in the window and started laughing again as I tried to move it out of sight.

"No, leave it, Ben! I think it is very funny!"

I have to say I was a bit put out by Katka finding my tree decorating so hilarious. I thought it looked okay; not 'tasteful' perhaps but bright and cheerful. It certainly cheered up Katka's mood. Every morning she'd walk into the sitting room, look at the tree and burst out laughing all over again. She said it set her up for the day almost as much as a good cup of coffee.

What didn't cheer either of us up was having to start looking for a bigger house for after the arrival of the twins. At first we thought it might be fun, but a few days of searching through the property pages and looking in estate agents' windows soon changed our minds. We quickly realised that finding somewhere we could afford that was big enough for all of us with room for me - and perhaps also Katka - to work from home, with as much character as the cottage and a bigger garden for the snowdrops was going to prove quite a challenge, if not impossible.

"These bigger houses are crazy prices, Ben! Especially ones with large gardens."

Katka sat staring sadly at the piles of newspapers and estate agents' particulars on the kitchen table.

"I know, Katka. We might have to just stay here and try to make a room for the twins in the attic or something."

"Ben, your attic is tiny. It is less than one-and-half metres high even in the middle. You cannot stand up in it."

"Yes, but the twins will be quite short to start with, right? Where are you going?"

"I am going to sitting room to look at your Christmas tree. I need a good laugh to cheer me up."

Hearing that Lady C had been given an ultimatum by the

bank didn't do anything to improve our mood either. We'd all hoped Lady C could see another snowdrop season out at Westcombe Manor, but the bank had decided that just before Christmas would be a good time to tell her the house, garden and woodland were to be sold at auction at the end of January. So Lady C, Alfred, Katka and I reluctantly started on the mammoth task of digging up Lady C's snowdrop collection, starting with the clumps of autumn snowdrops that had finished flowering, then moving on to the earliest Winter snowdrops that were starting to show through the ground. Luckily the mild winter meant it was going to be an early season and lots of snowdrops that would not normally appear until late January or early February were already pushing their noses above the soil. So at least we'd have no problem locating them all and getting them up ahead of the auction deadline - we hoped.

As we lifted the clumps, we carefully potted a few each of the very best varieties for Lady C in the hope that she could find somewhere to live with enough room to grow them. The rest were put into an assortment of large plastic bags, carrier bags and bin liners with leaf mould around their roots and stacked close together in a sheltered corner of the kitchen garden, ready to be divided up between Lady C's snowdrop growing friends.

At the same time, we sent out invitations to the very last 'Grand Snowdrop Giveaway Lunch', set for the third weekend in January. Everyone was asked to bring plenty of plastic bags to take their gifts home in, plus blank labels and pens, and their own bin bags and spades if they wanted to help themselves to any of the thousands of other lovely and rare plants and bulbs in the garden that Lady C couldn't take with her. The ghastly Humphrey Whimpleton-Pughe was definitely *not* on the invitation list for once. I'd half expected Lady C to invite him despite the ruckus at the last snowdrop lunch. She hated the idea of being rude to, or snubbing, anyone and was the most forgiving and considerate person I've ever known, so

I was surprised but pleased to see she'd stuck to her guns.

We also started contacting nurserymen to invite offers for the right to clear the woodland garden of the huge quantities of less rare but still very lovely and valuable snowdrop varieties, and other plants, that it contained. With planning permission already granted for most of the trees to be felled and the site levelled for house-building, Lady C was determined to leave not a single flower to be killed by the bulldozers.

The whole business was obviously heart-breaking for Lady C but she tackled it all with a cheery smile and endless pots of tea with hot buttered crumpets and whisky marmalade for her helpers. She even managed to put on a brave face when reporting back to us about her search for somewhere to rent after the eviction. While trying to keep the bank off their backs, she and the Colonel had run up a lot of other debts and when the cost of paying those off was subtracted from their state pension and the Colonel's Army pension, there wasn't a huge amount left for rent and other living costs. Everything they'd looked at in their price bracket so far had, she admitted, been decidedly pokey and with tiny gardens or none at all.

"I don't think I'll be able to take many snowdrops with me after all," she sighed after what had obviously been an especially disappointing house viewing. "Oh well, you'll just have to take a lot more of my special favourites, Ben. Then at least I can come and see them in *your* garden - that's if you have room for them of course."

Katka and I exchanged glances.

"Of course, Lady C. There's plenty of room in my garden. We'll squeeze them in if we need to - until you get somewhere with more space."

As Christmas approached, we were all getting more and more dispirited, so Katka decided we should have everyone round to the cottage for a Slovak-style Christmas celebration on Christmas Eve.

Katka and I spent a couple of days making Slovak cakes and baking honeybreads to hang on the tree so that, in Katka's words, at least it would *smell* like a Christmas tree should even if it looked like it ought to be standing on a street corner wearing fishnet stockings and smoking a cigarette. Then on the morning of Christmas Eve I squeezed a fat goose into my small oven, Katka prepared the Christmas soup, using her father's dried mushrooms, pearl barley and a jar of German sauerkraut I'd found in the supermarket, and we made the Slovak Christmas potato salad together. We thought about trying to get some carp, but in the end opted for breaded fish fillets as the simpler, less mud-flavoured option. There were also schnitzels and cold chicken, and of course plenty of roast spuds and steamed Brussels sprouts so the meal wouldn't be *too* much of a culture shock for the older guests. When we were planning the meal, Katka had jokingly offered to *pickle* some sprouts for me as a 'special treat' and looked surprised when I said okay and told her I'd quite enjoyed the ones her mother gave me; so I had my own special little bowl of those on the table as well.

Lady C, the Colonel, Alfred and Jeremy arrived together in Jeremy's car bearing bottles of wine. The Colonel, predictably, took one sip of the sauerkraut soup before pushing it away, ignored Katka's offer of potato salad and filled his plate with goose meat, roast potatoes and sprouts (most of which Lady C quickly confiscated, knowing from bitter experience what flatulent horrors the Colonel's digestive system could brew up if it had too many sprouts to work with).

After the main course, Katka and I sent the others through to the sitting room with their drinks while we cleared the kitchen table and took my pudding, a huge sherry trifle, out of the fridge. I know it's a bit old-fashioned, but it's one of my favourites, and I'd Slovak-icised this one by using Katka's granddad's slivovica instead of sherry. Yes, okay; I forgot to buy the sherry. Unfortunately Jeremy couldn't have any as Katka and I had calculated that one small bowlful would put him at least three times over the drink-drive limit. In fact the slivovica fumes were so strong as we spooned it into the bowls that I suspect we could have set fire to it like Christmas pudding and taken it through flaming festively.

Anyway, we were both in the kitchen so it was Lady C who answered the door and that's why, when we walked into the sitting room with the trifle, we found Katka's ex-boyfriend Radko sitting on the settee pouring the Colonel a large slug of whisky from the bottle that he'd brought with him and was now boasting loudly about.

"It is Johnnie Walker Blue Label, blend of best old malt whiskies; costs one-hundred-fifty pounds for single bottle. Drink, please! I have two more in car if we finish this one. Happy Christmas, Katka! I have present for you. Is jewellery. You will like. Ah, Bent, you are here? We need more whisky glasses, Bent."

"It's Ben, not *Bent*, and of course I'm here. I *live* here! *With Katka*!"

Katka nudged me and whispered in my ear.

"Radko is already drunk, Ben. He does not look or sound drunk but I can tell. I want this to be nice time for Primula, so we must try not to spoil it. Maybe he will go after he has had a drink. I will get glasses."

Radko poured more whisky for the Colonel, who beamed and put an arm around his shoulders, obviously keen not to see the bearer of such expensive and free-flowing whisky move from his side.

As it turned out, Radko wasn't as much of a problem as I'd expected. It quickly became clear that he was, as Katka had guessed, already a little drunk but not enough to become aggressive. Katka prised the bottle of Johnnie Walker away from him under the pretext of pouring herself some and then kept it out of his reach, only allowing him the occasional small top-up, while the Colonel occupied him with stories of the British Army's role in building a globe-spanning Empire on which the sun never set. After a while Radko's eyes glazed over, but every time he looked like he might nod off with boredom the Colonel would startle him back to attention with a stiff finger-poking and an admonition to "Listen to this! You'll like this one. Bloody good story."

The one time I noticed Radko show any real interest in what was being said was when Katka and Lady C, sitting together on the rug in front of the fire, were talking about the financial problems relating to Westcombe Manor; especially when Lady C mentioned just how much money they owed the bank. For the umpteenth time Katka was saying there must be *something* they could do to raise the money needed to save Lady C's house and garden.

"We've tried everything, dear," sighed Lady C. "Friends have offered to help, but we can't possibly raise what's needed to pay the bank off. Ben said he'd sell this cottage but that would be nowhere near enough even if he didn't have a mortgage on it."

"He did?"

"Oh not since he met you, dear. Before, when I first found out how much debt Oliver had got us into, Ben offered to sell up and live in the attic above our garage if it would help us keep the garden. Silly boy. As if I'd let him do that."

Lady C smiled a little tipsily and looked at the Colonel, who was in the middle of explaining to a bemused Radko the pivotal role of the British breaking of the German Enigma Code in winning the Second World War.

"Of course we *could* sell Oliver to the Russians, Katka. He's a bit past his sell-by date but I imagine they'd still be *quite* interested in what he knows even after all this time."

"Why would *Russians* want to *buy* the Colonel? Is this joke, Primula?"

Lady C took a large sip from her glass and leaned a little unsteadily towards Katka, lowering her voice to a stage whisper still more than loud enough for everyone in the room to hear. I think she'd had a little too much of the Johnnie Walker Blue Label by that point.

"Not at all, dear. You see, Oliver started out in the Army but later he was transferred to GCHQ in Cheltenham, and worked there until he retired, because he was so good at *codes*. He worked on some of the early computer code-breaking projects you know, and at the end he was one of their top experts. I think that's why he was so taken with our personal computer and thought he could work financial wonders with it. But his mind's not what it used to be, not by a long chalk. Poor old thing; these days he has trouble remembering his own birthday. You wouldn't believe he was responsible for a team at GCHQ that broke the Russians'…"

At that moment Jeremy returned from a trip to the toilet and stood frozen in the doorway, frowning at Lady C.

"Whoa! Hang on there, Lady C! Should you be talking about that kind of thing?"

"Oh stuff and nonsense, Jeremy. *Oliver* may have signed the Official Secrets Act, but I didn't. And who's going to tell the Russians? Katka? You think she's a spy? Everyone knows Oliver was at GCHQ and the sort of things he worked on. Even the Russians do. They tried to recruit him, you know, Katka. At a conference in Vienna in the sixties. The KGB, would you believe? Offered him a *lot of money* to be a mole for them. He told them where to go, didn't you, Oliver?"

The Colonel said nothing but I thought he looked a bit shifty, glancing almost worriedly in Jeremy's direction. Jeremy was too busy glaring at Lady C to notice. Or maybe I imagined it.

"Hee, hee! I know what we should do," chuckled Lady C. "We should put Oliver on *ebay*, like those people who auction their snowdrops. 'Rare British code-breaking expert for sale to highest bidder. A bit smelly but knows lots of secrets. Minimum bid one million pounds'. That would sort out our money problems!"

She laughed loudly and nudged Katka's arm jovially with her elbow, then held up her empty glass for a refill.

"That Johnnie Blue Label is rather good, isn't it? Can I have a teeny smidgen more, Ben?"

Katka looked decidedly unconvinced.

"But Cold War between East and West is over, Primula, so surely Britain and Russia do not need to spy on each other so much now?"

Lady C shook her head emphatically.

"Oh no, dear, there's *just* as much spying going on between Russia and the West as during the Cold War. At least that's what I get from the newspapers and some of Oliver's old friends who know about that sort of thing. Am I right, Jeremy?"

Reluctantly, Jeremy allowed himself to be drawn into the conversation, nodding agreement as he settled into an armchair.

"Yes. Probably even *more* than during the Cold War. Our government are very worried about energy security and having to rely on the gas pipelines from Russia, not to mention the Russians threatening to start a new arms race with the West. And for their part, the Russian leaders are equally concerned about NATO expanding and the Americans putting missile sites for their anti-ballistic-missile shield almost next door to them in Poland.

It looks like they're determined to become a superpower again. And now the Russians have the money, thanks to their huge natural gas revenues, for a massive military re-armament if that's what they decide to do."

Katka was gazing so admiringly at the hunky and handsome Jeremy, as he backed up Lady C so knowledgeably and authoritatively about international affairs, that I felt obliged to join in:

"Well, I think the Russians were pretty thoroughly humiliated when the USSR broke up and their economy crashed in the early nineties. American politicians spent a lot of time strutting around and crowing about having won the Cold War and claiming to be the only remaining superpower while treating Russia as nothing but a joke.

As I remember it, the Russians could barely *feed* themselves at first and the entire country was plunged into poverty, but they didn't get a lot of help. They were promised economic aid, but the West seemed more interested in grabbing their natural resources while they were down than helping them get back on their feet.

I'd say we're reaping what we sowed. If the Russians had been treated with a bit more diplomacy and respect, allowed a little more dignity in defeat and offered more of a helping hand, then they might not be so pissed off with us now. Jeremy, did you see all that stuff on the news back in the autumn about those Russian long-range nuclear bombers having to be turned back from entering British air space by RAF fighter planes? That's pretty scary."

"Yes, they were testing northern NATO air defence responses. Not something the Russians have done much of since the end of the Cold War.

It's difficult to say how much of the in-your-face new arms race confrontational stuff they really mean and how much of it is intended to make the Russian leadership look strong and commanding to their voters. They have presidential elections next month, remember. But I think you're right, Ben; the West could have been a bit less triumphal and a bit more helpful and conciliatory towards Russia in the nineties, and now the chickens are coming home to roost."

Jeremy made a show of looking at his watch then at the Colonel, who was nodding drunkenly, smiling to himself and quietly humming the Dam Busters theme tune, seemingly oblivious to the discussion going on around him - although the mention of bombers may well have been what sparked off the humming.

"Come on, Lady C. I'd better get you and the Colonel home. Radko doesn't look like he's in any fit state to drive. I suppose we'd better take him too. Radko? Are you staying nearby? In a hotel? Yes, I know the one. It's not much out of my way. No, you can't drive after what you've had to drink. I can easily drop you off. No trouble at all."

When they'd all gone, we decided to have an early night

and clear up in the morning. In the bedroom, Katka seemed impressed with my rant about East-West relations.

"You joke around so much, Ben, that it is easy to forget that you can also be quite serious and thoughtful. You should let people see this serious side of you more and be silly a little less."

As Katka climbed into bed, I lifted the duvet cover and pulled it over her head.

"Ben, what are you doing? What is that *smell*?! Oh God, I recognise it! Pickled Brussels sprouts! *That* is why you wanted them! You are so disgusting! I should never have married you!"

"Hah! That's for all those jokes you made about my Christmas tree looking like a tart!"

Christmas Eve was the last time I saw Radko. His car sat out in the street until Boxing Day, when Katka spotted a burly bodyguard type being dropped off to unlock the ridiculously expensive silver Aston Martin and drive it away. Presumably he took it to the ultra-posh country house hotel near Cheltenham where Radko had told Jeremy he was staying. I'd been to a wedding there once and knew the best rooms could cost up to five hundred pounds a night, and Katka was sure Radko would have the most expensive suite available.

By early January Katka was *really* getting fed up with the English winter weather. It was just as mild as it had been in November and there was no sign of any snow; just rain, drizzle and low grey clouds day after day. She was starting to seriously regret not staying in Slovakia for the birth, where she'd still have been tired, heavy and irritable but could at least have enjoyed the blue skies, refreshing cold and crisp white snow of the Tatras.

It got so bad that I even thought about hiring a fake snow machine to try to cheer her up. There's a company based not far from us which specialises in providing film makers with artificial snow and I knew someone who worked there. But I decided that, given how ratty Katka was getting, it would be taking a huge risk with my personal safety to let her wake up to a snow-covered garden only to find it was pretend snow and would be gone again almost as soon as the machine was turned off.

What I did do, on a particularly warm and almost sunny day not long before Katka's due date, when she seemed particularly down, was take her to visit Lady C and then suggest the two of us go for a walk in the woodland.

Katka still hadn't set foot in Lady C's snowdrop wood. She'd missed the afternoon walk at the previous year's lunch, and so far we'd been concentrating on lifting snowdrops from the garden and were nowhere near starting on those in the woodland. As we walked along the path towards the gap in the beech hedge that led to the wood, I told Katka I had a surprise for her and asked her to cover her eyes. She glared and said if it involved anything in my trousers then she wasn't in the mood and would probably hit me.

I led her carefully through the hedge, off the main path and along a side-track into the middle of Lady C's 'Atkinsii' patch. I say patch, but it was really a vast swathe amongst the trees, a small field almost, of a very early-flowering and tall-growing snowdrop, Galanthus 'Atkinsii', with large, long-petalled flowers. It's a very old and quite easily grown variety that Lady C had bulked up over more than half a century from a few dozen bulbs to thousands upon thousands.

The flowers were open wide and so thickly clustered together that you could barely see the leaves beneath them, and they stretched like a huge drift of fresh-fallen snow in a brilliant white carpet a good twenty or thirty feet in all directions. I told Katka she could open her eyes.

"Oh my God, Ben, it is beautiful! They are like snow on the ground. That is why you bring me here? Because they look like snow and I have been complaining about seeing no snow in England?"

"Yes."

"This is very nice thing to do. I really like it. "

"Good. Now wait here while I get you a spade. All these have to be dug up and put in bin bags."

"What? You are *joking*!"

"Yes, I am. Sorry. They're going to be lifted by a nurseryman who's buying them as a job lot. We'll only be taking up a few clumps. Look, I know it's no substitute for *real* snow and I'm sorry about the crap winter weather but..."

"Thank you for this, Ben. It was a very nice thought and I love you; even if you did let me trip over a tree root on way here with my eyes closed."

Katka hugged me and gazed, smiling, at the carpet of glistening white flowers, happier than I'd seen her for weeks.

"What, Ben? No! Lady C might come, or Alfred or the Colonel. No, I told you I would hit you if this had anything to do with anything in your trousers! Yes, I know I have been hoping the twins would come early so this bloody pregnancy could be over, and I know sex is a good way to help start labour, but.....hmmm, well okay, but we must be quick. Please find *large* tree for us to hide behind. I really, really do *not* want to be surprised by the *Colonel*."

As Katka's due date passed and we headed towards mid-January without any sign of the twins putting in an appearance, she grew more and more desperate for her labour to start. So when she got to six days overdue, we made an appointment to see the doctor. She checked Katka over and said that, although twins did usually arrive earlier rather than later, everything seemed fine and not to worry.

"Is there anything you can suggest to hurry things along?" I asked as Katka climbed off the doctor's couch. "We've been trying one or two things but obviously they haven't worked yet."

"What have you tried? Going for walks can help, and so can sex of course."

"We've tried walking in the woods *and* sex, and Katka's been doing a lot of digging, haven't you? And sawing and chopping firewood. And spicy food; hot curries, and lots of mustard on toast."

Katka smiled and nodded agreement.

"And she made me take her clubbing at the weekend. To a techno DJ dance night. I didn't think it was a good idea but she insisted. Then she got into a fight on the way home. Oh, and she's been trampolining. She did also mention bungee jumping at one point, but I think that was just a joke."

The doctor stared at us and Katka smiled back at her. The silence became a little uncomfortable, so I thought I'd better explain some more: That, for a start, it hadn't really been a proper fight and wasn't Katka's fault. She'd spent a couple of hours at the night club working up a sweat on the dance floor and enjoying herself more than she had done for a very long time. Everyone gave her plenty of room to dance. It was that or risk getting knocked sideways by her enormous bump. Then, walking through the town, we'd passed the local gay bar, where a pissed yob, egged on by his two mates, was haranguing a couple of young men having a cigarette on the pavement outside the door.

As we approached, the verbal piss-taking was becoming more and more physical and threatening until the yob pushed one of the kids, who couldn't have been more than eighteen or nineteen, up against the wall, banging his face on the brickwork and shouting and spitting at him while his friends laughed. Blood started to run from the kid's nose, dripping onto his jacket. A woman stuck her head out of the door to see what the noise was about and looked shocked by the sight of the blood.

"You fucking queers should all be put up against a fucking wall and fucking shot. Hello, darling! You a fucking lesbian then? You need some cock. That'd sort you out!"

The woman quickly stepped back inside.

"Come on, let's chuck these two queer cunts in the fucking canal. Then maybe we'll see if there are any lezzies in there who want a good seeing to, eh?"

It all happened very fast, and Katka's reaction was just as

quick. One second she was by my side and the next she wasn't. The yob's mates gawped at the sight of their friend lying face-down on the pavement with his arm up behind his back and a heavily pregnant woman gripping his wrist in one hand and his elbow in the other, her foot firmly stuck in the middle of his back. The door of the bar opened again and two very large transvestites wearing short, tight skirts and fishnet stockings stepped out into the street, both of them well over six foot in their high heels, followed by a whole crowd of the bar's regulars and the manager already on her mobile to the police. Katka kept the yob firmly on the ground as his mates ran off, then one of the transvestites hiked up his skirt a little and smiled at Katka.

"Thanks, love. You can let go of him now. We'll sit on him till the police get here. Might take a while. They get very busy on a Saturday night. Ever had a tranny sit on your head before, mate? It'll be a new experience for you then, won't it? Hold him down, Janine."

The trampoline incident wasn't as bad as it sounded either. I'd looked out of the back bedroom window one afternoon to see Katka in a baggy jumper and tracksuit bottoms jumping up and down on the trampoline that next door's kids had got for Christmas, while the children stood watching.

"I couldn't resist it," Katka told the doctor. "I was a trampoline champion at school."

"And a Kalashnikov-shooting champion too," I added. "Though presumably not both at the same time."

"I was only bouncing for a few minutes before Ben came out and shouted at me. Neighbours' kids said I could try it, but once they see me bouncing I think they were little bit worried I would break it, so I stopped. It is good trampoline. Did not break. Did not make my labour start either. I thought it might."

The doctor shook her head in disbelief, told us to keep up the walks and the sex but to cut out the dancing, the fighting and definitely the trampolining. And under no circumstances should there be any bungee jumping. As we walked to the car,

I grinned at Katka.

"So, more sex! Doctor's orders. Oh well, if it's on medical advice I suppose I'll just have to make the effort…"

"Ben, there must be somewhere round here that I can buy bungee rope."

"You heard the doctor. No more trampolines and definitely no bungee jumping."

"Not for jumping, Ben. I need something to *strangle* you with."

Christmas Eve may have been the last time I saw Katka's ex-boyfriend Radko, but it certainly wasn't the last time *she* saw him. I didn't know about it until later, but he turned up the day after our trip to the doctor's. I was in the town and Katka had walked over to Lady C's. She'd been eyeing the neighbours' trampoline again, so I'd suggested a bit of gentle snowdrop digging with Lady C and Alfred as a safer option.

Our neighbour had caught Katka on the way out to ask her, very nicely and apologetically, not to go on the trampoline again. Since the last time, she said, their four-year-old son had been having nightmares about an enormous whale-like pregnant Katka flying off the trampoline, landing on him and squashing him flat like a pancake.

Anyway, when Radko came calling, the neighbour was in the front garden, told him he'd just missed Katka, said she'd gone to Lady C's and gave him directions to Westcombe Manor. Katka went the long way round through the woods and Radko drove, so he got there before her. When she arrived, Radko had already opened the bag he had with him and shown Lady C the million pounds inside it; which had prompted Lady C to get out the best china, retrieved the Colonel's bottle of good malt whisky from its hiding place in the downstairs lavatory cistern and make Radko comfortable in the drawing room.

Radko, it transpired, had in a roundabout way contacted the Russian Federal Security Service, the FSB, as the KGB is apparently now called, about whether they'd be interested in someone with very detailed inside knowledge of Britain's Russian code-breaking activities over a great many years. It seems that one of the main activities of Radko's Bulgarian gangster father's organisation was smuggling hard drugs from Bulgaria, through Romania and Ukraine, into Russia and selling them for street distribution to elements of the Russian mafia, some of whom in turn had very 'unofficial' contacts in the FSB.

The FSB, he explained to Lady C and Katka, had responded very positively to the suggestion. Even their initial offer, without any need for bargaining, was enough to provide both him and his Russian mafia contacts with a very generous profit as the middle-men in the deal. All Radko had to do was raise one million to offer to Lady C so she could save Westcombe Manor and its garden. The Colonel would also be paid more than enough, in exchange for his co-operation with the Russians, to live a very comfortable life in Russia with all the malt whisky he could drink.

As I said, I knew nothing about all of this. Not until three days after Radko's visit with the bag of dosh. That was how long Lady C and Katka had persuaded Radko to give them to get the Colonel used to the idea that he'd be spending his last remaining years in Russia as a very well-paid guest of the Russian secret service. It was agreed that, after the three days were up, a couple of Radko's men would call round to pick up the Colonel and hand him over to the Russian mafia, presumably in exchange for a much bigger bag of cash than Radko had waved under Lady C's nose.

The exact moment I found out what was going on was when I turned up at Lady C's to find her and Katka laying out the Colonel, wearing his best Sunday suit, in the master bedroom with funereal black curtains cutting out the light and forced out-of-season white lilies in a bedside vase. I was supposed to be finishing the cartoons for a new book, so they weren't expecting me to get fed up with being indoors and drive over to lend a hand with the thousands of snowdrops still waiting to be dug up. Alfred was working in the front garden and told me they were all upstairs which, as I say, is where I found them and where they finally owned up to what was going on.

"You *really* thought this would work, Lady C?! And you, Katka?! In your wildest dreams, how could you *ever* have imagined this was a good idea?!"

"Radko showed Primula and me the money, Ben, and we just could not say no. It was enough to pay what is owed to bank. We thought we would invent some plan before Radko's gangsters come to take the Colonel."

"And *this* was the best you could come up with? Pretending the Colonel died of a heart attack? You really think they'll believe that? For crying out loud, you can see him *breathing*!"

Lady C pushed something under the bed then stood up, folded the Colonel's arms across his chest and laid some stems of pale lily flowers over them.

"It's not Katka's fault, Ben. I wanted to save the garden. We've filled Oliver up with so much whisky that he's pretty well sedated, and I've promised to buy him a whole case of Johnnie Walker Blue Label if he keeps still and plays dead when they turn up. Which should be any minute now."

"And what about the money? Radko won't just let you keep it! He'll want it back!"

"We will say that we already paid it to bank and cannot get it back," replied Katka. "Then we will offer to pay Radko instalments, like a loan."

"*Instalments*?! On a *million pound loan*?! From your Bulgarian gangster ex-boyfriend?! You're mad! Stark, staring bonkers, the pair of you! Shit! Is that the doorbell? Oh fuck! They're here!"

Katka went down to talk to the visitors. It turns out she speaks a little Bulgarian. Not much, but enough to explain to a couple of gangsters that the highly valuable code expert they'd come to collect had unexpectedly popped his clogs due to a massive coronary. They followed her upstairs to the semidarkened room where Lady C sat mourning by the Colonel's side, dressed in black and sniffling into a hankie. Seconds before they arrived, the semi-comatose Colonel let out a fart that luckily wasn't loud enough to be heard outside the room but which filled it with a revolting stench.

Katka later told us the gangsters were suspicious of her explanation about why the Colonel could not now accompany them to their lucrative appointment with the Russian mafia. But that changed the moment they entered the sickeningly stink-filled bedroom.

Katka, used by now to the Colonel's stupefying flatulent capabilities, took the vile smell in her stride, as did I, standing by Lady C's side, too terrified to breathe. The first gangster to walk into the room behind Katka, however, stopped dead and staggered back into the path of his colleague, holding his hand to his nose and mouth.

"Oh, Holy Mother of God! He stinks! He has been dead two, three days only? Smells like much more! You must bury him quickly or he will attract flies!"

That was the moment the Colonel chose to fart again, this time so thunderously that the noise woke him from his alcoholic stupor. He sat bolt upright, scattering the lilies, then saluted stiffly and bellowed:

"God bless you, Your Majesty! Any cheese left?"

That was also the moment that Lady C reached under the bed and pulled out the double-barrelled shotgun she'd stashed there as insurance, getting the drop on the stunned Bulgarian gangsters before they had the slightest idea what was going on. The three of us hauled the befuddled Colonel off the bed and dragged him down the stairs, Lady C covering the startled gangsters with the shotgun as they stared at us over the landing banisters. She grabbed her handbag from the hat-stand as she shouted at me:

"Is your car in the drive, Ben? You've got your keys? You're sure? Right, run for it!"

We sat in my new little pink car, alongside the gangsters'

large black BMW, as I frantically turned the key in the ignition again and again. The starter motor whirred but the engine wouldn't start.

"My old car started every time but you had to make me buy this one, Katka! Well thank you *very much*!"

Lady C pushed the Colonel back out of the car, pointing the shotgun at the Bulgarians as they appeared at the front door pulling their own guns from their shoulder holsters. She fired a barrel in their direction, which made them duck back inside, and shouted as she shoved the Colonel along in front of her:

"Come on, into the garage everyone! Hurry up, Oliver!"

So that's how we ended up cornered in Lady C's garage, escaping in the Colonel's Army-surplus armoured car and getting stuck on the front lawn of Westcombe Manor, surrounded by Radko's gun-toting Bulgarian gangster thugs and the equally heavily-armed and scary Russians, with the Colonel locked inside the armoured car and Katka about to give birth stuck in the driver's turret.

The leader of the black-coated Russians gathered on the lawn gazed up at Katka, her head and shoulders sticking up through the metal hatch and her huge pregnant tummy jammed inside, too big and awkwardly shaped to squeeze back out now the twins had changed position ready for the birth. He looked strangely concerned for a Russian mafia chief and his voice was unexpectedly warm and friendly.

"You are having your baby twins *now*, inside this thing? You cannot get out? I am sorry. It was not supposed to happen this way. We should have arrived sooner."

Katka winced with pain and gripped the edge of the hatch.

"Owww! Ben, babies are going to come. What if reason they are so late is because there is something wrong with them? What if they really do have two heads?"

This wasn't the first time Katka had raised this possibility and I was half expecting it to come up again as the births got closer.

"She was outside in her school's May Day parade in

Slovakia when the radioactive plume blew over from the Chernobyl nuclear power station explosion in Ukraine in eighty-six," I explained. "Since then she's always been worried that her children might have birth defects. Apparently the grass on some of the hills to the south of where she lived turned black and scorched just after Chernobyl. Katka, don't worry! If they have two heads we're fine. *Twins*, remember?"

"I mean two heads *each*! Sprostý chlap!"

While everyone's attention was fixed on Katka, the other Russians had slowly moved around behind the Bulgarians until suddenly the Bulgarian gangsters weren't holding their guns any more. Instead they were standing stiffly to attention with the Russians' guns to their heads and their own weapons on the ground at their feet.

A moment later, two more cars did sharp, tyre-squealing turns off the road and into the driveway, scattering gravel as they slid to a stop. The doors were flung open and yet more men leaped out with guns at the ready, lead by our very own *Jeremy*. Seeing that the Bulgarians were disarmed, he waved his group forward and walked across to us, looking us over worriedly, presumably checking for injuries.

"Sorry we're late! Is everybody okay? We had to go the long way round after we got stuck in a jam behind an overturned tractor trailer. So I called Yuri and told him not wait for us."

Jeremy exchanged a nod and a smile with the head Russian, who indicated for his men to hand the two gangsters and their weapons over to the new arrivals as Jeremy continued his apologetic explanations.

"We were tracking the Bulgarians, hoping Radko would meet up with them - and maybe even come with them to get the Colonel - so we could nab him too. We thought he might want to show off and play at being Mister Big in front of Katka, but he seems to have got wind of something and scarpered.

The plan was for Yuri and his lads to arrive just seconds

after Radko's thugs and pretend to be Russian mafia. And *we* were meant to be right behind *them*, as backup. By the way, you'd better tell your men to put their guns away, Yuri. You're not really supposed to be armed. That was our job."

"But you were not here Jeremy, and did you really think we would not have guns?"

All this time, I'd been staring at the Russian. There was something very familiar about him but I couldn't quite put my finger on it - until now.

"Yuri? Yuri Petrov? From the internet snowdrop forum? Yuri Petrov the snowdrop collector from Moscow? I thought you looked familiar. Not exactly like your photo on the forum but…"

The Russian held out his hand.

"Hello, Ben. Yes I am Yuri from the snowdrop forum. My forum photograph is quite old one and I have little less hair now. Nice to meet you. I liked the photographs you posted on the forum last week of your latest snowdrop seedlings, especially ikariae variety with green tips. But today I am *Major* Yuri Petrov of Russian FSB, which is of course the reason I am here. Although I would also very much like to see Lady Cherrington's famous snowdrop collection. Even if most of it is now in plastic bags waiting to be taken away."

Yuri smiled charmingly and made a short bow to Lady C, who smiled back and blushed a little before replying.

"Thank you, Yuri. You're very welcome to see the snowdrops. And you, Jeremy…MI5 I presume? I always *thought* you might be a spook. GCHQ security? So not a code person at all, but a spy catcher."

"Excuse me! I am still stuck in this bloody tank and I am still having babies! When you have all finished with introductions, could someone *do* something about this?"

"Sorry, Katka," answered Jeremy, his mobile to his ear. "I'll call the ambulance and fire brigade. They shouldn't be long."

"Keep breathing, Katka" I chipped in. "Like they showed

us in the classes. Y'know…the breathing? Okay, there's no need to swear like that. I'll come and hold your hand."

"Yes, please, Ben. Come where I can reach you. That's right. Come closer."

It turns out that when Jeremy, who was indeed with MI5, gave Radko a lift back to his hotel on Christmas Eve, Radko had started boasting that *he* could easily get a million pounds to save Lady C's house and garden if the Russians really would pay for her husband and his code-breaking secrets, and that *he* would have no problem contacting the FSB to negotiate a deal. He'd seemed very keen to know if Jeremy thought Katka would be impressed that he could pull all that off, and to find out just how concerned she was about 'the old lady' and her predicament.

At the hotel, Jeremy had joined Radko in the bar for a late drink, where the boasting and the obsessive interest in Katka had continued. Jeremy had carefully played Radko, agreeing that any woman would be impressed by someone who *did* have the power to pull the sort of strings Radko was talking about, but doubting that Radko could really pull it off.

Eventually Radko snapped open his mobile and made a long call in Bulgarian, announced to Jeremy that it was as good as done, shouted to the barmaid to bring another round of drinks and swaggered off to the toilets, leaving his jacket on the back of his chair. It only took Jeremy a moment to lift Radko's wallet and passport from the inside pocket and have a good look at them. When Radko got back, Jeremy made out he was impressed, exchanged mobile numbers with Radko and left him in the bar chatting up the barmaid.

With the information he'd gleaned at the hotel, Jeremy did some checking-up on Radko and didn't like what he discovered. Katka and I had already told him about her recurring problems with Radko and about Radko's father's reputation. The gangster stuff was confirmed and it also transpired that Radko had been the subject of a string of police investigations in Bulgaria involving allegations of date rape.

All the complaints had, it seemed, eventually been withdrawn, and there were suggestions that the women involved, including his ex-wife who'd made two complaints about sexual assault after their divorce, had been either intimidated or bought off. Radko obviously didn't like rejection and usually got what he wanted one way or another.

That's when Jeremy, concerned about me and Katka and worried that Radko could turn into a very serious problem, had contacted Yuri through the internet snowdrop forum. The moment Yuri joined the forum, Jeremy had checked him out - as he would have done with any Russian who 'accidentally' came into contact with him socially, even via an internet snowdrop discussion group - and quickly discovered that Yuri was with the FSB. At first Jeremy and his superiors had suspected an attempted infiltration of some kind but it seemed that Yuri was just a keen gardener and snowdrop collector who happened to join the same forum as Jeremy and was only interested in discussing snowdrops and other plants.

Together, Jeremy and Yuri concocted a plan for a 'sting' operation. While Radko's Bulgarians in Moscow were trying to contact the FSB through the Russian mafia, Yuri's FSB team was ready and waiting for the approach, all set to pretend to agree a deal and encourage Radko with offers of ridiculous amounts of money in exchange for the Colonel.

"Radko believed this because it was what he wanted to hear," said Yuri, sipping tea in Lady C's kitchen after the fire and ambulance people had managed to extricate Katka from the armoured car. Her contractions had immediately stopped again, so now she was sitting by the Aga listening to the conversation but looking incredibly grumpy. I was keeping my distance from her after she'd swatted me off the armoured car when I went to hold her hand and help her breathe.

"The man is a fool," Yuri went on, accepting another slice of fruit cake from Lady C. "And there is no fool like the one who thinks he is very clever. Radko is also careless. Normally it seems his father keeps an eye on him and makes sure he does not mess things up. But his father suffered a very serious illness over Christmas and was in hospital for a long time in an intensive care unit, so for a while Radko could do whatever he liked - except get into his father's bank accounts.

He pushed his father's people in Moscow to bring in unplanned shipments and make extra drug sales very quickly then channel money directly to him instead of through usual money laundering routes to Bulgaria. In the chaos he created, we were able to set up some of our people as 'buyers', record incriminating conversations on Radko's mobile and those of his father's men, also make secret videos of many transactions, and track money back through other gang members to Radko."

I offered Katka a plate of dark chocolate digestive biscuits, taking care to stay at arm's length from her. She glared but took three, and then a couple more, as I interrupted Yuri:

"I thought the KGB - sorry, the FSB - was all about spying and counter-espionage, not drugs smuggling and money laundering."

"HAPCHEE!!"

Everyone was startled by Katka's loud chocolate-allergy sneeze, including Yuri who had just opened his mouth to reply. Poor old Alfred, standing right beside her and obviously shaken by his recent experiences with gangsters and guns, let out a frightened squeak and dropped his cup and saucer on the quarry tiled floor.

"FSB has responsibility for drug smuggling and organised crime now, as well as for national security and counter-espionage," explained Yuri as Katka helped a very shaky Alfred to pick up the pieces of broken china.

"So this was quite normal kind of operation for us and it worked very well. Today we arrested all of Radko's father's men in Russia and we also make arrests amongst Moscow mafia. Some of the Bulgarians are giving us evidence against mafia in return for shorter sentences. Russian prisons are not good places to spend a long time."

Yuri paused to take a bite of cake and Jeremy took over the

story from him.

"If Radko had stopped to think about it, he'd have realised that computer systems and encryption have moved on so much since the Colonel's day that he'd be very little practical use to any foreign intelligence service now. Thirty or forty years ago it would have been a quite different story of course."

Once again, I could have sworn the Colonel looked very uncomfortable at the mention of his value to the Russians as an intelligence source in the sixties and seventies, but no-one else seemed to notice and Jeremy continued.

"We were lucky Radko was so stupid, and everything else just fell into place. He wanted a million in cash quickly to offer to Lady C before the house and garden were sold, plus another big chunk of money to tempt the Colonel to co-operate, and he had the opportunity to get it.

Unfortunately for him, Russian roubles still aren't worth very much so he needed a hell of a lot of them to get over a million pounds together in a rush, even selling drugs. Just one or two drug deals wouldn't do it. He had to make his men take risks they wouldn't normally even consider and deal with people they didn't have experience of. And then he had to change huge piles of Russian roubles, many of them marked notes, into pounds. It's a perfect paper trail of evidence leading right to him."

Lady C sighed sadly, opened a kitchen cabinet and pulled out a very large, heavy shoulder bag.

"You'll be wanting the money then? I really hoped we might be able to save the garden with it. Oh well, I suppose deep down Katka and I always knew it was a bit of a long shot. We just wanted it not to be. We were probably as stupid as Radko."

Jeremy looked at Yuri, took the bag and pushed it back out of sight.

"What money, Lady C? We didn't see anyone give you any money. The Colonel was never handed over to the Bulgarians, so as far as we know Radko still has all the proceeds from the drugs deals, which is what we'll make sure everyone else thinks too. If I was Radko's father and thought he was on the run after wrecking a major drug smuggling operation *and* had over a million in cash that belonged to me, I'd be especially keen to track him down. And if I was Radko, who knew his father was furious with him *and* thought he still had the money, I'd be especially keen to get as far away as possible and never be heard from again."

"So we can keep…"

"Keep something you never received? I have no problem with that. Do you, Yuri? There's just one proviso. Yuri and I, and our people, may just want to use your snowdrop lunches as an opportunity, a cover, for some very unofficial and rather unorthodox meetings between our respective organisations. You wouldn't have a problem with that would you?"

Yuri nodded in agreement.

"Yes, Lady Cherrington. These are once again difficult and dangerous times for our two countries. Perhaps quiet back-channel meetings such as we could have here between Jeremy and me, and perhaps some of our superiors, might help to prevent us sliding back into another Cold War.

There are a surprising number of keen gardeners in the FSB, people with dachas outside Moscow who love their gardens. And I am sure Jeremy cannot be the only person in your MI5 who would like to see your beautiful snowdrop woodland. Putting flowers into soldiers' gun barrels as a symbol of peace has a long tradition in the East as well as in the West. Maybe we should try it."

Lady C looked like she was going to cry, but instead took a deep breath, smiled and addressed the room.

"Well, if Westcombe Manor and the garden are saved after all, then I can say what I've been hoping I could tell Ben and Katka - that when the bank has been paid off, I want to swap houses with the two of you. If you agree. Legally, through solicitors, so Westcombe Manor is yours."

The Colonel, who had been quietly sipping his tea up to this point, sat up straight and spluttered.

"What did you say, Prim? Give the Manor away? Why? It's all sorted. We can stay, can't we?"

Lady C patted the Colonel on the shoulder.

"No, Oliver. We don't need this big old house and these huge gardens any more. You know it's become far too much for us to cope with, and we've no children to pass it on to; but Ben and Katka will look after it and this will be a wonderful place for them to bring up the twins.

We'll be much better off in Ben's cottage. It's perfect for the two of us, and we can walk into town any time we like. The garden's more than big enough for a few of my favourite snowdrops, and Ben and Katka won't mind if we visit them here sometimes, will you?

Anyway, my mind's made up. Westcombe Manor will be quite safe in Ben and Katka's hands. They'd never sell off the gardens or the woodland for building land, which is more than you could say about a lot of people these days. So, that's decided then!"

Katka looked at me, her face a mixture of delight and apprehension.

"Ben, we can *afford* to live here? I would love to, but it will be much more expensive than your cottage, I think."

"I don't know. I suppose so. Lady C, you mean just *swap*? You get our house and we get yours, and I transfer my mortgage across to Westcombe Manor? It'll be an expensive place to keep going, but I expect we could manage somehow, and Katka's good at repairing things."

Katka nodded and beamed.

"Yes, I can fix almost everything that needs mending, once the twins are born. Also, I was thinking I could easily build solar heating system for this house so there is not so much need for big, hungry boiler. All I need is some pipes and old radiators painted black to put on the outhouse roof. Also a wind turbine would be a good idea."

At that moment, two of Jeremy's MI5 officers walked in with Humphrey Whimpleton-Pughe supported between them, his podgy frame dressed all in black, covered in mud and shivering.

"Sir? We were checking the grounds and found this gentleman in what appears to be an elephant trap at the edge of the woodland. Says he's been in there since last night. We found another two traps, dirty great camouflaged holes in the ground, on a track along the far boundary with the lane. We think he's suffering from hypothermia. He had these with him."

Lady C took one look at Humphrey, and the spade and bag full of snowdrops the officers had found him with, and burst out laughing. She turned to the Colonel, who stuck his nose into his cup and pretended not to notice what was going on.

"Oliver, you *promised* not to make Alfred dig any more traps after the ramblers lost their way and fell into that one last year. You swore you'd had Alfred fill it in. But I have to admit I'm glad you didn't."

She turned to Humphrey, her hands on her hips.

"As for you, Humphrey, you have no idea how pleased I am to find out *you* are the Green Panther. I really would have *hated* for it to have been someone I *liked*."

The following day Lady C struck a deal with the bank and paid a very surprised manager at the local branch in used notes, Jeremy going along to flash his MI5 credentials and confirm it was all above board and not a case of money laundering. That afternoon Katka gave birth to healthy twins, a boy and a girl with just one head each, and the day after that I went with Lady C to her solicitor's office to get the house swap started. Then we sent out new invitations to the last 'Grand Snowdrop Giveaway Lunch', which had now become the 'Come and Help Replant the Snowdrops Lunch'.

On the day of the lunch, Yuri flew in from Moscow with three colleagues including, to the surprise of Jeremy and his MI5 section chief, a deputy director of the FSB. According to

Yuri, they were all members of the FSB Gardening Club, which Yuri had recently started. It seemed a shame that they'd changed the name to the FSB. I would have *loved* being able to tell people at parties that there was such a thing as the KGB Gardening Club.

Some urgent phone calls were made, and by the afternoon we were joined for the traditional snowdrop woodland walk by (according to Jeremy, in the strictest confidence) a *very* senior MI5 officer who collects ferns and someone high-up from the Foreign Office who breeds and shows daffodils. Both of them had recently - thanks to Jeremy getting them interested - also started to collect snowdrops in a small way, and they'd suddenly developed a keen desire to learn much more about the world of snowdrop growing. Keen enough to share a helicopter ride from London at short notice; which of course Katka, when she overheard how they'd travelled to Westcombe Manor, gave them both a good talking to about. From the looks on their faces, I don't think either of them had ever been called an eco-terrorist before.

By late afternoon everyone was back inside, gathered round a roaring log fire in the dining hall, warming up after the walk. It had suddenly turned very cold and the Colonel was being uncharacteristically generous with the case of incredibly expensive Johnnie Walker Blue Label whisky that Lady C had bought him out of the fairly decent lump of money she had left after some hard bargaining with the bank. The twins were sleeping in the drawing room, watched over lovingly by Alfred, who refused to leave their side. It looked like, along with Westcombe Manor, we were going to inherit a gardener *and* a nanny rolled into one. I edged my way over to where Katka and Lady C were standing talking by the fireside.

"Katka? Lady C? Can you put your coats back on for a minute? I want you to help me plant some things."

"Ben, Katka is tired. We've replanted enough snowdrops for one day and it's freezing out there. Have some of Oliver's whisky and relax."

"This is something special, Lady C. It'll only take a few minutes. Colonel, you'd better come too. And we'll get Alfred on the way out."

The sun had set and the light was fading by the time we reached the far end of the orchard. I'd already dug two holes and filled them with compost, and the pots with the seedlings were sitting on the grass. Katka looked at me and frowned.

"Ben, you bring us out here to plant these little trees? Why? What is so important about…"

"It's the walnuts your granddad gave me for my garden the autumn before last. I planted them just to see what would happen and these two came up. In all that wet weather last summer they shot up like magic beanstalks, so I lifted and potted them and now Alfred and I reckon they're just about big enough to plant out if we protect them from the squirrels. There was no way I could have grown them on in the garden at the cottage, but here...well, with any luck we might be harvesting our own nuts in about twenty years' time."

Katka took my hand and held it tight for a moment before letting go to reach for something fluttering down on the cold evening air.

"Oh, my God! Ben, look!"

Katka held out her hand to catch the snowflake, then another and another.

"It is snowing, Ben! At last!"

As the snow grew heavier and whirled around us, Katka hugged Lady C tightly to her with one arm and me with the other. Behind us, the Colonel farted loudly and sniggered. Katka, Lady C and I looked over our shoulders to glare at him and caught Alfred the gardener leaning on his spade with one muddy welly raised behind him, about to boot the Colonel up the bum. Alfred stopped, looking suddenly unsure and a little afraid, his boot poised. He raised his bushy eyebrows questioningly and, in unison, the three of us smiled and nodded.

Some other books by Martin Baxendale

......

Your New Baby – An Owner's Manual
Your Marriage – An Owner's Manual
The Cat Owner's Survival Guide
The Dog Owner's Survival Guide
The Relationship Survival guide
Your Pregnancy – A Survival Guide
Life After 40 – A Survival Guide for Women
Life After 40 – A Survival Guide for Men
Life After 50 – A Survival Guide for Women
Life After 50 – A Survival Guide for Men
How To Stay Awake During Sex
Martin Baxendale's Better Sex Guide
Your Man – An Owner's Manual
Your Woman – An Instruction Manual For Men
Your Willy – An Owner's Manual
The Hangover Survival Guide
A Very Rude Book About Willies
Calm Down! – A Stress Survival Guide
Your New Baby's First Adventures
Your New Baby's First Adventures No. 2
It's A Girl!
It's A Boy!
How To Be A Baby
How To Be Married

When Will My Baby Brain Fall Out?
(a cartoon humour book for children)

......

All these titles may be ordered from
bookshops or from Amazon.co.uk